For Michael Wincott—the greatest villain of all time

Torn

Amanda Hocking

TOR

First published 2012 by St Martin's Press, New York

First published in Great Britain 2012 by Tor
an imprint of Pan Macmillan, a division of Macmillan Publishers Limited
Pan Macmillan, 20 New Wharf Road, London N1 9RR
Basingstoke and Oxford
Associated companies throughout the world
www.panmacmillan.com

ISBN 978-1-4472-1030-6

Visit www.panmacmillan.com to read more about all our books
and to buy them. You will also find features, author interviews and
news of any author events, and you can sign up for e-newsletters
so that you're always first to hear about our new releases.

Torn

return

W hen Rhys and I showed up at my "brother" Matt's house at eight in the morning, he was happy . . . in the sense that he was glad I was alive and hadn't disappeared forever. Despite being angry, he listened while I put together a vague explanation, glaring at me the whole time with mystified rage.

At least I only had to face Matt. My aunt Maggie is my legal guardian, but she wasn't there when we arrived. Matt explained that she had gone off looking for me in Oregon. I have no idea why, but for some reason, she thought I'd run off there.

As Rhys and I sat on the shabby-chic couch in Matt's living room, surrounded by the boxes that he had yet to unpack from when we'd moved into the house two months ago, Matt paced back and forth in front of us.

"I still don't understand," Matt said. He stopped in front of us, arms folded over his chest.

"There's nothing to understand," I insisted, gesturing at Rhys. "He's your brother! It's pretty obvious when you look at him."

I have dark, wild, curly hair and mahogany eyes. Matt and

Rhys both have sandy hair and sapphire eyes. They had something much more open in their faces too, and they had the same easy smile. Rhys stared up at Matt with bemused wonderment, his eyes wide with awe.

"How could you possibly know that?" Matt asked.

"I don't know why you can't just trust me." I sighed and laid my head back on the couch. "I never lie to you!"

"You just ran away from home! I had no idea where you were. That's a major trust violation!"

Matt's anger couldn't cover up how hurt he still was, and his body showed signs of the strain he had been under. His face was gaunt and haggard, his eyes red and tired, and he had probably lost ten pounds. When I disappeared, he completely collapsed, I'm sure. I felt guilty, but I hadn't had a choice.

Matt had always been too preoccupied with my safety, a side effect from his mother having tried to kill me and all that. His life revolved around me to the point of being unhealthy. He had no friends, no job, no life of his own.

"I had to run away! Okay?" I ran a hand through my tangled curls and shook my head. "I can't explain it to you. I left for my safety and for yours. I don't know if I should even be here now."

"Safety? What were you running from? Where were you?" Matt asked desperately, not for the first time.

"Matt, I can't tell you! I wish I could but I can't."

I wasn't sure if it was legal for me to tell him anything about the Trylle or not. I assumed everything about them was secret, but nobody had expressly forbidden me from telling outsiders either. Matt would never believe me, though, so I didn't see the point in trying.

"You're really my brother," Rhys said in a hushed tone. He leaned forward to get a better look at Matt. "This is so weird."

"Yeah, it is," Matt agreed. He shifted uncomfortably under Rhys's stare before he turned to me, his expression serious. "Wendy, can I have a word with you? Alone?"

"Uh, sure." I looked over at Rhys.

Taking his cue, Rhys stood up. "Where's your bathroom?"

"Down that way, off the kitchen." Matt pointed to his right.

Once Rhys was gone, Matt sat down on the coffee table in front of me and lowered his voice.

"Look, Wendy, I don't understand what's going on. I have no idea how much of what you've told me is true, but that kid looks like a total weirdo to me. I don't want him in my house, and I don't know what you were thinking bringing him here."

"He's your brother," I said wearily. "Honest, Matt. I would never, ever lie about something this major. I am one hundred percent certain that he is your real brother."

"Wendy . . ." Matt rubbed his forehead, sighing. "I get that you believe that. But how could you actually know? I think this kid is feeding you a story."

"No, he's really not. Rhys is the most honest person I've ever known, except for you. Which makes sense, since you're brothers." I leaned in closer to Matt. "Please. Give him a chance. You'll see."

"What about his family?" Matt asked. "Who has been raising him all these years? Don't they miss him? And aren't they your 'real' family or whatever?"

"Trust me, they won't miss him. And I like you better," I said with a smile.

Matt shook his head as if unable to decide what to make of all this. I knew a large part of him didn't trust Rhys and wanted to throw him out of the house, so I admired him all the more for his restraint.

"I wish you would be straight with me about all of this," he said.

"I'm being as straight with you as I can be."

When Rhys came back from the bathroom, Matt leaned away from me and eyed him warily.

"You don't have any family pictures up," Rhys commented as he looked around the room.

That was true. We didn't really have decorations of any kind up, but we didn't particularly care to remember our family. Matt especially was not fond of our . . . er, his mother.

I had yet to explain to Rhys about his mother being a lunatic locked up in a mental institution. Stuff like that is hard to break to someone, especially someone as awestruck as Rhys.

"Yeah, we're just that way," I said and stood up. "We drove all night to get here. I'm pretty beat. What about you, Rhys?"

"Uh, yeah, I guess I'm tired." Rhys seemed a bit startled by my suggestion. Even though he hadn't gotten any sleep, he didn't look tired at all.

"We should get some sleep, and we can talk more later."

"Oh." Matt got to his feet slowly. "You're both going to be sleeping here, then?" He looked uncertainly at Rhys, then back at me.

"Yeah." I nodded. "He doesn't have anywhere else to go."

"Oh." Matt was clearly against the idea, but I knew he was afraid that if he kicked Rhys out, I'd go after him. "Rhys, I guess you can sleep in my room, for now."

"Really?" Rhys tried to tone down his excitement over staying in Matt's room, but it was obvious.

Matt awkwardly showed us up to our rooms. My room was still

my room, all my stuff the same as I had left it weeks earlier. As I settled in, I listened to Matt and Rhys talking across the hall in Matt's room. Rhys was asking him to explain the simplest things, like how to turn on the bedside lamp, and it made Matt frustrated and uncomfortable.

By the time Matt came into my room, I had already changed into my pajamas. They were worn and comfortable, and I loved them.

"Wendy, what is going on?" Matt whispered. He shut the door behind him and locked it, as if Rhys were some kind of spy. "Who is that kid really? Where did you go?"

"I can't tell you what happened while I was gone. Can't you just be happy that I'm here and I'm safe?"

"No, not really." Matt shook his head. "That kid is not right. He's so amazed by everything."

"He's amazed by *you*," I corrected him. "You have no idea how exciting all this is for him."

"None of this is making any sense." Matt ran a hand through his hair.

"I really do need to get some sleep, and this is a lot for you to process. I get that. Why don't you go call Maggie? Let her know I'm safe. I'll get some rest, and you can think about everything I've been saying."

Matt released a defeated sigh. "Fine," he said, then his blue eyes went hard. "But you better think about telling me what's really going on here."

"All right." I shrugged. I could think about it, but I wouldn't tell him.

Matt's gaze softened again, and his shoulders slackened. "I am glad you're home."

I could see just then how terrible this had all been for him. And I knew I could never disappear like that again. I went over and hugged him tightly.

Matt left me alone in my room, and I crawled into the familiar comfort of my twin bed. I had been sleeping in a giant king-sized bed in Förening, but somehow, my narrow bed felt so much better. I snuggled deeper in the covers, relieved to be somewhere that felt sane again.

I'd always had an inkling that I didn't fit in with my family, despite Matt's devotion to me. My mother had nearly killed me when I was six years old, claiming that I was a monster and not her daughter.

Turns out, she was right.

Less than a month ago, I found out I was a changeling—a child that is exchanged in secret for another child. Specifically, I was switched at birth with Rhys Dahl. It turns out that I'm a Trylle. Trylle are basically glamorous grifters with mild superpowers.

Technically, I'm a troll, but not in the creepy little green monster sort of way. I'm of normal height and fairly attractive. In Trylle culture, the use of changelings is a practice that dates back centuries. The custom's intention is to make sure Trylle offspring have the best childhoods possible.

I'm supposed to be a Princess in Förening—the compound in Minnesota where the Trylle live. My birth mother is Elora, the Trylle Queen. After spending a few weeks in Förening, I decided to head home. I had a falling-out with Elora, who had forbidden me from seeing Finn Holmes simply because he's not royalty.

I escaped and took Rhys with me. In Förening, Rhys had shown me genuine kindness, and I felt he deserved some of that in return.

I brought him here to meet Matt, since he is really Rhys's brother, not mine.

Of course, I couldn't tell Matt all of that. He'd think I was completely insane.

Growing drowsy, I thought again how good it felt to be home. It only took ten minutes for Rhys to shatter that comfort when he crept into my room. I was almost asleep, but the sound of my door opening made me alert. Matt had gone downstairs, presumably to make the phone call I suggested, and if he knew Rhys was in here, he'd kill us both.

"Wendy? Are you asleep?" Rhys whispered, sitting gingerly on the edge of my bed.

"Yes," I muttered.

"Sorry. I can't sleep," Rhys said. "How can you sleep?"

"It's not that exciting for me. I lived here before, remember?"

"Yeah, but . . ." He trailed off, probably because he had no argument for that. Suddenly he tensed and sucked in his breath. "Did you hear that?"

"You talking? Yes, but I've been trying not—" Before I could finish my sentence, I heard it too. A rustling sound outside my bedroom window.

Considering I had just had a horrible run-in with some very bad trolls known as Vittra, I was alarmed. I rolled over and peered at the window, but the curtains were drawn, blocking my view.

The rustling turned into actual banging, and I sat up, my heart pounding. Rhys shot a nervous glance at me. We heard the window slide open, and the curtains billowed out from the wind.

TWO

interruptions

He stepped into my room in one graceful move, as if entering through bedroom windows were nothing out of the ordinary.

His black hair was slicked back impeccably, but he had stubble growing along his jaw, making him look even sexier. His eyes were so dark they were nearly black, and he took one discerning look at Rhys before settling them on me, making my heart forget to beat entirely.

Finn Holmes had snuck into my room.

He still managed to stun me the same way he always did. I was so happy to see him that I almost forgot how angry I was with him.

The last time I had seen Finn, he was slinking out of my bedroom in Förening, per his deal with my mother. Elora told him that he could spend one more night with me before leaving. Forever.

We had only kissed, but Finn had failed to let me in on Elora's plan. He didn't even bother to say good-bye. He didn't fight it or try to get me to run away with him. He just crept out of my room, leaving Elora to explain to me exactly what had happened.

"What are you doing here?" Rhys asked, and Finn pulled his eyes off me to glare at Rhys.

"I came to collect the Princess, of course," Finn said, but irritation saturated his words.

"Well, yeah, but . . . I thought Elora reassigned you." Rhys seemed thrown by Finn's anger, and he fumbled for a minute. "I mean . . . that's what people were saying around Förening, that you weren't allowed around Wendy anymore."

Finn tensed noticeably at Rhys's words, his jaw flexing, and Rhys looked down at the floor.

"I'm not," Finn admitted after a moment. "I was preparing to leave when I heard that you two had vanished in the middle of the night. Elora was deciding who would be best suited to track Wendy, and I thought it would be in her best interest if I went after her, what with the Vittra *stalking* her."

Rhys opened his mouth to protest but Finn cut in.

"We all know you did a wonderful job of protecting her at the ball," Finn said. "If I hadn't shown up, you might've protected her right into getting murdered."

"I know the Vittra are a threat!" Rhys shot back. "I just . . . we came here to . . ."

Hearing his confusion, I got up off the bed, moving to intercede before Rhys figured out why he'd let me talk him into coming here.

The truth was, Rhys didn't agree to come here. He wanted to meet Matt, but he was adamant about my safety and had flat-out refused to let me leave the security of the compound. Unfortunately for Rhys, I had *persuasion*. When I looked at people and thought about what I wanted them to do, they would do it, whether they wanted to or not.

That's how I convinced Rhys to go with me when we ran away, and I needed to distract him before he caught on.

"The Vittra lost a lot of trackers in that fight," I interjected. "They're not eager to repeat it anytime soon. Besides that, I'm sure they're sick of trying to get me."

"That's highly unlikely." Finn narrowed his eyes, studying Rhys's bewilderment, and then he looked darkly at me. "Wendy, do you care nothing for your own safety?"

"I probably care more than you do." I crossed my arms firmly over my chest. "You were leaving to go on to another job. If I had waited one more day to leave, you wouldn't have even known I was gone."

"Is this about getting *my* attention?" Finn snapped, his eyes burning. I had never seen his anger directed at me this way before. "I don't know how many times I have to explain this to you! You are a Princess! I mean nothing! You need to forget about me!"

"What's going on?" That was Matt, shouting from the stairs. If he came up here and caught Finn in my room, it would be very, very bad.

"I'll go . . . create a diversion." Rhys glanced at me to make sure that was okay, and I nodded. He darted out the door, saying things to Matt about how awesome the house was, and their voices faded as they went downstairs.

I tucked my curls behind my ears and refused to look at Finn. It was hard to believe that the last time I had been with him, he had been kissing me so passionately, I could barely breathe. I remembered the way his scruff scraped against my cheeks and the way his lips pressed against mine.

I suddenly hated him for that memory, and I hated that all I could think about was how badly I wanted to kiss him again.

"Wendy, you are not safe here," Finn insisted quietly.

"I'm not going with you."

"You cannot stay here. I won't allow it."

"You won't allow it?" I scoffed. "I am the Princess, remember? Who are you to *allow* me to do anything? You're not even my tracker anymore. You're some guy being a creepy stalker."

That sounded much harsher than I'd meant it. Not that anything I said ever really seemed to hurt Finn. He just stared at me, his gaze level and unfazed.

"I knew I would find you faster than anyone. If you don't come home with me, that's fine," Finn said. "Another tracker will be here shortly, and you can go with him. I'll just wait with you until he arrives, to ensure your safety."

"It's not about you, Finn!"

He had played a larger part in my leaving Förening than I would ever admit, but it really wasn't just him. I hated my mother, my title, my house, everything. I wasn't meant to be a Princess.

Finn looked at me for a long moment, trying to understand where this was coming from. I had to fight the urge to squirm as he scrutinized me. His eyes flashed darkly for a second, and his expression hardened.

"Is this about the mänsklig?" Finn asked, referring to Rhys. "I thought I told you to stay away from him."

Mänsklig were the human children taken in exchange for Trylle babies. They were the lowest in the Trylle hierarchy, and if a Princess was caught dating one, they'd both be banished forever. Not that I cared, but I didn't have any feelings for Rhys that weren't purely platonic.

"It has nothing to do with Rhys. I just thought he'd like to see his family." I shrugged. "It has to be better than living in that stupid house with Elora."

"Good. He can stay here, then." Finn nodded. "Matt and Rhys are taken care of. Now you can come home."

"That is not my home. *This* is my home!" I gestured widely to my room. "I'm not going, Finn."

"You are not safe." He took a step closer to me, lowering his voice and staring into my eyes. "You saw what the Vittra did in Förening. They sent an army out to get you, Wendy." He put his hands on my arms, strong and warm on my skin. "They will not stop until they have you."

"Why? Why wouldn't they stop?" I asked. "There's got to be Trylle out there who are easier to get than me. And so what if I'm a Princess? If I don't come back, Elora can replace me. I'm meaningless."

"You are far more powerful than you know."

"What does that even mean?"

Before he could answer, there was a noise on the roof outside my window. Finn grabbed my arm and threw open my closet door, shoving me inside. As a rule, I don't enjoy being tossed into closets and having the door shut in my face, but I knew he was protecting me.

I opened the door a crack, so I could watch what happened and intervene if necessary. Even as mad as I was at Finn, I would never let him get hurt over me. Not again.

Finn stood a few feet from the window, his eyes blazing and his shoulders tense. But when the figure climbed through the window, Finn only scoffed.

The kid coming in tripped on the windowsill. He wore skinny jeans and purple shoes with the laces untied. Finn towered over him, looking down at him wearily.

"Hey, what are you doing here?" The kid flipped his bangs out of his eyes and pulled down his ill-fitting jacket. It was zipped all the way up, and the bottom met the top of his jeans. When he bent over or moved, it rode up.

"Getting the Princess. They sent you after her?" Finn arched an eyebrow. "Elora really thought you'd be able to bring her back?"

"Hey, I'm a good tracker. I've brought in way more people than you have."

"That's because you're seven years older than me," Finn replied. That made the clumsy kid twenty-seven. He looked much younger than that.

"Whatever. Elora picked me. Deal with it." The kid shook his head. "What? Are you jealous or something?"

"Don't be absurd."

"So where is the Princess anyway?" He looked around my room. "She ran away for *this*?"

"This is my room." I walked out of the closet, and the new tracker jumped. "You don't need to be condescending."

"Um, sorry," he stumbled, blushing. "My apologies, Princess." He offered me an unsure smile and did a low bow. "I'm Duncan Janssen, and I'm at your service."

"I'm not the Princess anymore, and I'm not going with you. I just finished explaining that to Finn."

"What?" Duncan looked uncertainly at Finn as he adjusted

his jacket again. Finn sat down on the edge of my bed and said nothing. "Princess, you have to come. It's not safe for you here."

"I don't care." I shrugged. "I'd rather take my chances."

"It can't be that bad at the palace." Duncan was the first person I had ever heard genuinely call Elora's house a palace, even though it sort of was one. "You're the Princess. You have everything."

"I'm not going. You can tell Elora that you tried your best, and I refused."

Duncan once again looked to Finn for help. Finn shrugged at Duncan, and his shift to indifference startled me. I had put my foot down on the subject, but I hadn't really expected him to listen.

"She can't possibly stay here," Duncan said.

"You think I don't agree with you?" Finn raised an eyebrow.

"I don't think you're helping." Duncan fidgeted with his jacket and tried to stare Finn down, a task I knew was impossible.

"What do you expect me to say to her that I haven't already said?" Finn asked, sounding surprisingly helpless.

"So you're saying we simply leave her here?"

"I'm right here, you know," I said. "And I don't really appreciate the way you keep referring to me like I'm not."

"If she wants to stay here, then she'll stay here," Finn said, continuing to ignore me. Duncan shifted and glanced over at me. "We're not going to kidnap her. That leaves little in the way of options."

"Can't you, like"—Duncan lowered his voice and fiddled with the zipper of his jacket—"you know, *convince* her somehow?"

Word of Finn's affection for me must have spread through the compound. Aggravated, I refused to let my feelings for him be used against me.

"Nothing is going to convince me," I snapped.

"Do you see?" Finn motioned toward me. Sighing, he got to his feet. "We should be on our way, then."

"Really?" I couldn't hide the shock in my voice.

"Yeah. Really?" Duncan echoed.

"You said there's nothing I can do to convince you. Has that changed?" Finn turned to me. His voice was hopeful, but his eyes were almost taunting. I shook my head firmly. "Then there is nothing left to say."

"Finn—" Duncan started to protest, but Finn held his hand up. "It is as the Princess wishes."

Duncan looked skeptically at Finn, probably thinking that this was some sort of trick, much as I was. There had to be something I wasn't getting, because Finn wouldn't just leave me here. Sure, that's exactly what he had done a few days ago, but that's when he thought leaving was what was best for me.

"But Finn—" Duncan tried again, but Finn waved him off.

"We must go. Her 'brother' will notice us soon," Finn said.

I glanced at my closed bedroom door, as if Matt would be lurking right there. The last time Matt and Finn had a run-in it had not gone well, and I was not eager to repeat the experience.

"Fine, but . . ." Duncan trailed off, realizing too late that he had nothing to threaten either of us with. He gave me another quick bow. "Princess. I'm sure we'll meet again."

I shrugged. "We'll see."

Duncan climbed out my bedroom window, practically falling onto the roof. After he was out, he half jumped, half fell off the roof. Finn watched him apprehensively for a moment, holding my curtain open, but he didn't follow after immediately.

Instead, he straightened up, looking over at me. My anger and resolution were fading, leaving me hopeful that Finn wouldn't really leave things this way.

"Once I'm out this window, lock it behind me," Finn commanded. "Make sure all the doors are locked, and never go anywhere alone. Never go anyplace at night, and if at all possible, always take Matt *and* Rhys with you." He looked past me for a moment, thinking of something.

"Although neither of them are really good for much of anything . . ." His dark eyes rested on mine once again. His expression was imploring, and he raised his hand as if he meant to touch my face, but he lowered it again. "You *must* be careful."

"Okay," I promised him.

With Finn standing right in front of me, I could feel the warmth of his body and smell his cologne. His eyes were locked on mine, and I remembered the way it felt when he tangled his fingers in my hair and held me so close to him I couldn't breathe.

He was so strong and controlled. In the brief moments he allowed himself to let go of his passion with me, it was the most wonderfully suffocating feeling I'd ever had.

I didn't want him to leave, and he didn't want to leave. But we had both made choices we were unwilling to change. He nodded once more, breaking eye contact, and then turned and slid out the window.

Duncan waited at the bottom of the tree, and Finn dropped gracefully to the ground. From the window, I watched Finn coax a hesitant Duncan away from the house.

When they reached the hedges separating my lawn from the neighbors', Finn looked around, checking to make sure no one was there. Without even looking at me, he and Duncan turned and disappeared.

I closed the window, locking it securely the way he'd said to. I felt a terrible ache watching him go. Even though he had done this kind of thing before, I couldn't wrap my mind around Finn really leaving and convincing Duncan to leave me too. If he was so concerned about the Vittra, why would he leave me so unprotected?

It finally dawned on me. Finn had *never* left me unprotected, no matter what I or anybody else wanted. As soon as he had realized I wasn't going with him, he hadn't wanted to waste any more time arguing. He would wait in the wings until I changed my mind or . . .

I shut the curtains tightly. I hated being spied on, but I also found it strangely comforting that Finn was watching over me. After having my window open for so long, my room felt chilly, so I went over to my closet and pulled on a heavy sweater.

The adrenaline rush from seeing Finn had left me wide awake, but I was looking forward to curling up in bed, even if I wouldn't be able to sleep.

I settled into my bed, trying futilely to forget about Finn. Within minutes, I heard a loud banging downstairs. Matt let out a yell, but it was cut short, leaving the house in total silence.

I jumped and ran to my bedroom door. With shaking hands, I opened it, hoping that Finn had tried to sneak back in and had a misunderstanding with Matt.

Then I heard Rhys screaming.

insentient

Rhys suddenly went silent. I barely took a step out of my room when I heard footsteps pounding up the stairs, and before I could react, she was there.

Kyra, a Vittra tracker I had dealt with before, appeared at the top of the landing. Her dark hair was in a pixie cut, and she wore a long black leather jacket. She hung on to the railing, crouching down. As soon as she saw me, she sneered, showing more teeth than any human would.

I rushed toward her, hoping for the element of surprise, but I was out of luck.

She dodged before I got close and sent a swift kick into my abdomen. I stumbled backward, gripping my stomach dramatically, and when she came at me again, I punched her in the face.

Unfazed, Kyra lunged at me and returned the blow much harder. When I fell down, she stood over me, smiling, with blood dripping from her nose.

I scrambled to my feet, and she grabbed my hair, yanking me up. I kicked at her as she lifted me, and she rewarded my moxie by kicking me in the side so hard I cried out. Kyra laughed at that and kicked me again.

This time I saw white and everything faded out for a moment. My hearing got wonky, and I barely hung on to consciousness.

"Stop!" a strong voice shouted.

When I blinked open my swollen eyes, I saw a man running up the stairs toward Kyra. He was tall, and beneath his black sweater he was well muscled. Kyra dropped me to the floor when he reached the top of the stairs.

"It's not like I can *really* hurt her, Loki," Kyra said, her voice bordering on whining.

I tried to get to my feet again, even though I felt dizzy, and she kicked me down.

"Knock it off," he snapped at her. She grimaced and took a step back.

He stood in front of me, towering above me, and then knelt down. I could scramble away from him, but I wouldn't get far. He cocked his head, looking at me curiously.

"So you're what all the fuss is about," he mused.

He reached forward, taking my face in his hands. Not painfully, but he was forcing me to look at him. His caramel eyes fixed on mine. I wanted to look away, but I couldn't.

This strange fog settled over me, and as terrified as I was, I felt my body relaxing, losing its ability to fight. My eyelids were too heavy to keep open, and, unable to stop it, I fell asleep.

I was dreaming of water. But anything more specific than that I couldn't remember. My body felt cold, like it should be shivering but wasn't. My cheeks were warm, though, resting against something soft.

"You're telling me that she's a *Princess*?" Matt asked, his voice a deep rumble above me. My head lay against his leg, and the more I woke up, the more I realized how terrible my body felt.

"It's not that hard to believe, really," Rhys said. His voice came from somewhere on the other side of the room. "Once you get all the Trylle stuff, the Princess part is pretty easy to take."

"I'm not sure what to believe anymore," Matt admitted.

I opened my eyes with a struggle. My lids felt unnaturally heavy, and my left eye was swollen from where Kyra had punched me. The room swayed, and I blinked it into focus.

When my vision finally cleared, I still didn't understand what I was seeing. The floor appeared to be dirt, and the walls were brown and gray stones, looking damp and weathered. It reminded me of an old cellar . . . or a dungeon.

Rhys paced the other side of the room, fresh bruises on his face. I tried to sit up, but my entire body hurt and my head felt woozy.

"Hey, take it easy," Matt said, putting his hand on my shoulder, but I didn't listen.

I pushed myself up until I was sitting, which took a lot more effort than it normally required. I grimaced and leaned against the wall next to him.

"You're awake!" Rhys grinned. He was probably the only person in the world who could look happy in this situation.

"How are you feeling?" Matt asked. For his part, he didn't have any visible bruises, but he was a better fighter than Rhys and me.

"Great." I had to lie through gritted teeth because it hurt to breathe. Based on the intense shooting pain in my diaphragm, I guessed I had a cracked rib, but I didn't want to worry Matt. "What's going on? Where are we?"

"I was hoping you could shed some light on that," Matt said.

"I already told him, but he won't believe me," Rhys said.

"Where are we, then?" I asked Rhys, and Matt scoffed.

"I'm not sure exactly." Rhys shook his head. "I think we're in the Vittra palace in Ondarike."

"Ondarike?" I asked.

"The Vittra capital," Rhys explained. "But I don't know exactly how far it is from Förening."

"I figured as much," I said, sighing. "I recognized the Vittra who attacked the house. Kyra went after me before."

"What?" Matt's eyes were wide and disbelieving. "These people went after you before?"

"Yeah, that's why I had to leave." I closed my eyes because it hurt too much to keep them open. The world wanted to spin out from under me.

"Told you," Rhys said to Matt. "I'm not lying about this stuff. After what happened, you would think you'd cut me a little slack."

"Rhys isn't lying," I said, wincing. It was getting harder to breathe, and I had to take very shallow breaths, which only made me more light-headed. "He knows more about all of this than I do. I wasn't there very long."

"Why are these Vittra people coming after you?" Matt asked. "Why do they want you?"

I shook my head, unwilling to risk the pain of speaking.

"I don't know," Rhys answered when I didn't. "I've never seen them go after anyone this way before. Then again, she's the first Princess I've been around, and they've foretold of her for a while."

I'd wanted to know what they were foretelling, but everyone gave me vague responses, so all I knew was that I'd be powerful someday. But I didn't feel very powerful, especially right now. It hurt too much to speak, and I was locked up in a dungeon.

And even worse, not only had I failed to save myself, but I'd gotten Rhys and Matt dragged into this mess along with me.

"Wendy, are you okay?" Matt asked.

"Yeah," I lied.

"You don't look okay," Rhys said.

"All your color is gone, and you're barely even breathing," Matt said, and I heard him getting to his feet next to me. "You need a doctor or something."

"What are you doing?" Rhys asked.

I opened my eyes to see what Matt was up to. His plan was simple and obvious—he went to the locked door and pounded on it.

"Help! Somebody! Wendy needs a doctor!"

"What makes you think they'd even want to help her?" Rhys asked, echoing my exact thoughts. Kyra had gone out of her way to hurt me when she captured me.

"They haven't killed her yet, so they probably don't want her dead." Matt had stopped pounding long enough to answer Rhys, then went back to hitting the door and yelling for help.

The sound of it echoed through the room, and I couldn't take it anymore. My head throbbed too much already. I was about to tell Matt to knock it off when the door opened.

This was the perfect time for Matt and Rhys to launch a counterattack, but it didn't occur to either of them. They both just moved away.

The Vittra from the house walked into the room, the one who had rendered me unconscious, and I dimly remembered Kyra calling him Loki. His shaggy hair was surprisingly light for a Vittra, almost blond.

Walking next to him was a troll, like an actual troll. All short and gobliny. His features were humanoid, but his skin was slimy and brown. He wore a hat, and tufts of grayish hair stuck out around the edge. He barely came up to Loki's hip, but the fact that he was an actual troll made him more intimidating somehow.

Rhys and Matt both gaped at the hobgoblin, and I probably would've too, if I'd been capable of gaping. I could barely keep my head up.

"You say the girl is in need of a doctor?" Loki asked, his eyes resting on me. He regarded me with the same mild curiosity he had before.

"Kyra did that?" the hobgoblin asked, his voice unexpectedly deep for such a small creature. He looked to Loki for confirmation, shaking his head at the damage she'd inflicted on me. "She needs to be put on a leash."

"I don't think Wendy can breathe," Matt said, his features hardening with self-restraint.

I was sure my condition was the only thing keeping him from attacking Loki. If he hurt them, they wouldn't be able to help me.

"Well, let me have a look." Loki walked over to me, his strides long and purposeful.

The hobgoblin stayed by the door, guarding it from Matt and Rhys, but they were too focused on me to consider escape.

Loki crouched down in front of me, looking me over with something that resembled concern. I was in too much pain to feel real fear, but I'm not sure I would have been afraid of him. Physically he was much stronger than me, and he had some kind of ability that could knock me out, maybe even more than that. But somehow, I knew he'd help me.

"What hurts?" Loki asked.

"She can barely breathe, let alone talk!" Matt snapped. "She needs immediate medical attention."

Loki held up his hand to silence him, and Matt sighed heavily. "Can you talk?" Loki kept staring at me.

When I opened my mouth, instead of speaking, an excruciating cough rose up in me. Closing my eyes, I tried to fight it. I coughed so hard, tears streamed down my cheeks, and I felt something wet. I opened my eyes to see bright red splattered all over my legs and Loki's feet. I was coughing up blood, and I couldn't stop.

"Ludlow!" Loki shouted at the hobgoblin. "Get Sara! Now!"

FOUR

vitriol

Loki crouched in front of me, keeping Matt back. He probably knew Matt's inclination would be to hold me, and Loki didn't want me moved, afraid that it might rupture something. Matt shouted frantically, but Loki kept insisting that everything would be all right.

Within moments a woman appeared in the room. Her long dark hair was pulled back in a ponytail, and she knelt down in front of me, pushing Loki to the side. Her eyes were almost as dark as Finn's, and I found something comforting in that.

"My name is Sara, and I'm going to help you." She pressed her hand hard against my abdomen, and I winced.

It hurt so bad I wanted to scream, but then the pain began to fade. A weird numbing tingle ran through me. It took me a second to figure out where I had felt the sensation before.

"You're a healer," I mumbled, slightly dismayed that she was helping me. The pain in my chest and stomach had disappeared, and she put her hand on my face, fixing my black eye.

"Does it hurt anywhere else?" Sara asked, ignoring my statement. She looked worn out, a temporary side effect from healing, but otherwise she was incredibly beautiful.

"I don't think so." I sat up, still a little unsteady, but that was lessening by the moment.

"Kyra went way overboard," Sara said, more to herself than me. "Are you okay now?"

"Yeah." I nodded.

"Excellent." Sara stood up and turned to Loki. "You need to control your trackers better."

"They're not *mine*." Loki crossed his arms over his chest. "If you have a problem with how they do their job, take it up with your husband."

"I'm certain my husband wouldn't like how this situation was handled." Sara looked at him severely, but he didn't back down.

"I was doing you a favor," Loki replied evenly. "If I hadn't been there, it would've been worse."

"I'm not having this discussion now." She glanced in my direction, then walked out of the room.

"Is that everything, then?" Loki asked us once she'd gone.

"Not even close." Matt had been sitting next to me but he got to his feet. "What do you want with us? You can't just keep us here!"

"I'll take that as a yes." Loki smiled emptily at me and turned to leave the room.

Matt tried to rush him, but Loki was already out the door before he got to him. He slammed the door and Matt flew into it. There was a loud clicking as bolts locked, and Matt sagged against the door.

"What is going on here?" Matt shouted and turned to look at me. "How come you're not dying anymore?"

"Would you rather I be dying?" I pulled the sleeve of my sweater down and wiped the blood away from my face. "I could get Kyra in here to finish the job."

"Don't be ridiculous." Matt rubbed his forehead. "I want to know what's happening. I feel like I'm in a bad dream."

"It gets easier," I said and turned to Rhys. "What the hell was that hobgoblin thing that came in? Was that an actual troll?"

"I don't know." Rhys shook his head, looking just as bewildered as I felt. "I've never seen one before, but everyone goes out of their way to make sure mänks don't know anything."

"I didn't think there were real trolls." I furrowed my brow, trying to remember what Finn had told me about trolls before. "I thought they were just myths."

"Really?" Matt asked. "After everything that's happened? So you pick and choose what mythology you believe in?"

"I'm not picking and choosing anything." I got to my feet. I still felt sore all over, but it was light-years better than I'd felt when I woke up. "I believe what I can see. I hadn't seen this before. That's all."

"Are you okay?" Matt watched me as I hobbled around the room. "Maybe you should take it easy."

"No, I'm fine." I brushed him off. I wanted to get my bearings in the space, maybe see if there was a way that we could get out. "How did we get here anyway?"

"They broke into the house and attacked us." Matt gestured to the door, referring to Loki and the Vittra. "That guy knocked us out somehow, and we woke up here. We hadn't been awake very long before you woke up."

"Lovely." I pressed my palms against the door, pushing on it as if I thought it would open. It didn't, but I had to try.

"Hey, where's Finn?" Rhys asked, echoing thoughts I was starting to have. "Why didn't he stop this?"

"What does Finn have to do with this?" Matt asked with an edge to his voice.

"Nothing. He used to be my tracker. It's sorta like a bodyguard." I took a step back, staring at the door and willing it to open. "He tried to protect me from all of this."

"That's why you ran away with him?" Matt asked. "He was protecting you?"

I sighed. "Something like that."

"Where is he?" Rhys repeated. "I thought he was with you when the Vittra came."

Matt started yelling about Finn being in my room, but I ignored him. I didn't have the energy to fight with Matt about propriety or his feelings for Finn.

"Finn left before they broke in," I said, once Matt had finished his tirade. "I don't know where he's at."

I wouldn't admit it, but I was surprised that Finn hadn't protected me. Maybe he had really left. I thought it had all been a bluff, but if it was, Finn would've been there when we were attacked.

Unless something bad had happened to him. The Vittra could have gotten to him before they came after me. He cared too much for duty, even if he didn't care enough for me. The only way he wouldn't keep me safe was if he *couldn't*.

"Wendy?" Rhys asked.

I think he'd been talking before that, but I hadn't heard anything he'd said. I'd been too busy thinking of Finn and staring at the door.

"We have to get out of here," I said and turned to Rhys and Matt. Matt sighed. "Obviously."

"I have an idea." I bit my lip. "But it's not a great one. When they come back, I can use my persuasion. I can convince them to let us go."

"Do you really think it's strong enough?" Rhys voiced the concern I'd had myself.

So far, I'd only used persuasion on unsuspecting humans, like Matt and Rhys, and Finn had told me that without training, my abilities weren't as strong as they could be. I hadn't begun my training yet in Förening, so I had no clue how powerful or weak I might be.

"I really don't know," I admitted.

"Persuasion?" Matt raised an eyebrow and looked at Rhys. "Is that the thing you were telling me about? That mind thing she can supposedly do?" Rhys nodded, and Matt rolled his eyes.

"It's not *supposedly*." I bristled at his skepticism. "I can do it. I've done it to you before."

"When?" Matt asked dubiously.

"How do you think I got you to take me to see Kim?" I asked, referring to when he'd taken me to see his mother, my "host" mother, in the institution.

He hated her and didn't want me to have anything to do with her. I'd used persuasion on him, even though I'd felt guilty about it, but it was the only way I could talk to her.

"You did that?" The shock and hurt in his eyes was instantly replaced by anger. He looked like he'd been slapped in the face. I lowered my eyes and turned away. "You tricked me? How could you do that, Wendy? You always say you never lie to me, then you go and do something like that!"

"It wasn't a lie," I said sheepishly.

"No, it's worse!" Matt shook his head and stepped away from

me, as if he couldn't stand to be near me. "I can't believe you did that. How often did you do that?"

"I don't know," I admitted. "For a long time, I didn't know I was doing it. But once I figured it out, I tried not to do it at all. I don't like doing it, especially to you. It's not fair, and I know it."

"Damn right it's not fair!" Matt snapped. "It's cruel and manipulative!"

"I'm really sorry." I met his eyes, and the hurt in them stung painfully. "I promise I won't ever do it again, not to you."

"I hate to break up this moment, but we need to figure a way out of here," Rhys interrupted. "So what is the plan?"

"We call someone," I said, happy for the reprieve from thinking about how much Matt must hate me.

"What do you mean, 'call someone'? Do you have your cell phone?" Rhys asked excitedly.

"No, I mean, summon someone. The way Matt did before." I pointed to the door behind me. "Knock on the door, say we're hungry or cold or dead or whatever. When they come, I can use my persuasion on them to get them to let us out."

"You think that will really work?" Matt asked, but the disbelief had dropped from his voice. He was only asking my opinion now.

"Maybe." I looked at Rhys. "But I have a favor to ask. Can I practice on you?"

"Sure." Rhys shrugged, trusting me immediately.

"What do you mean, 'practice'?" Matt asked with a concerned edge.

He moved a bit closer to Rhys, and I realized with some surprise that he finally believed Rhys was his brother. He wanted to protect Rhys from me. I felt some relief and happiness knowing that he'd started accepting him, but it hurt a little—okay, *a lot*—to know that Matt thought of me as a threat.

"I haven't done it very much." I didn't like the way Matt scrutinized me with his gaze, so I paced the room, as if that could deflect his attention somehow. "And it's been a while since I've done it at all."

That last part wasn't entirely true, since I'd just used it on Rhys the day before, but I didn't want him reacting the way Matt had. This whole process would go a lot easier the less people hated me.

"So what do you want to do?" Matt asked.

"I don't know yet." I shrugged. "But I just need to practice. It's the only way I can get stronger."

Despite Matt's obvious reservations, Rhys went along with it. It felt very odd to have someone witnessing persuasion, especially someone clearly against it, but I had no choice. It wasn't like I could send Matt into the next room or something.

I could see Matt watching me intently out of the corner of my eye. It was distracting, but that was probably better practice for me. I doubted I could get any of the Vittra to step aside to a quiet place while I tried to use a bit of mind control on the guard.

I decided to start simple. Rhys and I were standing, facing each other, so I started repeating in my head, *Sit down. I want you to sit down.*

His blue eyes met mine evenly at first, then a fog passed over them. His face seemed to slacken, and his expression went completely blank. Without a word, he sat down on the floor.

"Is he okay?" Matt asked nervously.

"Yeah, I'm fine." Rhys sounded like he'd just woken up. He looked up at me, his eyes dazed. "So, are you gonna do it or what?"

"I already did it." I had never talked to anybody about it after using persuasion on them, and it felt strange to be open about it.

"What are you talking about?" Rhys's brow furrowed, and he looked back and forth between Matt and me, trying to understand.

"You got all spaced out, then you sat on the floor," Matt said.

"Why did you sit down?" I asked.

"I . . ." His face scrunched up in concentration. "I don't know. I just . . . I sat down." He shook his head and looked up at me. "You did that?"

"Yeah. You didn't feel anything or sense anything?" I asked.

I had never known if what I did hurt people. They never complained of pain or anything, but maybe they couldn't because they didn't understand what was happening.

"No. I didn't even . . ." He shook his head again, unable to articulate what he meant. "I expected there to be a blackout or something. But . . . I knew that I was sitting. It was more like a reflex. Like, I breathe all the time, but I don't think about it. This was the same."

"Hmm." I looked at him thoughtfully. "Stand up."

"What?" Rhys asked.

"Stand up," I repeated. He stared up at me for a second, then looked around. His eyes hardened and his eyebrows pinched up.

"What's going on?" Matt asked, moving closer to us.

"I . . . I can't stand up."

"Do you need me to help you up?" Matt offered.

"No. It's not like that." Rhys shook his head. "I mean, you could pull me up. You're stronger than me, and I'm not physically pinned to the floor. I just . . . forgot how?"

"Weird." I watched him with fascination.

Once before, I had made Matt get out of my room, and it'd been a while before he'd been able to go in there again. Which meant my persuasion had lingering effects, but it did eventually wear off.

" 'Weird'?" Matt scoffed. "Wendy, fix him!"

"He's not broken," I said defensively, but Matt glared at me in a way that made me want to crawl under a rock. I crouched down in front of Rhys. "Rhys, look at me."

"Okay?" He met my eyes uncertainly.

I wasn't even sure if I could reverse the process. I had never tried to undo persuasion before, but I didn't think it'd be that hard. And if I couldn't, then he'd just have to sit down for a week or two. Maybe.

Instead of worrying about the possible repercussions, I focused all my energy on him. I just said, *Stand up*, in my head over and over again. It took longer than it did last time, but eventually his face started to fog over. He blinked at me a few times and got to his feet.

"I am so glad that worked." I let out a sigh of relief.

"Are you sure it worked?" Matt asked me, but his eyes were on Rhys. Rhys stared blankly at the floor, looking more out of it than he had last time. "Rhys? Are you okay?"

"What?" Rhys lifted his head. He blinked at us, as if he'd just noticed we were there. "What? Did something happen?"

"You're standing up." I pointed to his legs, and he looked down.

"Oh." He lifted one of his legs, making sure it still worked, and didn't say anything for a minute. Then he looked up at me. "I'm sorry. Were we talking about something?"

"You couldn't stand up. Remember?" I asked, but my stomach twisted. I might really have broken Rhys.

"Oh. Yeah." He shook his head. "Yeah, I remember. But I can stand now. Did you do that?"

"Wendy, I don't like you playing with him like this," Matt said quietly.

Matt faced Rhys, but he gave me a sidelong glance. He tried to keep his face hard, but his eyes betrayed his fear.

I had scared Matt, and not in the same way as when I'd run away. Then he'd been scared for me, but now he seemed scared *of* me, and it created a painful knot in my chest.

"I'm done now." I stepped away from Rhys.

My dark hair hung around my face. I had a tie around my wrist, so I pulled my hair up into a loose bun.

"What?" Rhys asked, sounding alert.

He had fully come out of the trance I'd had him under, but I didn't want to look at him. Matt made me feel ashamed about using persuasion, even if Rhys was aware of what I had done.

"Sit down," Matt suggested.

"Why? I don't wanna sit down."

"Sit down anyway," Matt said, more firmly this time. When Rhys didn't respond, Matt repeated his command. "Rhys, sit down."

"I don't get why it's so important to you that I sit down." Rhys grew more agitated as Matt pressed him, which was strange, since I'd never really heard him sound irritated with anyone. "I'm fine standing up."

"You can't sit down." Matt sighed, looking over at me. "You broke him a different way, Wendy."

"Wendy did this?" Rhys furrowed his brow. "I don't understand. What did you do? You told me not to sit?"

"No, I told you to sit, and you couldn't stand. Then I told you to stand, and you can't sit." I sighed in frustration. "Now I don't know what to say! I don't really wanna say anything anymore. I might make it so you stop breathing or something."

"Can you do that?" Matt asked.

"I don't know!" I threw my hands up. "I have no idea what I'm capable of."

"I can't sit down for a while." Rhys shrugged. "Big deal. I don't even wanna sit down."

"That's probably a side effect of the persuasion," I told him as I paced our cell.

"Whatever, I don't care if it is," Rhys said. "It doesn't matter. I'm not in a situation that calls for sitting down, anyway. The important thing is that you know that you can do this. You can use this, we can get out of here, and somebody in Förening can fix me. Okay?"

I stopped pacing and looked uneasily at Matt and Rhys. Rhys was right. I needed to get us out of here. It wasn't safe here, and Rhys's inability to sit was a secondary concern. If anything, it just made me want to get us out of here quicker.

"Are you guys ready?"

"For what?" Matt asked.

"To run. I don't know what's on the other side of the door, or how long I can hold them off," I said. "As soon as they open the door, you have to be ready to run as fast as you can, as far as you can."

"Aren't you just gonna *Star Wars* them?" Rhys asked, completely unfazed by the idea. "When Obi-Wan's like, 'These aren't the droids you're looking for.'"

"Yeah, but I don't know how many guards there are, or how dangerous they might be." My thoughts flashed back to Finn and how he hadn't been at my house during the attack. I shivered involuntarily and shook my head.

"Let's just get out of here, okay? There's no way to know what we're up against, so let's deal with it as it comes. Anything's better than sitting around waiting for them to figure out what they want to do with us. Because when they do decide, I have a feeling it won't be good."

Matt didn't look convinced, but I doubted anything could've convinced him. This whole thing had turned into a giant horrible mess, all because I hadn't wanted to stay in Förening and be a stupid Princess.

If I had, none of this would've happened. Matt and Rhys would be at their respective homes, safe and sound, and Finn would be . . . well, I didn't know where he'd be, but it had to be better than where he was now.

With that thought burning in my mind, I pounded on the door, knocking as loudly as I could. My fist hurt from how hard I hit, but I didn't care.

hobgoblin

W hat?" a deep, craggy voice asked, and a slot slid open in the middle of the door.

I bent over to peer through, and I saw the hobgoblin that had come in with Loki. His eyes were buried under bushy eyebrows, and I wasn't sure if I had a good enough view to persuade him. Or if it even worked on actual trolls. They appeared to be an entirely different species.

"Ludlow, is it?" I asked, remembering the name Loki had shouted when sending for help.

"Don't try to sweet-talk me, Princess." The hobgoblin coughed, retching up phlegm and spitting it on the ground. He wiped his face on the back of his sleeve before turning back to me. "I've turned down far prettier girls than you before."

"I need to go to the bathroom." I dropped any pretense of being friendly. I had a feeling that honesty and cynicism would go further with him.

"So go. You don't have to ask me for permission." Ludlow laughed, but it wasn't a pleasant sound.

"There's no bathroom in here. I'm not gonna squat on the ground," I said, genuinely disgusted by the idea.

"Then hold it." Ludlow started to shut the slot, but I put my hand out, blocking it.

"Can't you get a guard or something to take me to the bathroom?" I asked.

"I am the guard," Ludlow snapped, sounding huffy.

"Oh, really?" I smirked at him, realizing this might be far easier than I thought.

"Don't underestimate me, Princess," Ludlow growled. "I eat girls like you for breakfast."

"So you're a cannibal?" I wrinkled my nose.

"Ludlow, are you harassing the poor girl?" came a voice from behind Ludlow. He moved to the side, and through the slot I saw Loki swaggering toward us.

"She's harassing *me*," Ludlow complained.

"Yes, talking to a beautiful Princess—what a rough lot you have in life," Loki said dryly, and Matt snorted behind me.

Ludlow muttered something, but Loki held up his hand, silencing him. Then he was too close to the door for me to see his face. The slot was at Ludlow's eye level, which came up to Loki's waist.

"What seems to be the problem?" Loki asked.

"I need to go to the bathroom." I leaned in closer to the slot, peering up at him. I wanted to catch his eyes, but they remained out of my vision.

"And I told her to go inside the cell," Ludlow said with pride.

"Oh, come, now. She's not a common mänks. We can't leave her in squalor!" Loki chastised the troll. "Open the door. Let her out."

"But sir, I'm not to let her out until the King calls for her." Ludlow looked up at him nervously.

"You think the King would want her treated this way?" Loki asked, and the hobgoblin wrung his hands. "You can explain to the Majesty that this is all my fault, if it comes to it."

Ludlow nodded reluctantly. He slid the slot shut, and I let him this time. I stood up and listened to the sounds of the bolts and locks clicking and turning.

"I don't like this," Matt said in a low voice.

"We don't have much of a choice," I whispered. "I got us into this, and I'll get us out."

The door opened a bit, and I stood back, expecting it to open farther. I thought Loki would step in, I would use persuasion, and we would be off. But he and Ludlow remained hidden outside.

"Well?" Ludlow asked. "I'm not holding this door open all day."

Ludlow had left the door open a few inches, giving me barely enough room to slide my body through. I squeezed my way out, and as soon as I had, Ludlow slammed the door shut. I stared down at him, already busying himself with locking it up.

"The bathroom is this way," Loki said.

He gestured down the hall, which was made of the same dank bricks as the cell I'd been in. The floors were dirt, and torches on the wall lit the way.

"Thanks." I smiled at Loki and caught his eyes easily. They were really quite beautiful, a dark golden color, but I pushed that thought from my mind.

Concentrating as hard as I could, I started chanting silently, *Let them go. Let us go. Open the cell and let us go.* It took a few seconds before I saw any response, but the one I got wasn't at all what I was expecting.

A bemused smile crossed his lips, and his eyes sparkled with wicked pleasure.

"I bet you don't even have to go to the bathroom, do you?" Loki smirked at me.

"I—what?" I fumbled, startled that nothing had happened.

"I told you we shouldn't let her out!" Ludlow shouted.

"Relax, Ludlow," Loki said but kept his eyes on me. "She's fine. Harmless."

I redoubled my efforts, thinking I hadn't tried hard enough. Maybe I'd weakened myself by using persuasion on Rhys so recently. Healers were tired and aged after they used their abilities. I was probably the same way, even though I didn't feel tired.

I started repeating it in my mind again when Loki waved his hand, stopping me.

"Easy, Princess, you're going to hurt yourself." He laughed. "You're persistent, though. I'll give you that."

"So, what? You're immune or something?" I asked.

No point in pretending I hadn't been trying to use persuasion on him. He obviously knew what I was doing.

"Not exactly. You're far too unfocused." He crossed his arms over his chest, watching me with that same curious expression he always seemed to have. "You're quite powerful, though."

"I thought you said she was harmless," Ludlow interjected.

"She is. Without training, she's almost useless," Loki clarified. "Someday she'll be a great asset. Right now she's little more than a parlor trick."

"Thanks," I muttered.

I hurried to rethink the plan. I could probably take down Ludlow, but I didn't understand how all the locks worked. Even if I got him out of the way, I wasn't sure that I could open the door to Matt and Rhys's cell to free them.

But Loki was my biggest problem, since I already knew how well I'd fare against him. Besides being taller and stronger than me, he had the ability to knock me out just by looking at me.

"I can see your mind spinning," Loki said, almost in awe. I tensed up, afraid he might be able to read my mind, and I tried to think of nothing. "I can't see what's *on* your mind. If I had, I wouldn't have let you out. But now that you are, we might as well make the best of it."

"What do you mean?" I asked warily, moving away from him.

"You overestimate my interest in you." Loki grinned broadly. "I prefer my Princesses in unsoiled pajamas."

My clothes would've been relatively clean if it weren't for the blood on my sweater and some dirt on my knees. I was sure I was a mess, but it wasn't my fault.

"I'm sorry. I usually look much nicer after I take a beating," I said, and his smile faltered.

"Yes, well, I don't think you'll have to worry about that now." Loki recovered quickly, his cocky edge returning. "I think it's time you went and saw Sara."

"Sir, I really think that's unwise—" Ludlow interrupted, but Loki glared at him and he shut up.

"What about my friends?" I pointed at the cell.

"They're not going anywhere." Loki smiled at his own joke, and I resisted the urge to roll my eyes.

"I know that. But I'm not leaving without them."

"You're in luck. You're not leaving." Loki took a step back, still facing me. "Don't worry, Princess. They're perfectly safe. Come on. Talking to Sara is in your best interest."

"I've already met Sara," I said, attempting some kind of a protest.

I looked apprehensively back at the cell door, but Loki took another step away. I sighed, deciding that talking to higher-ups would probably be the only way I could barter for Matt and Rhys's release. Even if I couldn't ensure my own.

"How did you know?" I asked as I fell into step with him.

We walked side by side down the hall, passing several more doors like the one on my cell. I didn't hear much of anything or see any other hobgoblins standing guard, but I wondered how many other prisoners were here.

"Know what?"

"That I was . . . you know, trying to persuade you," I said. "If it wasn't working, how did you know?"

"Because you're powerful," Loki reiterated and gestured to his head. "It's like a static. I could feel you trying to push your way inside my head." He shrugged. "You'll feel it too, if anyone tries it on you. I'm not sure if it'd work, though."

"So it doesn't work on Trylle or Vittra?" I asked, doubting he would give me a straight answer. I wondered why he was telling me anything in the first place.

"No, it does. And if you were doing it well, I wouldn't have felt anything at all," Loki explained. "But we're harder to control than mänks. If you do a sloppy job of digging around in our heads, we'll feel it."

We reached some concrete steps, and Loki bounded up them, barely waiting for me. He showed no concern for me escaping, and he had divulged more information than he needed to. As far as I could tell, Loki was a really terrible guard. Ludlow should've had more authority over him.

He pushed through the massive doors at the top of the stairs, and we stepped out into a grand hall. Not a hallway kind of hall, but hall as in a large room with vaulted ceilings. The walls were dark wood with red accents, and an ornate red rug lay in the center of the floor.

It had the same kind of opulence as the palace in Förening, but the tones were deeper and richer. It felt more like a luxurious castle.

"This is really nice," I said, not hiding the surprise and awe in my voice.

"Yes, of course it is. It's the King's home." Loki looked at me, bemused by how stupefied I appeared. "What else would you expect?"

"I don't know. After being downstairs, I assumed something creepier and dirtier." I shrugged. "You didn't even have electricity down there."

"It's for dramatic effect. It's a dungeon." He led the way down a corridor decorated the same as the hall.

"What would happen if I tried to escape?" I asked.

I didn't see anyone else. If I outran Loki, I could probably get away. Not that I knew where to go, and I still wouldn't be able to free Matt and Rhys.

"I would stop you," he replied simply.

"The same way Kyra did at my house?" A pain flared up in my rib, as if reminding me of the damage she'd caused.

"No." Something dark flickered across his face for a second. He quickly erased it and smiled at me. "I would simply take you in my arms and hold you there until you swooned."

"It sounds romantic when you say it that way." I wrinkled my nose, remembering how he'd made me pass out by staring into my eyes. It hadn't been painful, but it hadn't exactly been pleasant either.

"It is when I envision it."

"That's a little twisted," I said, but he shrugged in response. "Why did you kidnap me and take me here?"

"I fear you have too many questions for me, Princess," Loki said, almost tiredly. "You'd do better saving them all for Sara. She's the one with the answers."

We walked the rest of the way without saying anything. He led me down the hall, up a flight of stairs carpeted in red velvet, and down another hall before stopping at ornate wooden double doors. Vines, fairies, and trolls were carved into them, depicting a fantasy scene in the vein of Hans Christian Andersen.

Loki knocked once with dramatic flair, then opened the doors without waiting for a response. I followed behind him.

"Loki!" Sara shouted. "You are to wait to be let into my chambers!"

Her room was much the same as the rest of the house. A large four-poster bed sat in the center, with unmade crimson sheets on top of it.

A dressing table sat on one side of the room, and she was perched on a small stool in front of it. Her hair was pulled up in the same tight ponytail as before, but she'd changed out of her clothes. A long black satin robe hung about her.

When she turned to look at us, the fabric moved as if it were liquid. Her brown eyes widened with shock at the sight of me, but she hurried to compose herself.

A hobgoblin stood next to her, the same kind as Ludlow. He

had attempted to dress up, wearing a small butler's uniform, but he had the same horrible skin and haggard appearance. Long necklaces, layered in diamonds and pearls, hung from his hands. At first I didn't understand why, but soon I realized he was holding them for her, like a living jewelry box.

A yapping ball of fur jumped off the bed when we came into the room. It stopped just short of us, and I saw it was only a Pomeranian. The majority of its rage seemed directed at me, and when Loki told it to be quiet, it fell silent. Eyeing me warily, the dog walked toward Sara.

"I didn't expect to see you so soon." Sara forced a smile at me, and her eyes turned icy when she looked at Loki. "I would've dressed if I had known you were coming."

"The Princess was getting restless." Loki lounged on a velvet couch near the end of the bed. "After the day she's had, I thought she deserved a break."

"I understand that, but I'm a tad unprepared at the moment." Sara continued glaring at him and gestured to her robe.

"Well, then you shouldn't have sent me to retrieve her so soon," Loki said, returning her stare evenly.

"You know that we had to do—" Sara cut herself off and shook her head. "Never mind. What's done is done, and you're absolutely right."

She smiled at me, her expression leaning toward something warm. Or at least something far warmer than my mother Elora ever managed.

"What's going on?" I asked.

Even after all they'd done, I still had no idea what the Vittra really wanted with me. I knew only that they refused to stop coming after me.

"Yes, we should talk." She tapped her fingers on the table for a minute while she thought. "Can you give us a minute, please?"

"Fine." Loki sighed and got to his feet. "Come on, Froud." The little dog ran happily to him, and Loki scooped him up. "The grown-ups need to talk."

The hobgoblin carefully set the jewelry on the table, and then headed toward the door. He walked slowly, his gait wobbly thanks to his stature, but Loki loitered so that the troll made it out of the room before him.

"Loki?" Sara said when he reached the doors, but she didn't look at him. "Make sure my husband is ready for us."

"As you wish." Loki made a small bow, still carrying the dog. When he walked out, he shut the doors behind him, leaving me alone with Sara.

"How are you feeling?" Sara offered a smile.

"Better. Thank you." I wasn't certain that I should be thanking her. She had healed me, but she had something to do with me getting hurt in the first place.

"You'll want to get changed." Sara nodded at my clothes as she stood up. "I might have something in your size."

"Thanks, but I don't really care about my clothes. I want to know what's going on. Why did you kidnap me?" I felt exasperated, and I knew it came out in my tone, but she didn't seem to notice.

"I'm sure I have something," Sara continued, as if I hadn't said anything. She walked over to a large closet in the corner and opened the door. "It might be a little big on you, but I'm sure it'll work." After looking for a matter of seconds, she pulled out a long black dress.

"I really don't give a damn about the clothes!" I snapped. "I want to know why you keep chasing after me. I can't give you what you want if I don't know what it is."

As she walked to the bed, I realized she was uncomfortable looking at me. Her eyes seemed to go everywhere but to me. And anytime they did land on me, she was quick to look away. She went over to the bed, laying my dress on it.

"You sent them out so we can talk and now you won't say anything?" I asked, growing even more frustrated.

"I've imagined this day for a long time." Sara lovingly touched the dress, smoothing it out on the bed. "Yet here it is, and I feel so unprepared."

"Seriously, what does that mean?"

Her expression grew pained for a minute, then returned to the same blank, serene look she'd worn before.

"I hope you don't mind, but I'm going to get dressed." She turned her back to me, walking over to a folding screen in the corner.

A fantasy scene similar to the one on the doors had been painted on it, and a black-and-red ball gown hung from the edge. Sara took the dress and went behind the screen to change in private.

"Do you know where Finn is?" I asked with a painful ache in my chest.

"That's your tracker?" Sara asked, draping the robe over the screen. I could only see the top of her head above it.

"Yes." I swallowed hard, fearing the worst.

"I'm not sure where he is. We don't have him, if that's what you're asking."

"Then why hasn't he come for me? How did he let you take me away?" I demanded.

"I assumed they detained him until they got away with you." She slipped the dress over her head, so her words were muffled for a moment. "I'm not certain of the specifics, but they had orders not to hurt anyone unless it was absolutely necessary."

"Yeah, and Kyra's orders were not to hurt me, right?" I asked wryly, but Sara didn't say anything. "Can you just tell me if he's okay?"

"Loki didn't report any fatalities," Sara said.

"He was in charge of bringing me here?" I looked at the closed doors behind us, realizing too late that I should've been asking him these questions. I thought about going after him, but then Sara came out from behind the screen.

"Yes. And other than Kyra's . . . outburst, Loki recounted that everything went well." She ran her hands along her skirt, then pointed to the dress on the bed. "Please. Get dressed. We're going to see the King."

"And he'll answer my questions?" I raised my eyebrow.

"Yes. I'm certain he'll tell you everything." Sara nodded, keeping her eyes locked on the floor.

I decided to go along with it. If he tried to give me the runaround, I would bolt. I didn't have time to waste on vague answers and evasive language. Matt and Rhys were captive, and Rhys couldn't even sit down.

But I also needed them to like me so that maybe I could talk them into letting Matt and Rhys go. If that meant I had to put on a silly little dress, so be it.

I went behind the screen and changed, while Sara continued getting ready. She put on one of the necklaces that the hobgoblin had left on the table and let down her hair. It was black and straight, shining like silk down her back. It reminded me of Elora's.

I wondered what Elora would make of all this. Would she send out a rescue mission to get me? Did she even know I was gone?

After I put on the dress, Sara tried to tie a loose ribbon on the back, but I wouldn't let her. She had reached out to touch it, and when I snapped at her to leave it alone, her expression fell into something tragic. Her hands hovered in the air for a moment, as if she couldn't believe what had just happened. Then she let them fall to her side and nodded.

Without saying anything, she led me down the hall. At the end, we came to another set of doors that mirrored the ones on her chamber. She knocked, and while we waited for a response, she smoothed down her crimson and black lace skirt again. It already lay perfectly flat, so I suspected this was some kind of nervous habit.

"Come in," a strong gravelly voice boomed from the other side of the doors.

Sara nodded, as if he could see her, then pushed open the doors.

The room was windowless, as had been every room I'd seen, and the walls were dark mahogany. Despite its massive size, the room had a cavelike quality. One wall was covered floor-to-ceiling with bookcases, and a heavy wooden desk sat nearby. Several elegant red chairs were the only other furniture.

The largest one, with intricate designs on the wooden feet, sat directly across from us, and a man sat in it. His dark brown hair ran long, past his shoulders. He wore all black—pressed pants, a dress shirt, and a long jacket that resembled a robe. He was handsome, in a battled kind of way, and he appeared to be in his forties.

Loki had been sitting in a chair, but he stood up when we came in. Froud the small dog had disappeared entirely, and I hoped they hadn't eaten it or something equally horrible.

"Ah, Princess." The King smiled when he saw me but didn't get up. His gaze flitted over to Loki for the briefest of seconds. "Loki, you are dismissed."

"Thank you, sire." Loki bowed and hastily departed. He left me with the impression that he didn't enjoy the company of the King, and that made me all the more nervous.

"So are you gonna tell me what's going on?" I asked the King directly, and his smile widened.

"I suppose we should start with the basics," he said. "I'm the King of the Vittra. My name is Oren, and I am your father."

kings & pawns

M y first thought was the most obvious: *He's lying.*

This was quickly followed by: *What if he isn't lying?*

Elora, by all accounts, had been a horrible mother who cared very little for me. I thought of the encounter I'd had a few minutes earlier with Sara. She had lovingly caressed my dress, saying, *I've imagined this day for a very long time.*

Sara stood nearby, wringing her hands. She met my eyes for the first time and smiled hopefully at me, but there still seemed to be a sadness in her face that I didn't understand.

I didn't look like her, not any more than I looked like Elora. They both far surpassed me in beauty, but Sara appeared much younger, only in her early thirties.

"So . . ." I swallowed, forcing my mouth to work, and turned to Oren. "You're saying that Elora isn't my mother?"

"No, unfortunately, Elora is your mother," he said with a heavy sigh.

This confused me even more. His admission gave more credence to his words, though. It would be simpler for him to lie to me. He could've told me that he and Sara were my parents, if his plan was to entice me into staying and taking his side.

But he'd told me that Elora was my mother, which left me with an alliance to her, which couldn't possibly benefit him.

"Why are you telling me this?" I asked.

"You need to know the truth. I know how fond of games Elora is." Every time Oren said her name, it came out bitterly, as if it hurt to speak it. "If you have all the facts, it will be easy for you to make a decision."

"And what decision is that?" I asked, but I thought I knew.

"The only decision that matters, of course." His lips twitched with a strange smile. "What kingdom you will rule."

"To be perfectly honest, I don't want to rule any kingdom." I twisted a stray curl that had come loose from my hair tie.

"Why don't you sit down?" Sara gestured to a chair behind me. After I sat, she took a seat nearer to the King.

"So . . ." I looked at her smiling sadly at me. "You're my step-mother?"

She nodded. "Yes."

"Oh." I sat in silence for a minute, taking it all in. "I don't understand. Elora told me my father was dead."

"Of course she did." Oren laughed darkly. "If she told you about me, she'd have to give you a choice, and she knew you'd never choose her."

"So how did you . . ." I floundered for the right word. "How exactly did the two of you . . . get together to . . . you know, conceive me?"

"We were married," Oren said. "This was long before I married Sara, and it was a rather brief union."

"You married Elora?" I asked and anger boiled up.

Initially, when he'd told me he was my father, I'd thought it was an illicit affair, like the one Elora had had with Finn's father. I didn't imagine that it'd be something of public record, something that every single person I'd met in Förening would've known about.

Including Finn. When he'd been going over the Trylle history, giving me a crash course on everything I needed to know about being a Princess, he'd failed to mention that my mother had been married to the Vittra King.

"Yes, briefly," Oren said. "We were wed because we thought it would be a good way to combine our respective kingdoms. Vittra and Trylle have had their disagreements over the years, and we wanted to create peace. Unfortunately, your mother is the most impossible, irrational, horrible woman on the planet." He smiled at me. "Well, you know. You've met her."

"Yes, I'm aware of how impossible she can be." I felt a strange urge to defend her, but I bit my tongue.

Elora had been cold, bordering on cruel at times, but for some reason, when Oren put her down, it offended me. But I nodded and smiled like I agreed completely.

"It's amazing I even managed to conceive a child with her," he said, more to himself than to me, and I cringed at the thought of it. I didn't need to picture Oren and Elora being intimate. "Before you were even born, the marriage was over. Elora took you, hid you, and I've been searching for you all these years."

"You did a horrible job of it," I said, and his expression hardened. "You do realize that your trackers have beaten me up on three separate occasions? Your wife had to come in and heal me so I didn't die."

"I am terribly sorry about that, and Kyra is being dealt with,"

Oren said, but he didn't sound apologetic. His words were hard and angry, but I hoped that was directed more at Kyra than at me. "But you wouldn't have died."

"How do you know that?" I asked sharply.

"Call it a King's intuition," Oren answered vaguely. I would've pressed further, but he continued, "I don't expect you to greet us with open arms. I know Elora's already had a chance to brainwash you, but I'd like you to take a few days to get to know our kingdom before making a decision to rule here."

"And what if I decide not to stay?" I asked, meeting his eyes evenly.

"Look around our kingdom first," Oren suggested. He smiled, but the edge to his voice was unmistakable.

"Let my friends go," I blurted out. That had been my motivation for speaking to him in the first place, but all this talk of parentage had gotten me sidetracked.

"I'd rather not," he said with that same weird smile.

"I won't stay here if you don't let them go," I said as firmly as I could.

"No, you won't leave if they're here." The gravel in his voice made his words carry greater severity. "They're insurance, so I can be sure that you take my offer *very* seriously."

He smiled at me, as if that would counteract the veiled threat, but the wicked edge to his smile made it worse somehow. The hair on the back of my neck stood up, and I was finding it harder to believe this man was my father.

"I promise you, I won't go anywhere." I struggled to hide the tremor in my voice. "If you let them go, I will stay as long as you want."

"I'll let them go when I believe you," he countered reasonably.

I swallowed hard, trying to think of another way to barter. "Who are these people that you have such concern for?"

"Um . . ." I considered lying to him, but he already knew I cared for them. "It's my brother, er, my . . . host brother or whatever, Matt, and my mänsklig, Rhys."

"They're still doing that practice?" Oren frowned in disapproval. "Elora absolutely despises change. She refuses to break from tradition, so this shouldn't come as a shock. But it's so outdated."

"What?" I asked.

"The whole mänsklig business. It's a total waste of resources." Oren gave a dismissive wave at the whole idea of it.

"What do you mean?" I asked. "What do you do with the baby you take when you leave a changeling?" When a baby is left with the host family then the family's original baby has to be taken.

"We don't take a baby," he said. My stomach twisted when I imagined them killing the infant, the way I had once feared the Trylle did. "We simply leave them behind, at human hospitals or orphanages. It's none of our concern what happens to them."

"Why don't Trylle do that?" I asked. Once he said it, it made sense, and I wondered why everyone didn't do that. It would be easier and cheaper.

"At first they took them as slave labor. Now they do it out of tradition." He shook his head, as if he thought nothing of it.

"It's a moot point, anyway." Oren exhaled deeply. "We rarely even practice changelings anymore."

"Really?" I asked. For the first time since I'd met him, it felt like I might actually agree with him about something.

"Changelings can get hurt, lost, or simply refuse us," Oren said. "It's a waste of a child, and it's killing our lineage. We're far more powerful than the humans. If we want something, we can take it. We don't need to risk our progeny in their clumsy hands."

He had a point, but I wasn't sure it was much better than Elora's. She worked more of a con job, and Oren proposed outright theft.

"She was unwilling to change the old ways." His face grew darker when he spoke of her. "She was so set on keeping the humans and trolls separate that she made their lives irrevocably tied, but she couldn't see the hypocrisy of it. She saw it as nothing more than having your children raised by nannies."

"It's entirely different," I said.

I thought of my childhood with the host mother who had tried to kill me, and my bond with Matt. I couldn't imagine any nanny taking care of a child in the same way.

"Exactly." He shook his head. "And that's why our marriage didn't work. I wanted you. She gave you away."

I knew his reasoning was twisted by some sort of flawed logic I couldn't quite pinpoint. But I felt myself surprisingly moved, even if I didn't entirely believe him. This was the first time any of my parents, host or real, had ever said they wanted me.

"Do I . . ." I said, refusing to let myself be overcome by emotion. "Do I have any siblings?"

Oren and Sara exchanged a look I couldn't read, and Sara stared down at her hands folded in her lap. She was the opposite of Elora in almost every way. Physically they were strikingly similar, with long black hair and beautiful dark eyes, but that's where the parallels ended. Sara spoke little, but conveyed a warmth and submissive nature that Elora would be incapable of.

"No. I have no other children, and Sara has no children at all," Oren said.

This fact seemed to sadden Sara further, so I had a feeling the lack of children had not been her choice.

"I'm sorry," I said.

"She's infertile," Oren announced without provocation, and Sara's cheeks reddened.

"Um . . . I'm sorry. I'm sure it's not her fault," I fumbled.

"No, it's not," Oren agreed heartily. "It's the curse."

"Pardon?" I asked, hoping I'd misheard him.

I didn't think I could take any more of the supernatural. Trolls and abilities were enough without adding curses on top of it.

"Legend has it that a spurned witch cursed the Vittra after we stole her child for a changeling." He shook his head as if he didn't believe it, which gave me some relief. "I don't give much credence to that. It is all part of the same thing that gives us abilities, the thing that we're descended from."

"What is?" I asked.

"We're all trolls. The Vittra, the Trylle, you, me, Sara. All of us are trolls." He gestured around. "And you've seen the trolls that live around here, the ones that look like hobgoblins?"

"You mean Ludlow?"

"Exactly. They're trolls, Vittra, the same as you and me," Oren explained. "But they're an abnormality that only seems to plague our colony."

"I don't understand. Where do they come from?"

"Us." He said it as if it made sense, and I shook my head. "Infertility runs rampant among us, and of the few births we have, over half of them are born as hobgoblins."

"You mean . . ." I wrinkled my nose, feeling a bit grossed out. "Vittra like you and Sara give birth to trolls like Ludlow?"

"Precisely," Oren said.

"That's actually kinda creepy," I said, and Oren wagged his head like he didn't entirely disagree.

"It's a curse of our longevity, not a bitter old woman's spell, but here we are." He sighed and smiled. "You, obviously, are far lovelier than anything we could've hoped for."

"You can't imagine how pleased we are to have you with us," Sara agreed.

Looking at her hopeful face, it finally dawned on me. I understood why the Vittra had been coming after me so aggressively and so relentlessly. They didn't have a choice. I was their only hope.

"You didn't marry Elora to unite your people," I said, sizing Oren up. "You did it because you couldn't have kids with a member of your own tribe. You needed an heir to the throne."

"You are my daughter." He raised his voice, not so he was shouting, but enough to make it boom through the room. "Elora has no more right to you than I do. And you will stay here because you are the Princess, and it is your duty."

"Oren. Your Majesty," Sara said, imploring him. "She has been through a tremendous amount today. She needs to rest and recuperate. It's impossible to have a reasonable conversation when she hasn't fully healed."

"Why hasn't she fully healed?" Oren gave her an icy glare, and she lowered her gaze.

"I did everything I could for her," Sara said quietly. "And it was not my fault she was injured in the first place."

"If Loki could keep the damn trackers in line," Oren growled. His temper didn't come as a surprise. I'd sensed it lying just below the surface.

"Loki did you a favor, Your Majesty," Sara argued politely.

"This is far beyond what his title dictates. If he hadn't been there, I'm certain things would've gone much worse."

"I'm done arguing with you about that idiot," he said. "If the Princess needs to rest, then show her to her room and leave me be."

"Thank you, sire." Sara stood up, doing a curtsy before him, and turned her attention to me. "Come, Princess. I'll show you to your room."

I wanted to protest, but I knew this wasn't the best time. Oren was ready to strike out against someone simply because he could, and I didn't want to give him any reason for it to be me.

Once we left the King's chambers and the doors were safely shut behind us, Sara began making apologies for him. All of this had been so trying for him. He'd spent nearly eighteen years trying to reach me, and Elora had made it as hard on him as she could. It had all come to a head tonight.

Sara wanted me to believe that he wasn't always this way, but I had a feeling that couldn't be further from the truth. Oren had given me the impression that this was him in a good mood.

When we reached a room nearer to hers, Sara let me in. It was a smaller, more sparsely furnished version of hers, and she expressed regret for the lack of clothing. So their home wasn't stocked the way Förening had been for me. Not that I minded. Clothing and accommodations weren't my priority.

"You don't really expect me to stay here, do you?" I asked. She went about my room, turning on the lights and showing me where things were. "Not when my friends are being held prisoner in the dungeon."

"I expect that you don't have a choice," Sara said carefully. Her words didn't carry the same threat as Oren's. Rather, she was stating a fact.

"You have to help me." I went over to her, appealing to her obvious maternal instinct. "They're down there without food or water. I can't let them stay that way."

"I can assure you that they are safe and will be taken care of." She met my eyes, impressing upon me that she told the truth. "As long as you are here, they will be fed and clothed."

"That's not good enough." I shook my head. "They don't have a bed or a bathroom." I didn't mention that Rhys couldn't sit, and I had no clue how to break the spell I'd accidentally put him under.

"I am sorry," Sara said sincerely. "I can promise you that I will check on them myself to ensure they are being properly cared for, but that's the best I can do."

"Can't you put them in another room or something? Lock them in a spare bedroom." I wasn't thrilled about them being captive no matter what, but getting them out of the dungeon would be a step in the right direction.

"Oren would never allow it." She shook her head. "It'd pose too great a risk. I'm sorry." She looked helplessly at me, and I realized that was the best I could get from her. "I'll get you some appropriate clothing to sleep in."

I sighed and sat on the bed. Once she left, I let my body sag from exhaustion. The emotional roller coaster I'd been on had left me depleted and worn out.

But as tired as I was, I knew I couldn't sleep. Not until I knew that Matt and Rhys were safe.

SEVEN

dungeons & heroes

It's not as if I had a plan or even knew where I was going. Sara had brought me clothes—yoga pants and a tank top, both in black. I changed because sneaking around in a dress didn't sound like much fun, and then I crept out into the hall.

I tried to remember the way Loki had led me up here, but they had dimmed the lights, making it even harder for me to recognize my unfamiliar surroundings. As I recalled, we didn't take that many turns. It should be fairly simple.

The hardest part would be figuring out what to do once I found the dungeon. Maybe I could use persuasion on the guard. Or if it was another hobgoblin, I could overpower him and get him to open the door.

I found the winding staircase. It only led down to the main floor, so I still had to find the rest of the route to the dungeon.

When I reached the bottom of the steps, I heard voices. I froze, debating whether I should run or hide, before deciding that staying in the shadows would be the way to go. I hurried behind the staircase and crouched down, making myself as small as possible.

The voices got louder as they came closer, and they appeared to be arguing about how to make the best squash. My heart pounded so loudly I was certain they could hear it, and I held my breath. Moments later, I saw the feet of two hobgoblins walking past.

One of them appeared to be female, with long ratty hair in a braid down her back. They really were unattractive creatures, but based on the way they talked, they seemed harmless. They sounded more human and normal than some of the Trylle I'd encountered in Förening.

I waited a few minutes until I was sure that the hobgoblins had disappeared down the hall before I started breathing again. I figured I could take them, but I didn't want to beat up random strangers. Besides that, they could make noise and alert everyone else in the palace, including Oren.

I stepped out from underneath the staircase and almost ran into Loki. He leaned casually against the stairs, his elbow resting on the railing and his legs crossed at the ankles. I nearly screamed, but I caught myself, knowing that drawing further attention would only make things worse.

"Hello, Princess." Loki grinned at me. "Couldn't sleep?"

He and Ludlow had been calling me "Princess" from the beginning, and I thought they were taunting me about my standing with the Trylle. But I realized I was their Princess too, and he was actually giving me some form of reverence.

Unfortunately, I knew that my title pulled no weight with him. Right now I was a prisoner too.

"Yeah, I just . . . I needed something to eat," I fumbled.

"A likely story," he said, and his expression became skeptical. "If only I could believe you."

"I haven't had anything to eat all day." While that was actually the truth, my nerves had my stomach too racked to even think about eating.

"What do you plan to do?" Loki asked, ignoring my feeble excuse. "Even if you find the dungeon, how will you get them out?"

"I won't, now. You're gonna run and tell on me, aren't you?" I studied his eyes, trying to get a read on him, but he looked as amused as he always did.

"Maybe." He shrugged as if he hadn't decided yet. "Let me hear your plan. It's probably not even worth bothering anyone with."

"What makes you say that?" I asked.

"You seem like a self-saboteur," he said. I opened my mouth to protest, and he laughed at my obvious indignation. "Don't take it personally, Princess. It happens to the best of us."

"I'm not going to stop until I get my friends out of here."

"Now that I believe." He leaned in toward me. "This all goes so much easier when you're honest."

"Like I'm the one being devious," I scoffed.

"I haven't lied to you yet," he said, sounding oddly serious.

"All right, then," I said. "How do I break my friends out of the dungeon?"

"Just because I don't lie doesn't mean I'll answer you." Loki smiled.

"Fine. I'll find them myself."

I felt confident he wouldn't stop me, although I didn't know why he wouldn't. If Oren found out that he was even indulging my plans for escape, I'm sure it wouldn't bode well for him.

When I brushed past him, walking down the corridor to where I thought the main hall was, he followed me. I tried to walk quickly, but he matched my pace with ease.

"You think it's this way, do you?" Loki asked, a teasing lilt in his voice.

"Don't try to confuse me. I know my directions. I don't get lost," I lied. I got lost a lot. "Isn't that a Trylle affinity or something?"

"I don't know. I'm not Trylle," he replied. "And neither are you."

"I'm half Trylle," I said defensively.

Why was I defending it? I didn't even want to be Trylle, or Vittra, or anything. Plain ordinary human had suited me just fine my whole life. Now that I found myself in this ethnic quagmire, I felt strangely protective of the Trylle and Förening. Apparently, I cared more than I thought I did.

"You're rather feisty for a Princess," Loki remarked, watching me as I walked purposefully down the hallway.

"How many Princesses have you met?" I countered.

"None." He tilted his head thoughtfully. "I suppose I thought you'd be more like Sara. She isn't feisty at all."

"Sara's not my mother," I said.

When we reached the main hall, I wanted to jump up and down, but it didn't seem appropriate. Besides, I'd only found the doorway to the dungeon. I still had to actually rescue Matt and Rhys.

"Now what?" Loki asked, pausing in the center of the hall.

"I go down and get them." I pointed to the large doors leading down to the basement.

"No, I don't very much care for that idea." He shook his head.

"Of course you don't. You don't want me to get them out," I said. My heart beat rapidly, and I wondered exactly how far Loki would let me take this.

"That's not why. It just doesn't seem very interesting." He pushed up the sleeves of his sweater, revealing his tanned forearms. "In fact, I'm rather bored with the whole thing. Why don't we do something else?"

"No, I'm getting them out," I said. "I won't let you keep us prisoner here."

He laughed darkly at that and shook his head.

"Why is that funny?" I demanded, crossing my arms over my chest.

"You say that as if *I'm* the one holding you captive." He'd glanced away from me, but when he looked back, he smiled bitterly and his eyes were sad. "This is Ondarike. We're all prisoners here."

"You expect me to believe that you're being held against your will?" I raised a skeptical eyebrow. "You're roaming around the castle freely."

"As are you." He turned away from me then. "Not all prisons have bars. You should know that better than anyone, Princess."

"So you're not the King's head henchman?" I asked.

"I didn't say that either." Loki shrugged, apparently tiring of the conversation. "I'm saying that since I can't help you with your friends, we ought to find something else to do."

"I'm not doing anything else until I get them," I insisted.

"But you haven't heard what I'd like to do instead." His expression changed from morose to playful, and there was something in his eyes that made me feel funny.

Not bad, and not the same as when he made me pass out. It wasn't a magic Vittra power or anything. It was just a look that made me feel sort of . . . fluttery inside.

Before I had time to analyze what I felt or what he meant, a loud banging at the main doors interrupted us. The hall where we stood contained two sets of doors—the ones leading to the lower level, and the massive ones leading outside. These dwarfed the ones in the King's and Queen's chambers.

The banging came again, making me jump, and Loki moved in front of me. Was he protecting me? Or hiding me?

The doors flew open, and joy surged through me.

Tove had blown the doors open with his abilities, and he stood on the other side of them, looking astonishingly badass. Tove was a rather foxy and very powerful Trylle I'd known in Förening. His quirky, antisocial personality had endeared him to me, but he was also the last person I'd expected to see here. His abilities did allow him to move objects with his mind, though, so he was a very powerful ally to have.

Then I caught sight of who he had with him. Duncan and Finn stood behind him, letting him throw open the doors while they waited to rush in. As soon as I saw Finn, my heart wanted to explode.

I'd been so afraid he had been hurt or I might never see him again, and there he was.

"Finn! You're okay!" I rushed past Loki and ran to Finn.

I threw my arms around him, and for a brief second he hugged me. The strength of his embrace let me know how worried he had been about me. But almost as soon as I felt it, he cut it short, and pushed me away.

"Wendy, we have to get out of here," Finn said, as if I'd suggested that we vacation here.

"Matt and Rhys are here. We have to get them first."

I turned to start telling Finn about the dungeon, and I saw that Tove had Loki pinned up high on the wall. Tove stood several feet back, holding his hand out at Loki, and Loki hung suspended in the air, his face grimacing in pain.

"No, Tove! Don't hurt him!" I yelled.

Tove glanced at me but didn't question my command. He lowered Loki to the floor and released him, leaving Loki gasping for breath. Loki held his side, bending over.

Tove wasn't a violent guy by nature, but after the horrible battle he'd had with the Vittra a few days ago, I didn't blame him for being a little preemptive.

"Let's get you out of here," Duncan said, grabbing my arm as if he meant to drag me out. I glared at him, and he instantly dropped his hand. "Sorry, Princess. But we need to hurry."

"I'm not leaving without Matt and Rhys," I reiterated, and turned to Loki. "Will you help me get them?"

His eyes met mine, and his cocky demeanor had completely disappeared. He looked conflicted and pained, and I knew it wasn't just from Tove hurting him. A few moments ago, he'd seemed to understand what I was going through, but he'd felt unable to help. Now he had a chance, an excuse, and I hoped he would take it.

"We can come back for them," Finn said.

Nobody had rushed to the hall yet to investigate the commotion, but it was only a matter of time before someone did. And I knew it would serve us well not to tangle with Oren.

"No. We can't leave. If we do, he'll kill them." I kept my eyes on Loki, pleading with him. "Loki, please."

"Princess . . ." Loki let his voice trail off.

"Tell the King we overpowered you. Blame it all on us," I said. "He never needs to know you helped us."

Loki didn't answer immediately, and that was too long for Finn. He left my side and went over to Loki, grabbing his arm roughly.

"Where are they?" Finn demanded, but Loki didn't respond.

Knowing we had to hurry, I ran toward the dungeon and everyone followed, Finn dragging Loki along with us. "This way," I said with anxious fervor.

I threw open the basement door and almost tumbled down the stairs in my hurry, but Finn caught my arm before I fell. Duncan actually did trip, thanks to his shoelaces, and I rolled my eyes as I waited for him to catch up.

"What the heck is that?" Duncan asked when he saw the hobgoblin guarding Matt and Rhys's cell. It wasn't Ludlow, but a hobgoblin just like him.

They all stopped short at the sight of him. The shocked reaction of Duncan, Finn, and Tove pleased me. Apparently I wasn't the only one unfamiliar with this particular type of Vittra. I wasn't sure if that meant Oren was very good at keeping secrets or if Elora was, but I had a feeling it was probably both.

"Never mind him." I walked over to the door, pushing the troll out of my way easily.

He didn't put up much of a fight. At the sight of the four of us, with Loki as a hostage, he knew he didn't stand a chance. He started to take off, but Tove stopped him, pinning him against a wall and preventing him from alarming anyone.

"This is pretty weak security," Duncan said. He watched the hobgoblin wiggle against the wall, while I went over to unlock the door.

"We didn't really expect anyone to break in," Loki said. He enunciated his words more than he needed to, as if he were in pain or talking to a small child, but he made no attempt to free himself from Finn's grip.

"Well, that was pretty stupid." Duncan laughed. "I mean, she's the Princess. It's not rocket science that we'd come after her."

"No, I suppose not," Loki said tightly.

"I don't understand this!" I said after futilely twisting at things that did nothing. It had to be the most labyrinthine system of locks I'd ever encountered. I looked to Loki. "Can you do this?"

He sighed, and Finn jerked on his arm. Both Loki and I glared at him, but Finn only acknowledged mine.

"Just help her," Finn said, reluctantly releasing him.

Wordlessly, Loki went over to the door and began unlocking it. I watched him, and I still didn't completely understand what he did. The bolts clicked loudly, and I could hear Rhys shouting something from inside the cell. Finn kept his eyes on Loki, watching for a wrong move, and Duncan looked around, commenting on the dankness of the dungeon.

As soon as the door opened, Matt and Rhys shot out, nearly knocking over Loki in the process. Rhys hugged me in his enthusiasm, and while I couldn't see the angry look I'm sure Finn gave him over that, I could see the way Matt glared at Finn.

This whole situation could become an awful mess, but we didn't have time for it.

"You had something to do with this, didn't you?" Matt asked, his eyes locked on Finn.

"Matt, knock it off," I said, untangling myself from Rhys's hug. "He's here to rescue us, and we have to get out of here. So shut up, and let's go."

"Somebody has to come after us soon, right?" Duncan asked, bewildered by the lack of a counterattack.

"Let's just get out of here," Matt said, taking the cue.

Tove released the hobgoblin pinned to the wall, and the guys all rushed ahead, leading our escape from the dungeon.

I paused, looking back at Loki. He stood in front of the cell door, looking weirdly forlorn. His earlier bravado had completely disappeared, and his golden eyes settled on me.

"Wait a few minutes to tell Oren we're gone, okay?" I asked.

"As you wish," Loki said simply. Something in the way he looked at me stirred up that fluttery feeling I'd had upstairs.

"Thank you for letting us go," I said, but he didn't say anything to that. After hearing what he'd said earlier, I considered asking him to come with us. In fact, I almost did, but then Finn jarred me from the idea.

"Wendy!" Finn snapped.

I ran to catch up, then Finn took my hand. That small touch felt strong and safe, and sent warm tingles running through me. As we raced up the stairs, holding his hand almost made me forget that he'd hurt me or that we were escaping from an enemy prison.

The cold night air hit me when we ran outside. Duncan led the way, stumbling through the dark with Rhys at his heels. Both Tove and Matt kept stopping to make sure that Finn and I were coming, with Matt's gaze particularly wary.

The ground felt icy, and branches and rocks stung my bare feet. Whenever I slowed down, Finn squeezed my hand, and that spurred me on. The air smelled of winter, like ice and pines, and I heard an owl hooting in the distance.

I glanced behind me once, but since the palace had no windows to light it up, I could hardly make out its dark shape looming behind us.

Finn's silver Cadillac waited for us at the edge of the trees. The moon filtered through the branches, glinting on the car, and I quickened my pace. I didn't have the stamina to run all the way to Förening, and I had become a little afraid I might have to.

When we reached the car, Duncan had already jumped in back, and Matt stood next to the open car door, waiting for me to get there. Rhys stood next to him, but he was far more anxious, shifting his weight from one leg to the other.

"Get in the car! Let's go!" Finn commanded, looking at them like they were idiots. Tove was the only one who complied, climbing in the front passenger's side.

"Wendy," Rhys said. "I can't sit down."

"What?" Finn looked irritated, his eyes bouncing between Rhys and me.

"I used my persuasion on him, and I got him stuck—" I tried to explain lamely, but Finn cut me off.

"Just tell him to get in the damn car," Finn said. I didn't understand, so he elaborated. "Use the persuasion. Make him sit in the car. We'll sort it out when we get home."

I looked at Rhys, barely able to make out his eyes in the moonlight, but I didn't know if seeing him actually mattered. Using all my concentration, I told him to get in the car. A few seconds later, he got in the car and let out a massive sigh of relief.

"It feels sooo good to sit down!" Rhys said, and a fresh guilt washed over me.

Matt got in the car after him, but he didn't close the door. He was waiting for me to get in back with him, but Finn still had my hand. He led me around the front of the car, and I got in the driver's side. I slid over so he could drive and sat on the armrest hump in the middle.

Matt started to voice his complaints, but Finn put the car in drive. Matt swore, slamming the car door shut as Finn sped off down the road. The rest of us settled into a tense silence. I think we all had expected the Vittra to put up more of a fight, especially after the way they'd pursued me. This felt almost . . . too easy.

"That's weird," Duncan said. "They didn't do anything. They didn't even try to stop us."

"We did just damage their army," Tove said, offering some kind of an explanation. "I'm sure most of their people are recuperating or . . ." He trailed off, unwilling to verbalize that the Trylle had been forced to kill some of the Vittra in the attack.

Duncan made a few more comments about how strange it was and how Ondarike was different from how he'd thought it'd be. Nobody said anything in response, so eventually he stopped talking.

I got as comfortable as my seat would allow. Once I felt safe, my exhaustion really had a chance to take hold, and it no longer mattered where I was sitting.

I rested my head on Finn's shoulder, taking a small, private glee in being close to him. As I drifted off to sleep, I could hear him breathing, and that definitely helped me relax.

EIGHT

predictions

It may have felt good falling asleep next to Finn, but it did not feel good waking up. My body still felt sore from Kyra's recent attack, and the uncomfortable way I'd slept had left me full of kinks and aches.

When Finn pulled up in front of the house, I stretched, and my neck screamed at me. I got out of the car, rolling my shoulders, and Matt stared up at the mansion with shock.

Opulent and gorgeous, it really was a palace, resting on the bluffs of the Mississippi River, vines covering the white exterior. It hung off the edge, held up by thin pillars, and the entire wall facing the river was made of glass. I remembered how the mansion's elegance had hit me when I first arrived, but now I was too angry to even look at it.

I wanted to talk to Matt about everything, but I had to talk to Elora first. She had lied to me, again. If I had known that the Vittra King was my father, I never would've taken Rhys to see Matt. I would never have put them in danger that way.

When we went into the house, I left Rhys to help show Matt

around. I hadn't figured out how to fix him yet, so I'd settled for telling him to stand up, and leaving Finn and Tove to help him sort it out.

Finn told me I should calm down first, but I ignored him and stormed down the hall to see Elora. She didn't scare me anymore, not in the slightest. Oren would actually hurt me. At her worst, Elora would just humiliate me.

The palace was divided into two massive wings, separated by a rotunda that served as the front hall. All of the official business took place in the south wing, where there were meeting rooms, a ballroom, a massive dining hall, offices, the throne room, as well as staff quarters and the Queen's bedroom.

The north wing held the more casual rooms in the house, like my room, guest bedrooms, and the kitchen. Elora's sitting parlor was at the far end of the north wing. It was a corner room, so two walls were made entirely of windows. She spent most of her free time there, painting and reading, and whatever else she did to relax.

"When were you gonna tell me that Oren is my father?" I demanded, throwing open the door.

Elora lay on her chaise lounge, her dark gown flowing out around her. Even in repose, she had an innate elegance to her. Her poise and beauty were qualities I'd been envious of when I first met her, but now I saw them as nothing more than a weak façade. Everything she did was for appearance, and I doubted that anything went deeper than that with her.

I stood just inside her parlor, my arms crossed over my chest. She held her arm over her eyes, as if the light were too painful to deal with. She was plagued by regular migraines, so that might have been the case now. Or maybe not, since she left the blinds open on the glass walls, letting the morning light stream in.

"I'm glad to see you're safe," she said but didn't move her arm so she could actually see me.

"I can tell." I walked over and stood directly in front of her. "Elora. You need to tell me the truth. You can't keep hiding stuff from me this way, not if you want me to rule someday. I'd make a very horrible Queen if I was ignorant to everything."

I decided to play it reasonable, instead of shouting all the things I really wanted to say.

"And now you know the truth." She sounded tired of the conversation already, and it'd only just begun. She finally lowered her arm, wearily meeting my angry stare with her dark eyes. "Why are you looking at me that way?"

"That's all you have to say to me?" I asked.

"What more do you want me to say?" Elora sat up in one smooth, graceful move. When I didn't back down, she stood up, apparently not fond of the idea of me looking down on her.

"I was just kidnapped by the Vittra, the King of whom is my father, and you have *nothing* to say to me?" I stared at her incredulously, and she walked away, putting her back to me as she went over to the window.

"I'd feel more sympathetic to your plight if you hadn't run away." She folded her arms over her chest, almost hugging herself as she stared out at the river flowing below. "I specifically forbade you from leaving the compound, and we all told you it was for your own protection. After the attack, you knew firsthand the dangers of leaving, and you left. It's not my fault you put yourself in that situation."

"Because of the attack I thought they'd be too injured and afraid to try anything like that again!" I yelled. "I didn't think the Vittra would have any reason to keep coming after me, but I would've if I had known about my father."

"You took your life into your own hands when you left, and you knew it," Elora said simply.

"Dammit, Elora!" I shouted. "This isn't about placing blame, okay? I want to know why you lied. You told me my father was dead."

"It was far simpler and cleaner than telling you the truth." She said that like it would make everything okay. It was easier lying to me, so that's fine. I wouldn't want to make her life complicated or anything.

"What is the truth?" I asked her directly.

"I married your father because it was the right thing to do." She didn't say anything more for so long I thought she might not continue, but then she said, "The Vittra and Trylle have been fighting for centuries, maybe forever."

"Why?" I stepped closer to her, but she didn't look at me.

"Various reasons." She gave a slight shrug. "The Vittra have always been more aggressive than we, but we're more powerful. It led to an odd power structure, and they were always jostling for more control, more land, more people."

"So you thought marrying Oren would end centuries of fighting?"

"My parents thought so. They had arranged it before I even came to Förening." Elora had been a changeling, like I had, though she rarely spoke of it. "I could've contested it, of course, the way you contested your name."

She said that last part somewhat bitterly. As part of returning to the Trylle, I was supposed to undergo a christening ceremony and change my name to something more fitting. I hadn't wanted to, and thanks to the Vittra busting up the ceremony, I hadn't had to. Elora had relented and allowed me to keep my own name, and I'd been the first Princess to do so in our history.

"But you didn't contest it?" I asked, ignoring her little jab at me.

"No. I had to put my own wants behind the greater good of the people. That's something you'll have to learn to do." The light shone on her hair as if she had a halo. She turned back to the window, and it was gone.

"If a simple wedding would end the abhorrence, then I had to do it," Elora continued. "I had to think of the lives and wasted energy of both the Trylle and Vittra."

"So you married him," I finished for her. "Then what happened?"

"Not a lot. We weren't married for very long." She rubbed her arm, stifling a chill only she felt. "I'd met him a handful of times before the wedding, and he'd been on his best behavior. I hadn't loved him, but . . ."

She didn't finish her thought, and the way she let it hang in the air led me to believe that she had cared for him.

I couldn't imagine Elora caring for anyone. When she flirted with Garrett Strom, it seemed like a show. I'm not sure if they were actually dating or not, but he seemed to like her and hung around a lot. Plus, he was a Markis, so she could marry him if she wanted.

Both Finn and Rhys had told me of a secret, long-standing affair that Elora had had with Finn's father, after my own father was gone. He'd been a tracker and was married to Finn's mother, so they could never be together openly, but Rhys claimed that she truly loved him.

"What happened after you were married?" I asked.

Elora had been lost in thought for a moment, and when I brought her out of it, she shook her head.

"It didn't go well," she said simply. "He wasn't outright cruel, which made things harder. I couldn't leave him, not without just cause. Not with so much riding on it."

"But you did eventually?"

"Yes. After you were conceived, he . . ." She paused, searching for the right word. "He became too much for me to bear. Right before you were born, I left him, and I hid you. I wanted a strong family to protect and shelter you, should he come looking."

"Is that why Finn started tracking me so early?" I asked.

Trackers usually waited to retrieve changelings until they were eighteen or so, once they were legal adults with access to trust funds. Finn had been following me around since the beginning of my senior year, making me one of the youngest changelings ever to return.

He'd claimed it was because I moved around so much, they were afraid of losing me, but now I suspected that they'd been afraid the Vittra would get to me first.

"Yes." Elora nodded. "Thankfully, I wasn't yet Queen of the Trylle when we separated. Oren may have been King of the Vittra, but he was only a prince here. He had no standing over the kingdom. Otherwise things could've gone a lot differently."

"When did you become Queen?" I asked, momentarily distracted from information about Oren.

I couldn't imagine Elora as a Princess. I knew she must've been young and inexperienced at one time, but she had the regality of someone who had always been Queen.

"Not long after you were born." Elora turned to me. "But I am glad that you're here."

"I almost didn't make it back," I said, trying to elicit some concern from her. She raised an eyebrow but said nothing. "Their tracker, Kyra, beat the crap out of me. I would've died if Oren wasn't married to a healer."

"You wouldn't have died." She brushed me off, the same way everybody seemed to when I told them of Kyra hurting me.

"I was coughing up blood! I think a broken rib punctured a lung or something." My ribs still ached, and I'd been certain that I would die in that dungeon.

"Oren would never let you die," Elora said dismissively. She stepped away from the window and sat down on the chaise lounge, but I stayed standing.

"Maybe not," I admitted. "But he could've killed Matt and Rhys."

"Matt?" She was confused for a minute, an expression that looked unusual on her.

"My brother. Er, my host brother, or whatever you wanna call him." I grew tired of trying to explain him as anything else and decided that from here on out, I'd just call him my brother. As far as I was concerned, he still was.

"Are they here now?" Her expression shifted from confusion to irritation.

"Yeah. I wasn't going to leave them there. Oren would kill them to spite me." I wasn't sure if that was true or not, but it felt true.

"You all made it out of there, then?" For a second she sounded and looked as if she actually cared. It was nowhere near Matt's level of concern, but at least it resembled something human and loving.

"Yeah. We did. Finn and Tove got us out of there without any problem." I furrowed my brow, remembering how easy it had been to escape.

"Did something happen?" Elora asked, homing in on my unease.

"No." I shook my head. "And that's just it. *Nothing* happened. We practically walked right out of there."

"Well, that is Oren for you." She rolled her eyes. "He's too arrogant, and that's always been his downfall."

"What do you mean?"

"He's powerful, *very* powerful." Elora's tone held a sense of awe I hadn't witnessed from her before. "But he's always thought that he could take anything he wanted and no one would stop him. It's true most trolls are too afraid to cross him. He incorrectly assumed I would fall into that category."

"But I'm your daughter. He didn't think you'd even try?" I asked dubiously.

"Like I said, he's too arrogant." She rubbed her temple and settled back on the chaise.

Elora had the gift of precognition, as well as some other telekinetic powers. I didn't know the extent of them all, but I hoped to get a better grasp soon.

I turned to look at her paintings more closely, which she used to predict the future. She only had two completed in the room, and one she'd recently started. The new one only had a swatch of blue painted in the corner, so I couldn't get anything from that.

The first finished one showed the garden behind the house. It started under the balcony and ran down the bluff, surrounded by a brick wall. I'd only been in it once, and it had been idyllic, thanks to the Trylle magic that kept it perpetually in bloom.

In her painting, the garden was covered in a light snow that glimmered and sparkled like diamonds. But the stream, flowing like a waterfall to a fountain in the center, hadn't frozen over. Despite the wintry scene, all the flowers were still in full bloom. Petals of pink and blue and purple glistened with a light frost, making it all look like an exotic fairyland.

Elora had a breathtaking skill for painting, and I would've commented on it if I'd thought my opinion mattered to her. The beauty of the garden painting enraptured me so much it took me a moment to realize there was something dark lurking in it.

A figure stood by the hedge. It appeared to be a man with hair far lighter than my own, but the shadows made it hard to tell. He stood in the distance, making his face too blurry to be distinguishable.

Even though I couldn't see much, there was something menacing about him. Or at least Elora thought so when she painted him. I got that vibe from the canvas.

"When did you know the Vittra had gotten me?" I asked, realizing she might've known all along.

"When Finn told me," she answered absently. "He came and retrieved Tove, and then left to get you."

"And you just . . ." I was about to ask why she let them go without sending along help, like an army, perhaps. But my gaze had moved on to the other painting and I stopped.

This one showed me, a close-up from my waist up. The background was a blur of blacks and grays, giving no indication of where I stood. I appeared much the same as I did now, except dressed much better. My hair was down and the dark curls were arranged beautifully. I had on a gorgeous white gown, decorated with diamonds that matched my necklace and the ones in my earrings.

But what was most striking was that on my head I wore a crown, ornately twisted silver adorned with diamonds. My face looked expressionless, and I couldn't tell if I was pleased or upset to be crowned, but there it was. A picture of me as Queen.

"When did you paint this?" I pointed to the picture and turned to Elora. She had her arm draped over her eyes, but she lifted it up to see what I was asking about.

"Oh, that." She dropped her arm. "Don't concern yourself with that. You'll drive yourself mad trying to discern and prevent the future. It's much better letting things unfold."

"Is this why you never seemed worried about me dying?" I asked, surprised at how angry I felt.

She knew I wouldn't die. She had proof that I'd someday be Queen, and she hadn't bothered letting me in on that.

Elora sighed. "Among other things."

"What does that mean?" I snapped. "Why do you always have to be so damn cryptic all the time?"

"It doesn't mean anything!" She sounded exasperated. "For all I know, that painting means you'll be the Vittra Queen. The future is far too fluid to ever understand or change. And just because I paint something doesn't mean it'll come true."

"But you predicted the attack at my christening ceremony," I countered. "I saw the painting. You painted the ballroom on fire."

"Yes, and I couldn't stop it," she said icily.

"You didn't even try! You didn't warn me or cancel the ceremony!"

"I tried to stop it!" She shot me an angry glare that would've made me cringe before, but not anymore. "I met with people. I discussed it with everyone. I told Finn and all the trackers. But I had nothing to go on. I only saw fire and chandeliers and smoke.

No people. Not the room. Not even a time frame. Do you know how many chandeliers there are in the south wing alone? What was I supposed to do? Tell everyone to avoid chandeliers forever?"

"No. I don't know," I stammered. "You could've done . . . something."

"It's not until after that I understand what the vision means," Elora said, more to herself than me. "It's that way with all of them. It's almost worse being able to see the future. I don't know what it means, and I can't stop it. Only after, it all seems so obvious."

"So then what are you saying?" I asked. "I won't be Queen?"

"No. I'm saying that the painting doesn't mean anything." She closed her eyes and rubbed the bridge of her nose. "I'm getting a terrible migraine. I'd rather not continue this conversation."

"Fine. Whatever." I threw my hands up in the air, knowing I couldn't force things with Elora. I was lucky she hadn't summoned Finn to drag me out of here.

Then I remembered him, Finn. I hadn't been able to say much of anything in the car ride to Förening, but I definitely still had a lot to say to him.

I left the parlor to go track down Finn. I should have been more concerned with other things, but right then I only wanted to find a moment alone with him. A moment when we could really talk and I could . . . I don't know. But I had to see him.

Instead of Finn, I found Duncan waiting a little ways down the hall. He'd been leaning against the wall, playing with his phone, but when I came out of the room he straightened up. He offered a sheepish smile, and his attempt at quickly shoving his phone in his pocket only made him drop it.

"Sorry." Duncan scrambled to pick it up as I approached. "I just wanted to give you alone time with your mother."

"Thanks." I continued down the hall, and he followed along. "Why were you waiting for me? Did you need something?"

"No. I'm your tracker now. Remember?" He looked embarrassed. "And the Vittra are really after you, so I'm on guard all the time."

"Right." I nodded. I'd been hoping that since Finn had saved my life—again—he'd be reinstated as my tracker. "Where's Finn? I need to talk to him."

"Finn?" Duncan's steps faltered. "Um, he's not your tracker anymore."

"No, I know that. And it's not a condemnation of your ability." I forced a smile. "I wanted to talk to Finn for a minute."

"No, yeah." He shook his head. "It's just that . . ." Unsure why he was so flustered, I stopped walking. "I mean, he's not your tracker. So . . . he left."

"He left?" I felt that familiar pang shoot through my heart.

I shouldn't be surprised, and I shouldn't let it hurt me anymore. But the wound sprang open fresh, just like when he'd left before.

"Yeah." Duncan stared at his feet and fiddled with the zipper on his jacket. "You're safe and everything. His job's done, right?"

"Right," I said numbly.

I could've asked where Finn had gone, and maybe I should've. He couldn't have gotten too far that fast. I was sure Finn would say he left to protect me, or protect my honor, or something like that. But I didn't care.

Right then, it didn't matter what his reasons were. All I knew was that I was sick of him breaking my heart.

NINE

underrated

Tove couldn't fix Rhys because that wasn't how his abilities worked. When I went upstairs after my talk with Elora, I had to send Rhys down for her to fix him. I could've gone with him, but I figured Elora had had her fill of me for the day.

Tove went to his house to get some rest, and I thanked him for everything he'd done. Without him, I'm not entirely sure we could've gotten out. Even though Oren's security was lax, it was Tove who had gotten in and kept the trolls at bay.

Rhys had started getting Matt settled in one of the spare rooms down the hall from mine. I went to see how he was doing, and Duncan seemed far too content to follow at my heels. It took a lot of convincing, but I managed to get him to wait outside. Duncan didn't trust Matt because he was human, but if he was going to be my tracker, he had to learn to deal with it.

Matt stood in the middle of the room looking lost, and he'd never been the kind of guy who got lost. He'd changed into a pair of sweatpants that fit okay, but his T-shirt was snug, so I assumed he'd borrowed them from Rhys.

"How are you doing with all of this?" I asked, closing the bedroom door quietly as I came in. I knew Duncan was keeping his post outside, and I didn't want him listening. Not that I planned on saying anything secret. I just wanted a moment alone with my brother.

"Um . . . great?" He gave me a sad smile and shook his head. "I don't know. How am I supposed to be doing?"

"About like this."

"None of this seems real, you know?" Matt sat down on the bed and sighed. "I keep thinking I'll wake up and this will all be a very strange dream."

"I know the feeling *exactly*." I remembered how confusing and scary everything had seemed when I first got here. It still seemed that way most of the time.

"How long am I staying here?" Matt asked.

"I don't know. I hadn't really thought about it." I came over and sat on the bed next to him. Honestly, I wanted him to stay here forever, but that'd be selfish. "I guess until this all blows over. When the Vittra stop being a threat."

"Why are they coming after you?"

"It's a very long story, and I'll tell you later." I wanted to tell him, but I didn't have the strength for a lengthy explanation. At least not right now.

"But they will stop, won't they?" Matt asked, and I nodded as if I actually believed it.

"Until then, I want you to stay here. I need to know you're safe," I said. I wasn't sure how Elora would feel about that, but I didn't care.

"Yeah, I know the feeling," he said with an edge to his voice, and guilt tightened my heart.

"I'm really sorry, Matt."

"You could've told me about all of this."

"You wouldn't have believed any of it."

"Wendy. This is me, okay?" He turned to face me, and I finally looked at him. "Yeah, this is really hard to believe, and I know that if I hadn't seen it for myself, I'd find it even harder. But I've *always* been on your side. You should've trusted me."

"I know. I'm sorry." I lowered my eyes. "But I'm glad you're here and that I'm telling you stuff now. It was hard for me, keeping things from you. I don't wanna do it again."

"Good."

"But you should call Maggie," I said. "She needs to know where we are, and she can't go home. Not now. I don't know if they would take her to get at me."

"Are you safe here?" Matt asked. "Like, really safe?"

"Yeah, of course I am." I said it with more conviction than I really had. "Duncan's outside standing guard right now."

"That kid's an idiot," Matt said seriously, and I laughed.

"No, we're safe. Don't worry," I assured him as I stood up. "But you should call Maggie, and I should shower and put on my own clothes."

"What should I tell her?"

"I don't know." I shook my head. "Just make sure she doesn't go home."

I promised Matt I'd see him later and explain more to him then, but now I needed a moment to decompress. Duncan tried to follow me down the hall into my room, but I wouldn't let him in.

It wasn't until I was in the shower, with the sound of the water drowning me out, that I let myself cry. I don't even really know why I was crying. Part of it had to do with Finn, leaving me that way again, but mostly it was because it was all just too much.

After I got dressed, I felt better. Everything had turned out all right, as in we all survived with only minor injuries. On top of that, I got to have Matt around again. I didn't know for how long, but at least he knew the truth now.

And I finally knew why the Vittra were so fixated on me. Sure, the answer didn't make things any easier, but I understood, and that was something.

When I thought about it, the only real dark spot was Finn's absence. It left a dull ache inside my chest, but I had to ignore it. There were too many other things going on for me to sit around missing him.

I hated that he'd even come at all. It would've been easier if he'd just left me alone and I'd never seen him again.

I went over to Matt's room and discovered Rhys keeping him company. Elora had fixed him, much to my relief, and Rhys said that I'd have to begin my "training" soon to harness my abilities. I didn't know exactly what that would entail, but I didn't want to pump him for information.

I sat down in an overstuffed chair in Matt's room and decided to tell him everything. Rhys had told him some in the Vittra dungeon, but I wanted to fill in the blanks. More important, I thought Matt needed to hear it from me.

I started from the beginning, explaining how Elora had switched me for Rhys. I told him how Finn had been sent to track me and bring me here, about what it meant to be a Princess, and about the Trylle and their abilities.

The whole time I talked, Rhys said nothing, but watched with rapt interest. I'm not sure how much of this he already knew.

Matt didn't say much of anything either, only asking the occasional question. He began pacing when I started talking, but he didn't seem anxious or confused. When I finished, he stood silently for a minute, absorbing it all.

"So?" I asked when he still didn't say anything.

"So . . . do you guys still eat?" Matt looked over at me. " 'Cause I'm starving."

"Yeah, of course we do." I smiled, feeling relieved.

"I wouldn't call what they eat *food*," Rhys scoffed. He'd been sitting on the bed, but now he stood, since the conversation appeared to be wrapping up.

"What do you mean?" Matt asked.

"Well, you lived with Wendy. You have to know how she eats." Rhys seemed to realize he might have said something wrong, and he hurried to correct it. "Trylle are more careful eaters than us. They don't drink pop or eat meat, really."

Matt stared at Rhys for a moment longer, then glanced at me. There was something new in Matt's eyes, something I was feeling for the first time myself. Rhys had just put Matt and himself into an "us," a club I didn't belong to.

I had never and *could* never think of Matt as less than me, but we were different. We were separate. And despite all the differences between us that had been so obvious, it felt weird to know just how different we actually were, to have someone articulate that we weren't even the same species.

"Fortunately, I have a fridge stocked with real food," Rhys pushed on, trying to change the mood in the room. "And I'm a pretty decent cook. Ask Wendy."

"Yeah, he's pretty good," I lied, but I wasn't that hungry anymore. My stomach had tightened, and I was amazed that I could even force a smile at them both. "Come on. Let's get some food."

Rhys thought that talking nonstop would make up for his small blunder, and neither Matt nor I contradicted him. We walked down to the kitchen, with Duncan tagging along as soon as we'd left Matt's room.

Duncan's constant presence irritated me far more than Finn's ever had, even though Duncan hadn't really done anything. Maybe it was simply because he was there and Finn wasn't.

I pulled up a stool at the kitchen counter and watched Matt and Rhys interact. Rhys kept playing up his cooking skills, but once Matt saw him in action, he realized that he'd better take the lead. I propped my chin up on my hand, feeling all sorts of conflicting emotions as they talked and laughed and teased each other.

Part of me was thrilled that they got to have each other in their lives, the way they should've from the beginning. Depriving Rhys of a wonderful big brother like Matt had been a very cruel side effect of the changeling process.

But part of me couldn't help but feel like I was losing my brother.

"Do you mind if I have a water?" Duncan asked, pulling me from my thoughts.

"Why would I care if you had a water?" I looked at him like he was an idiot, but he didn't notice. Or maybe he got it so often, he thought that was just how people looked at him.

"I don't know. Some Trylle don't like when trackers use their stuff." Duncan went over to the fridge to get a bottled water, while Matt attempted to teach Rhys how to flip blueberry flapjacks.

"Well, how do you eat and drink if you don't use their stuff?" I asked Duncan.

"Buy our own." With the fridge still open, Duncan held a water toward me. "Do you want one?"

I shrugged. "Yeah, sure." He walked over and handed it to me. "You've been doing this for a long time?"

"Almost twelve years, I think." Duncan unscrewed his bottle and took a long drink. "Wow. It's weird it's been that long."

"Are you really the best they have?" I asked, trying to keep the skepticism out of my voice.

He seemed a little too amazed by Matt's ability to make pancakes. He didn't exude any of the confidence or formality that Finn had, but then again, it was probably better for him to be as different from Finn as possible.

"No," Duncan admitted, and if my question shamed him, he didn't show it. He just played with his bottle cap. "But I'm pretty close. My appearance is deceiving, but that's part of why I'm good. People underestimate me."

Something about the way he said that made me flash on to *Scream*. Maybe Duncan had a bit of that clumsy, unassuming boyish charm.

"Did anybody ever tell you that you remind them of Deputy Dewey from the *Scream* movies?" I asked.

"You mean David Arquette?" Duncan asked. "But I'm better-looking, right?"

I nodded. "Oh, yeah, definitely." I could never see myself being attracted to him, but he was kinda foxy. In his own way.

Rhys swore as a flapjack landed on the floor with a splat. Matt patiently tried to explain what he'd done wrong and how to correct it, using the same tone of voice he'd used to teach me how to tie my shoes, ride a bike, and drive a car. It was so strange seeing him be the older brother to somebody else.

"Wendy!" Willa shouted from behind me, and I'd barely turned around when she came running over. She threw her arms around me, shocking me with a fierce hug. "I'm so glad you're all right!"

"Um, thanks," I said, untangling myself from her hug.

Willa Strom was a few years older than me, and the only Trylle other than Finn who actually called me "Wendy" instead of "Princess," so I guess that made us friends. Her father, Garrett, was Elora's only friend, and Willa had been insanely helpful and kind after Finn left the first time. Without her, the christening ceremony would've been a disaster even before the Vittra broke in.

"My dad was telling me that the Vittra had kidnapped you, and nobody knew for sure what was going on." Willa could be snobby, but the concern on her face was sincere. "I rushed over here as soon as I heard you were back. I'm so glad you're here."

"Yeah, me too," I said, but I wasn't sure if that was true or not.

"Duncan?" Willa looked at him, as if noticing he was here for the first time. "You've got to be kidding me. There is no way Elora would let you be her tracker."

"See? Underrated." Duncan smiled. He seemed to take some pride in it, so I let him have it.

"Oh, my god. I'm gonna talk to my dad." Willa shook her head, tucking her perfectly tamed light-brown waves of hair behind her ears. "There's no way he can do this."

"It's fine. I'm fine." I shrugged. "I'm in the palace. What can happen here?"

Willa gave me a knowing look, but thankfully, before she could say something, Matt announced breakfast was done. When I had been regaling him with the tales of being Trylle, I had conveniently left out the part about the Vittra busting in here and Oren being my father. I thought it would freak him out too much.

"Are you gonna eat some too?" Matt asked Willa. He dished up the flapjacks, and, polite as ever, he included her. "We've got plenty to go around."

"Are those blueberry?" Willa wrinkled her nose, looking totally disgusted by the prospect of eating them. "Eww. No way."

"They're really good." Matt slid a plate toward her.

For reasons I didn't completely understand, there were few foods we actually enjoyed. We mostly ate fresh fruits and vegetables. I didn't like juice of any kind, although I did like some wine. Pancakes were made with processed flour and sugar, so they were never that appealing, although I had been eating them for years to appease Matt.

"You're not gonna eat those, are you?" Willa was completely aghast as I picked up my fork and prepared to dig in.

Matt had given Duncan a plate too. I'm sure the pancakes sounded as appealing to him as they did to Willa and me, but Duncan followed suit and picked up his fork.

"They're pretty good," I said.

I had been assured by many people over the years that they were really good, although I'm not sure how anyone could taste them after they drowned them in syrup the way Matt and Rhys were doing. Duncan and I declined syrup. There was no way we could ever force them down like that.

"I've cooked for Wendy for years," Matt said, unfazed by Willa's reaction. "I know how to make food that she likes."

In general, he had gotten pretty good at it, but there were a lot of times when I ate things just to make him happy. And also, I'd starve if I didn't.

"Oh, yeah, right," Willa scoffed. "Like I'm gonna trust a mänks in sweats and a baby tee to make me *pancakes*."

"Willa," I said. "He's my brother, okay? So lay off."

"What?" She tilted her head, not fathoming what I meant. "Oh. You mean he's your host brother?"

"Yeah." I took a big forkful of the pancake and shoved it in my mouth.

"You know he's not your *real*—"

"Willa!" I snapped with a mouthful of food, and I choked it down. "I understand the semantics. Now drop it."

"I can understand how that dweeb Duncan can eat that." Willa smoothed out her designer outfit, trying not to look offended that I'd snapped at her. "But you're a Princess. He's too stupid to—"

"Hey!" Matt said. He had been sitting next to Duncan, eating, but he stopped and glared at her. "I get it. You're fancy and pretty and rich. Good for you. But unless you wanna go over there and make us all breakfast, then I suggest you quit your bitching and sit down."

"Whoa!" Rhys laughed. He loved seeing her put in her place.

Willa made a face at Rhys but didn't say anything. When Matt went back to eating his pancakes, she sat down on the stool next to me.

Since I'd first met Willa, it was clear she walked around with a sense of entitlement. She was nice to me because she thought we were equals, but she definitely didn't feel the same way about everyone else.

"I am thirsty," Willa said after a minute, sounding pouty.

Automatically, Duncan stood to get water for her, but Matt shook his head, stopping him. Uncertainly, Duncan sat back down. As a tracker, he spent a lot of his life waiting on changelings. Trackers were considered staff and treated as such by royalty.

"You know where the fridge's at," Matt said between bites.

Willa opened her mouth but didn't say anything. She turned to me, hoping I would come to her aid, but I only shrugged. She did know where the fridge was at, after all.

After a minute of deliberating, she got up and went over to the fridge. Rhys snickered under his breath, but Matt shushed him.

I found the whole thing kind of amazing. Finn had been Willa's tracker, and a strict one at that. But she never listened to him or treated him with as much respect as she did Matt, who by Trylle standards was much lower in rank than Finn.

In the five minutes he'd known her, Matt had managed to whip her into shape better than anyone else ever had.

Willa hung around me for the rest of the afternoon, and she seemed relieved when we split off from Matt and Rhys. Rhys wanted to play some war video game or something, and I didn't feel like it.

Instead, Willa and I stayed in my room. Duncan stood outside my door for a bit, but eventually I felt sorry for him, so I had him come in and sit down.

She sorted my clothes because she liked doing that, and I lay on the floor, watching Willa and thinking about how weird it was that this was my life. She organized them in some way that I didn't understand, even after she'd explained it to me.

All the while, she talked about how great her training had been going. Willa had power over the wind, and she hadn't thought anything of it before the attack.

Now she wanted to be as prepared and strong as she possibly could. She figured that my training would start right away too, since I needed to be more prepared than anyone else here.

The night went on much the same way, and I was surprised when she joined us for supper. This time she even ate what Matt cooked, and I felt as if the whole world were turning upside down.

I went to bed shortly after, but I tossed and turned all night. My mind raced too much to really sleep. It felt like I'd only just fallen asleep when someone shook me awake. I pushed the person off, snuggling deeper in my covers.

It wasn't until I had buried my face in my pillow that I realized I should probably be alarmed that someone was in my room. What with evil trolls trying to kidnap me and all that.

repositioning

H oly hell!" Tove Kroner shouted and jumped back from the side of my bed.

I'd sat up, almost leaping out of bed, preparing to attack whoever had just woken me up. It turned out to be Tove, and I didn't understand what I'd done to him.

As far as I knew, I hadn't even reacted yet, other than sitting up. But Tove stood off to the side of the room, pressing his palms to his temples. He was bent over, his dark hair falling over his face.

"Tove?" I swung my feet over the edge of the bed and stood up. He didn't respond, so I stepped closer to him. "Tove? Are you okay? Did I do something?"

"Yeah." He shook his head and straightened up. His eyes were closed, but he'd dropped his hands from his head.

"I'm sorry. What did I do?"

"I don't know." Tove opened his mouth wide and stretched his jaw, reminding me of someone who had just been slapped in the face. "I came in to wake you up for your training. And you . . ."

"Did I hit you?" I supplied when he trailed off.

"No, it was in my head." Tove stared ahead thoughtfully for a minute. "No, you were right. It was like you slapped me inside my head."

"What are you talking about?"

"Have you ever done anything like that before? Maybe when you were scared?" He turned to look at me, ignoring my confusion to satisfy his.

"Not that I know of, but I don't even know what I did."

"Hmm." He sighed and ran his hand through his hair. "Your abilities are still developing. They should fully present themselves soon, and maybe this is part of that. Or maybe it's just because I'm me."

"What?"

"Because I'm psychic," Tove reminded me. "Your aura is very dark today."

He couldn't read minds or anything, but he could sense things. I projected, so I could get in people's minds like Elora could and use persuasion, and Tove received, so he could see auras and was more sensitive to emotion.

"What does that mean?" I asked.

"You're unhappy." Tove sounded distracted, and he made for the door. "Hurry. Get dressed. We have much to do."

He left my room before I could ask him more, and I didn't understand what Willa saw in him. I wasn't sure if she really had a crush on him, or if her interest only stemmed from the fact that his family was powerful. The Kroners were next in line for the crown, Tove specifically, if I couldn't fulfill my duties.

Tove was attractive, though. His dark hair had soft natural highlights coursing through it, although it was longish and unruly, settling below his ears. His skin had a distinct mossy undertone, the green complexion that occurred in some powerful Trylle. Nobody here had skin like that, except maybe his mother, but hers was even fainter than Tove's.

I didn't know why Tove would be training me. I'm not sure that Elora approved of him, even if he had connections. Besides that, he was scatterbrained and a little strange.

Tove did have the strongest abilities out of any of the Trylle I'd met. This was particularly weird since men usually had weaker abilities than their female counterparts.

But I wanted to get a handle on my abilities, so I figured it'd do me good to spend the day doing something other than moping around. I dressed quickly and left my room to find Tove chatting with Duncan.

"Ready?" Tove asked without looking at me. He started walking before I answered.

"Duncan, you don't need to come with us," I told him as I hurried after Tove. Duncan followed me the way he always did, but he slowed.

"It's probably best if he does," Tove said, tucking his hair behind his ears.

"Why?" I asked, but Duncan smiled, excited to be included.

"We need someone to test on," Tove replied matter-of-factly, and Duncan's smile instantly faded.

"Where are we going?" I nearly jogged to keep up with Tove, and I wished he would slow down.

"Did you hear that?" Tove stopped abruptly, and Duncan almost ran into him.

"What?" Duncan looked around, as if expecting an attacker to be waiting behind a closed door.

"I didn't hear anything," I said.

"No, of course you didn't." Tove waved me off.

"Why wouldn't I? What's that supposed to mean?"

"Because you're the one that made the sound." Tove sighed, still focused on Duncan. "Are you sure you didn't hear anything?"

"No," Duncan said. He looked over at me, hoping I could shed light on Tove's random behavior, but I shrugged. I had no idea what he was talking about.

"Tove, what's going on?" I asked, speaking loudly so he'd pay attention to me.

"You need to be careful." Tove cocked his head, listening. "You're quiet now. But when you're upset, angry, scared, irritated, you send things out. You're not controlling it, I don't think. I can pick it up, because I'm sensitive. Duncan can't and the average Trylle can't, because you're not directing it at them. But if I can hear it, others might too."

"What? I didn't say anything," I said, growing more frustrated with him.

"You thought, *I wish he'd slow down,*" Tove said.

"I wasn't using persuasion or anything." I was dumbfounded.

"I know. You'll get a handle on it, though," he assured me, and then started walking again.

He led us downstairs. I'm not sure where I thought he'd take us, but I was definitely surprised by where we ended up—the ballroom that had been devastated by the Vittra attack. It had once been luxurious, very much like a ballroom from a Disney fairy tale. Marble floors, white walls with gold detailing, skylights, diamond chandeliers.

After the attack, it looked very different. The glass ceiling had been crashed in, and to keep the elements out, blue and clear tarps had been laid over it, giving the room an odd glow. Shattered chandeliers and glass were still on the floor, as well as broken chairs and tables. The floor and walls were blackened with damage from the fire and smoke.

"Why are we here?" I asked. My voice still echoed, thanks to the room's massive size, but it wasn't as crisp thanks to the tarps.

"I like it here." Tove held his hands out, using his telekinesis to push the debris to the sides of the room.

"Does the Queen know where we are?" Duncan asked. He was uncomfortable being here, and I tried to remember if he'd been present during the attack. I hadn't been paying that much attention, and I'd met far too many people that night to say for certain.

Tove shrugged. "I'm not sure."

"Does she know you're training me?" I asked. He nodded, looking around with his back to me. "Why are you training me? Your abilities aren't the same as mine."

"They're similar." Tove turned around to face me. "And no two people are exactly alike."

"Have you trained anyone before?"

"No. But I'm the best suited to train you," he said and started rolling up the sleeves of his shirt.

"Why?" I asked, and I could see Duncan wearing the same dubious expression I was.

"You're too powerful for everyone else. They wouldn't be able to help you tap into your potential because they don't understand it the way I do." He'd finished rolling up his sleeves and put his hands on his hips. "Are you ready?"

"I guess." I shrugged, unsure what I needed to be ready for.

"Move this stuff." He gestured vaguely to the mess around the room.

"You mean with my mind?" I shook my head. "I can't do that."

"Have you tried?" Tove countered, his eyes sparkling.

"Well . . . no," I admitted.

"Do it."

"How?"

He shrugged. "Figure it out."

"You're really good at this training thing," I said with a sigh.

Tove laughed, but I did as I was told. I decided to start small, so I picked a broken chair nearby. I stared at in concentration. The only thing I knew how to use was persuasion, so I thought I'd go that way. In my mind, I repeated, *I want the chair to move, I want—*

"Nope!" Tove said, snapping me out of it. "You're thinking about it wrong."

"How am I supposed to think about it?"

"It's not a person. You can't tell it what to do. *You* have to move it," Tove said, as if that clarified his point.

"How?" I asked again, but he didn't say anything. "It'd be easier if you told me."

"I can't tell you. That's not how it works."

I grumbled a few unseemly remarks under my breath then I turned to the chair, preparing to get down to business.

So I couldn't tell the chair to move. *I* had to move it. How did that translate to thought? I squinted, hoping that might help somehow, and repeated, *Move the chair, move the chair.*

"Now look what you've done," Tove said.

I didn't think anything at all had happened, and then I saw Duncan walking toward the chair.

"Duncan, what are you doing?" I asked.

"I, uh . . . moving the chair. I guess." He seemed confused but coherent, and once he picked up the chair, he gave me an even more bewildered look. "I don't know where to, though."

"Set it anywhere," I told him absently and turned to Tove. "I did that?"

"Of course you did that. I could hear you chanting loud and clear, and if you'd harnessed it better, I'd be the one picking up the chair." He crossed his arms over his chest, giving me a look that bordered on disapproving.

"I didn't try to do that. I wasn't even looking at him."

"That makes it even worse, doesn't it?" Tove asked.

"I don't understand," Duncan said. He'd set down the chair, and, now free of his duty, walked over to us. "What are you expecting her to do?"

"You need to control your energy before someone gets hurt." Tove looked at me solemnly, his mossy eyes bravely meeting mine for almost a minute before he turned away. He gestured around his head, in much the same way Loki had when he explained how he knew I had persuasion. "You have so much going on. It comes off like a . . ."

"Static?" I suggested.

"Exactly!" He snapped his fingers and pointed at me. "You need to tune it, get your frequencies in check, like a radio."

"I would love to. Just tell me how."

"It's not a matter of turning a dial. You have no on or off switch." He walked around in a large lazy circle. "It's something you have to practice. It's more like being potty-trained. You have to learn when to hold it and when to release."

"That's a pretty sexy analogy," I said.

"You can move the chair." Tove stopped suddenly. "But that can wait. You need to learn to rein in your persuasion." He looked at Duncan. "Duncan, you don't mind being experimented on, do you?"

"Um . . . I guess not?"

"Tell him to do something. Anything." He tilted his head, still watching Duncan, then turned to me. "But make sure I can't hear."

"How? I don't even know how you're hearing," I pointed out.

"Focus. You have to focus your energy. It's imperative."

"How?" I repeated.

He kept telling me to do things without giving me any clue how. He might as well have been telling me to build a damn rocket ship. I had no idea what to do.

"You were more focused when you were around Finn," Tove said. "You were more grounded, in the way electricity is grounded."

"Well, he's not here," I snapped.

"It doesn't matter. *He* didn't do anything," Tove continued, unfazed. "You're the one with the power. You grounded yourself around him. You tell me how."

I didn't want to think about Finn or the way I had been around him. One of the reasons I had been excited for this training was because it would distract me from thoughts of him. Now Tove was telling me that Finn was the key to my success. Perfect.

Instead of yelling at Tove, I walked away. I hated the way he seemed to know everything, but lacked the ability to articulate anything. I stretched my arms and rolled my neck, working out the tension. Duncan started to say something, but Tove shushed him.

Finn. When I was around Finn, what did I do differently? He made me crazy. He made my heart beat too fast and my stomach swirl, and it was hard to take my eyes off him. Whenever he was around, I'd hardly been able to think of anything.

And that was it. It was almost too simple.

When Finn was around, my focus had been on him. That restrained my energy somehow. If my conscious mind focused on something, the rest of my mind would pull itself in. Maybe my energy was going crazy now because I was trying *not* to think of Finn.

Finn wasn't the key. But when he'd been around, I had let my mind focus. When he wasn't, I tried not to think of anything, because everything reminded me of him. Everything scattered all over, latching on to anything it could.

I closed my eyes. *Think of something. Focus on anything.*

Finn came to my mind first, the way he always did, but I pushed him away. I could think of something else. The first thing I thought of after him was Loki, and that shocked me, so I discounted him instantly. I didn't want to focus on him. Or anyone, for that matter.

I thought of the garden behind the palace. It was gorgeous, and I loved it. Elora had painted a beautiful picture of it, but it didn't really do the place justice. I remembered the way the flowers smelled, and the way the grass felt cool on my bare feet. Butterflies had flown about, and I could hear the stream babbling past me.

"Try it now," Tove suggested.

I turned to look at Duncan. He had his hands shoved in his pockets, and he gulped, as if he were afraid I might slap him. Keeping the image of the garden in my mind, I started repeating, *Whistle "Twinkle, Twinkle, Little Star."* It seemed mundane, but that was the point. I didn't want to hurt him.

His face relaxed, his eyes went blank, and then he started whistling. Feeling pleased with myself, I looked over at Tove.

"Well?" I asked hopefully.

"I didn't hear it." Tove smiled. "Excellent work."

I continued trying things out on Duncan the rest of the day. After the first few didn't turn out painful, Duncan became more at ease with the whole thing. He was a terrific sport about it, considering I made him whistle, dance, clap, and do a whole number of silly things.

Tove went on to explain what had gone wrong with Rhys and his inability to sit. Apparently, the more focus and intensity I used when trying to persuade people, the more permanent the command would become.

Rhys was human, so his mind was already more malleable than a Trylle's, and he was open to persuasion. I'd barely have to try to get it to work on him. I'd used far more energy than I needed to. I needed to learn to control the doses of my persuasion to match my target.

Of course, I could undo any command I made, like how I redirected Rhys from sitting to standing, and vice versa. But with unfocused energy, it was possible I could persuade people without even trying, the way I had gotten Duncan to move the chair.

I spent the rest of the day trying to restrain my energy, since it was potentially very dangerous. By the end of the day, I felt completely drained. It didn't help matters that I hadn't stopped for a lunch break, not that I felt like eating anyway.

Tove tried to assure me that eventually this would all be second nature, like breathing or blinking. But the way I felt right now, I didn't believe him.

I walked Tove to the front door, then I headed up to my room for a shower and a nap. Duncan went down to his quarters, daring to leave me alone so he could get in a nap himself. Being the guinea pig had been tiring for him too.

On the way to my room, I got sidetracked.

"This is Queen Sybilla," Willa was saying, pointing to a painting on the wall. Matt stood next to her, admiring the artwork as she explained it. "She's one of the most revered monarchs. I think she ruled over the Long Winter War, which I guess is much worse than it sounds."

"A long winter?" Matt smirked, and she laughed. It was a nice sound; I don't think I'd heard her laugh that way before.

"I know. It's silly." She had her hair up in a ponytail, making her look more playful, and she smoothed out a flyaway hair. "To be honest, most of this stuff is rather silly."

"Yeah, I can tell." Matt smiled.

"Hey, guys," I said tentatively, walking toward them.

"Oh, hey!" Willa smiled wider, and they both turned to face me.

As usual, she was dressed to the nines and looked stunning. Her top was low cut, and a diamond pendant rested just above her cleavage. She wore lots of jewelry—a charm bracelet, anklet, earrings, and rings—but that was all part of being Trylle. We had a fascination with trinkets. I wasn't as bad as Willa, but I'd always had a penchant for rings.

"Where have you been?" Matt asked, but he didn't sound concerned or angry. Merely curious.

"Training with Tove." I shrugged, downplaying the event. I expected Willa to squeal and press me for details about him, but she didn't register any excitement. "What are you guys doing?"

"I came to see if you wanted to do anything, and your brother was wandering around here like a lost puppy." She laughed a little, and he shook his head and rubbed the back of his neck.

"I was not a lost puppy." He grinned, but his cheeks reddened. "I had nothing to do here."

"Right. So I thought I'd show him around." Willa gestured to the halls. "I've been trying to explain your formidable ancestry."

"I really don't get it," Matt said almost wearily.

"I don't really either," I admitted, and they both laughed.

"Are you hungry?" Matt asked, and I was pleased to see him returning to a subject that felt more normal. Like worrying if I'd eaten. "I was about to go downstairs and make supper for me and Rhys and that girl with a weird name."

"Rhiannon?" Willa suggested.

"Yeah, that's her." Matt nodded.

"Oh, she's real nice," Willa said, and my jaw dropped.

Rhiannon was Willa's mänsklig, meaning she was the girl that Willa had been switched at birth with. Rhiannon was friends with Rhys and incredibly sweet, but I'd never heard Willa talk about her that way.

"Are she and Rhys dating or something?" Matt asked, looking at Willa.

"I don't know. She has a big crush on him, but I'm not sure how he feels about her." Willa sounded happy about the prospect. Normally, when she talked about Rhys or any mänks, she sounded bored.

"So what do you think?" Matt turned to me. "Are you gonna eat supper?"

"No, thanks." I shook my head. "I'm pretty beat. I need a shower and a nap."

"Are you sure?" Matt asked, and I nodded. "What about you, Willa? Do you have dinner plans?"

"Um, no." She smiled at him. "I'd love to eat here."

"Awesome," Matt said.

I extricated myself from the conversation as quickly as possible.

It was too weird for me to handle. Willa was being way too nice, and now she was willingly eating food prepared by a mänks.

That said nothing for the way Matt acted, which felt . . . not quite right. It was hard to put my finger on what exactly was going on, but I was relieved to be away from them.

ELEVEN

little star

A nother long day of training did nothing to improve my mood. My control was getting better, and that was good. But it was getting harder not to think of Finn. I thought time would make it easier, but it didn't. The ache only seemed to grow.

We spent the morning in the throne room, where I'd never been before. It was really an atrium, with a domed skylight stretching high above. The room was circular, the rounded wall behind the throne made entirely of glass. Vines grew over the ornate silver and gold designs etched on the walls, reminding me of the outside of the palace.

Given the height of the ceiling, the room itself didn't seem that large, but it didn't need to be. Tove offhandedly said it was only used for meeting dignitaries.

A solitary throne sat in the center of the room, padded with lush red velvet. Two smaller chairs sat on either side, but they weren't as elegant. Instead of wood, the throne was made of platinum that wove itself into lacy designs. Diamonds and rubies were inlaid into the metal.

I walked over to it, gingerly touching the soft velvet. It felt brand-new, too plush to have ever been used. The heavy metal arms were surprisingly smooth under my fingertips. I ran my hand over it, tracing the swirling patterns of the latticing.

"Unless you plan to move that with your mind, I suggest you get practicing," Tove said.

"Why are we practicing in here?" I turned to look at him, pulling myself away from the chair. I don't know why, but something about it captivated me, made this all the more real.

"I like the space." He gestured vaguely at the airiness of the room. "It helps my thoughts. The ballroom is being worked on today, so we had to move."

Almost reluctantly, I walked away from the throne and went over to Tove to see what cryptic lesson he had in store for me. Duncan stood off to the side of the room for most of the morning, getting a reprieve from being my test subject. Tove wanted me to work on restraining my thoughts again, this time using tactics that made even less sense to me.

I stood facing a wall, and while I counted up to a thousand, I was supposed to picture the garden and use my persuasion. Since I wasn't using it on anyone, I wasn't exactly sure how I'd be able to tell if it was working or not, but Tove said the point was that I learn to flex my psychic muscles. My mind would have to learn to juggle a lot of ideas, some of them conflicting, in order for me to get control over this.

While I practiced, he sprawled on the floor, lying on the cold marble. Duncan eventually tired and went over to the throne, sitting in it with one of his legs draped over the side. I felt a little irritated by that, but I wasn't sure why, so I didn't say anything. I didn't support aristocracy, and I wasn't going to enforce it on Duncan.

"How are you doing?" Tove asked, speaking for the first time in about a half hour. We'd all been silent as I tried to master whatever it was I was supposed to master.

"Fantastic," I muttered.

"Great. Let's add a song." He stared up at the skylight, watching the clouds roll over us.

"What?" I stopped counting and let go of my persuasion so I could turn to face him. "Why?"

"I can still hear you," Tove said. "It's getting fainter, but it's like the hum you hear from power lines. You need to quiet the noise in your head."

"And doing a million things at once will do that?" I asked skeptically.

"Yes. You're getting stronger, which means you're learning to hold things in." He lay down, closing the matter. "Now add a song to it."

"What should I sing?" I sighed, turning to face the wall.

"Not 'Twinkle, Twinkle, Little Star.'" Duncan grimaced. "I've had that stuck in my head for some reason."

"I've always been partial to the Beatles," Tove said.

I glanced over at Duncan, who smirked with surprise. Sighing again, I started singing "Eleanor Rigby." I messed up the words a couple times, but Tove didn't complain, which was good. It was hard enough trying to do this *and* remember the lyrics to a song I hadn't heard in years.

"I hope I'm not interrupting." Elora's voice ruined any semblance I had of concentration, so I stopped singing and turned to face her.

Duncan scrambled out of the chair, but not before I caught

sight of the nasty glare she shot him. He looked down so his hair would cover the crimson blush on his cheeks.

"Not really." I shrugged. For once, I was actually happy to see Elora, since her arrival meant a reprieve from all of this.

Elora surveyed the room with disdain, but I wasn't sure what met her disapproval, since she had to at least have had a hand in the design. She stepped into the room, her long gown pooling around her feet. Tove didn't get up and watched her with offhanded interest.

"Can I have a moment alone with the Princess?" Elora asked without looking at anyone. She managed to stand in such a way that her back was to all three of us.

Duncan mumbled apologies as he hurried out of the room, stumbling over his own feet. Tove left more slowly, always content to do things at his own pace. He ran a hand through his disheveled hair and made a vague comment about coming to find me when I was done.

"I've never cared for this room," Elora said once they'd gone. "It always felt more like a greenhouse to me than a throne room. I know that was the idea behind it, helping us maintain our more organic roots, but it never felt right to me."

"I think it's nice." I understood what she meant, but it was still a beautiful room. All the glass gave it a sleek yet opulent feel.

"Your 'friend' is staying with us." She chose her words carefully and walked over to the throne. She ran her fingers along the arms much the same way I had, letting her black manicured nails linger on the details.

"My friend?"

"Yes. The . . . boy. Matt, is it?" Elora lifted her head, meeting my eyes to see if she was correct.

"You mean my brother," I said deliberately.

"Don't call him that. Think of him however you'd like, but if someone hears you say that . . ." She trailed off. "How long will he be staying with us?"

"Until I feel it's safe for him to leave." I stood up straighter, steeling myself for another fight, but she didn't say anything. She simply nodded once and looked out the window. "You're not gonna try to stop me?"

"I've been Queen for a while, Princess." She smiled thinly at me. "I know how to pick my battles. This is one I suspect I couldn't win."

"So you're okay with it?" I asked, unable to hide the shock in my voice.

"You learn to tolerate the things you cannot change," Elora told me simply.

"Do you want to meet him or anything?" I felt unsure about what I should do.

I didn't know why she'd come to talk to me, if it wasn't to stop me from doing something or tell me I'd done something wrong. That seemed to be the only time she sought me out.

"I'm certain I'll see him in due time." She smoothed her black hair and walked a bit closer to me. "How is your training going?"

"Fine." I shrugged. "I don't get it, really, but it's okay. I guess."

"You're getting along all right with Tove?" Her dark eyes met mine again, as if studying me.

"Yeah. He's fine."

Whatever she saw in me must've pleased her, because she nodded and smiled. Elora stayed and chatted with me a few minutes longer, asking more about the training, but her interest waned almost immediately. She excused herself, citing business to attend to.

Once she had gone, Tove returned to continue the training, but I suggested we get lunch instead. We went down to the kitchen to discover Matt making something for him and Willa. Rhys was at school, so it was just the two of them.

Willa threw a grape at Matt, and when he tossed it back, she giggled. If Tove noticed anything unusual about their banter, he didn't say anything, but he hardly looked up from his plate. He ate in total silence, while I watched Matt and Willa with confused fascination.

I ate in a hurry, then Tove and I went back to training while Matt and Willa were still eating. Not that either of them really seemed to notice or care about our departure.

The rest of the day didn't afford me much time to think about how strange Matt and Willa were acting. Training went on in the throne room much the way it had in the morning. Toward the end of the day I began feeling tired, but I didn't stop until Tove called it quits.

After Tove left, Duncan followed me upstairs, because I couldn't seem to ditch him no matter what I said. I wanted to be alone, but I let Duncan in my room. I felt weird and mean making him stand out in the hall all the time.

I know he supposedly was a bodyguard, but he wasn't some stiff in a suit with an earpiece. He was a kid in skinny jeans, which made it hard for me to treat him like staff.

"I don't understand why you hate it here so much," Duncan said, admiring my room.

"I don't hate it here," I said, but I wasn't sure if that was true.

My hair had been up in a messy bun, and I took it down, running my fingers through the kinks and curls. Duncan looked at the stuff on my desk, touching my computer and CDs. I would've been mad, if any of it were really mine. Everything had come with the place when I moved in. Even though this was my room, very little in it felt like it actually belonged to me.

"Why'd you run away?" Duncan picked up a Fall Out Boy CD and investigated the track list.

"I thought you knew why." I got into my bed, immersing myself in the overflow of blankets and pillows. I folded a pillow under my head so I could see him better. "You seemed to have it all figured out."

"When?" He set the CD down and turned to look at me. "I never seem like I have anything figured out."

"That's true," I said, pushing a dark curl off my forehead. "But at my house, when you came to get me. I thought you knew."

When I'd first met him, he'd said something. I couldn't remember exactly what it was, but he'd implied he knew what had happened between Finn and me. Or at the very least, he'd known why Finn had been dismissed, which was because of the way Finn felt about me.

Although I wasn't so sure about Finn's feelings anymore. I doubted they were real now, if they had ever been. We had lain in this very bed, kissing and holding each other. I'd wanted to do more, but Finn had stopped things, saying he didn't want to disturb me. But maybe he'd never really wanted me at all.

If he had, he wouldn't have just left that way. He couldn't have.

"I don't know what you're talking about." Duncan shook his head. "I don't think I ever understood why you left."

"I must've imagined it, then." I rolled onto my back so I could stare up at the ceiling. Before he could ask me more about it, I changed the subject. "What happened to you guys anyway?"

"When?" He'd moved on from the CDs to perusing the small book collection I had.

They weren't terrible, but they'd all been Rhys's and Rhiannon's choices, so they weren't really my tastes. Other than a book by Jerry Spinelli, there was nothing I would have picked out for myself.

"Back at my house. You guys left, and the Vittra kidnapped me. What'd you do? Where'd you go?"

"We didn't get very far. Finn planned on sticking around. He thought you'd come around eventually." Duncan picked up a book and absently flipped through it. "But we only made it a block away, and they jumped us. This guy with scraggly blondish hair, he just looked at us, and we were out."

"Loki," I said with a sigh.

"Who?" Duncan asked, and I shook my head.

The Vittra must have been watching, waiting for the opportunity to surprise Finn and Duncan. They snuck up on them, and Loki took care of them. Finn was lucky that they'd only knocked him out. Kyra seemed way too keen on destroying me.

She must've been sent ahead to get me, leaving Loki behind to neutralize Finn and Duncan. Loki hadn't seemed that big into violence. In fact, if he hadn't intervened, Kyra might've actually killed me.

"Wait." Duncan narrowed his eyes at me, as if figuring something out. "Did you think we left you there?"

"I didn't know what to think," I said. "You just left, and I hadn't expected you to. I didn't want to go with you, but you left without much of a fight. I thought maybe—"

"Is that why you've been so mopey?"

"I have not been mopey!" I had been a little depressed since I'd gotten back. Well, since before then, really, but I didn't think I'd been *mopey*.

"No, you have," he assured me with a smile. "There's no way we'd leave you that way. You were an easy target. Finn would never let anything happen to you." He'd turned to my stuff and picked up my iPod. "I mean, he can't even leave you now, and you're completely safe here."

"What?" My heart raced in my chest. "What are you talking about?"

"What?" Duncan belatedly realized he'd said too much, and his skin paled. "Nothing."

"No, Duncan, what do you mean?" I sat up, knowing I should at least pretend not to care so much, but I couldn't help it. "Finn's here? You mean like *here* here?"

"I shouldn't say anything." He shifted uneasily.

"You have to tell me," I insisted, scooting to the edge of the bed.

"No, Finn would kill me if he knew I said anything." Duncan stared down at his feet and fiddled with a broken belt loop. "I'm sorry."

"He told you not to tell me he's here?" I asked, once again feeling a painful stab in my heart.

"He's not here, like in the palace." He groaned and looked sheepishly at me. "If I get mixed up in whatever sordid thing it is you have with him, I'll never get a job again. Please, Princess. Don't make me tell you."

It wasn't until the words were out of his mouth that I realized I *could* make him tell me. While my persuasion might not be strong enough for the likes of Tove and Loki, I'd been practicing on Duncan. He was easily susceptible to my charms.

"Where is he, Duncan?" I demanded, looking directly at him.

I didn't even have to chant it in my head. As soon as I'd said it, his jaw sagged and his eyes glassed over. His mind was awfully pliable, and I felt bad. Later on, I'd have to make this up to him somehow.

"He's in Förening, at his parents' house," Duncan said, blinking hard at me.

"His parents?"

"Yeah, they live down the road." He pointed south. "Follow the main road towards the gate, then take the third left on a gravel road. Go down the side of the bluff a little ways, and they live in a cottage. It's the one with goats."

"Goats?" I asked, wondering if Duncan was pulling my leg.

"His mother raises a few angora goats. She makes sweaters and scarves from the mohair and sells them." He shook his head. "I've said way too much. I'm gonna be in so much trouble."

"No, you'll be fine," I assured him as I jumped out of bed.

I ran to the closet to change my clothes. I didn't look bad, but if I was gonna see Finn, I had to look good. Duncan kept groaning about what an idiot he was for telling me anything. I tried to calm him, but my mind raced too much.

I couldn't believe how stupid I was. I'd imagined that as soon as he was unassigned from me, Finn had been sent to track someone else. But now I realized he had to have some turnaround time before his next job, and he had to stay somewhere. If he wasn't living at the palace, his parents were the next logical choice. He'd spoken very little of them, and it never occurred to me that they might be neighbors.

"Elora will find out. She knows everything," Duncan muttered as I exited the closet.

"I promise. I won't tell anyone." I looked at myself in the mirror. I was pale, scattered, and terrified. Finn liked my hair better when it was down, so I left it that way, even though it was messy.

"She'll still find out," Duncan insisted.

"I'll protect your job," I said, but he still looked skeptical. "I'm the Princess. I have to have some pull around here." He shrugged, but I could tell I'd managed to alleviate some of his fears. "I've gotta go. You can't tell anyone where I am."

"They'll freak out if they don't know where you're at."

"Well . . ." I looked around, thinking. "Stay here. If anyone comes looking for me, tell them I'm in the bath and can't be disturbed. We're each other's alibis."

"You sure?" He raised an eyebrow.

"Yes," I lied. "I have to go. And thank you."

Duncan still didn't seem convinced this was a good idea, but I'd left him with little choice. I raced out of the palace, trying to be as inconspicuous as possible. Elora had a few other trackers wandering around to keep watch on things, but I slid past them without any notice.

When I pushed open the front doors, I realized I didn't even know why I was in such a hurry to see Finn. What did I plan on doing once I saw him? Convince him to come with me? Did I even want that?

After the way things had been left between us, what was I going after?

I couldn't answer that for sure. All I knew was I had to see him. I hurried down the winding road, going south, and tried to remember Duncan's directions.

TWELVE

kinfolk

The gravel road wound down at a steep incline. I wouldn't have known I was going the right way if I hadn't heard the goats bleating.

When I rounded the bend, I saw the small cottage nestled into the side of the bluffs. Vines and bushes covered it so much that I might not have noticed it if it weren't for the smoke coming out of the chimney.

The pasture for the goats leveled out a bit more than the rest of the bluff, so it was sitting on a plateau. A wooden fence kept them enclosed. The long fur on the goats was dingy white.

The overcast sky and the chill in the air didn't help bring out the color, though. Even the leaves, which had turned golden and red, appeared faded as they littered the yard around Finn's house.

Now that I was here, I wasn't sure what I should do. I wrapped my arms around myself and swallowed hard. Did I go knock on the door? What did I even have to say to him? He left. He made his choice, and I already knew that.

I looked toward the palace, deciding it might be better if I went home without seeing Finn. A woman's voice stopped me, though, and I turned to Finn's house.

"I've already fed you," a woman was telling the goats.

She walked through the pasture, coming from the small barn on the far side of the field. Her worn dress dragged on the ground, so the hem was filthy. A dark cloak hung over her shoulders, and her brown hair had been pulled up in two tight buns. The goats swarmed around her, begging for a handout, and she'd been too busy gently pushing them back to notice me right away.

When she saw me, her steps slowed so much, she nearly stopped. Her eyes were as black as Finn's, and while she was very pretty, her face was more tired than any other I had seen here. She couldn't be more than forty, but her skin had the worn, tanned look that came from a lifetime of hard work.

"Can I help you?" she asked, quickening her pace as she came toward me.

"Um . . ." I hugged myself more tightly and glanced up the road. "I don't think so."

She opened the gate, making a clicking sound at the goats to get them to back off, and stepped outside of it. She stopped a few feet in front of me, sizing me up in a way that I knew wasn't approving, and she wiped her hands on her dress, cleaning them of dirt from the animals.

Nodding once, she let out a deep breath.

"It's getting cold out here," she said. "Why don't you come inside?"

"Thank you, but I—" I started to excuse myself, but she cut me off.

"I think you should come inside."

She turned and walked toward the cottage. I stayed back for a minute, debating whether or not I should escape, but she left the cottage door open, letting the warm air waft out. It smelled deliciously of vegetable stew, something hearty and homemade and enticing in a way that food hardly ever smelled.

When I stepped inside the cottage, she'd already hung up her cloak and gone over to the large potbellied stove in the corner. A black pot sat on top of it, bubbling with that wonderful-smelling stew, and she stirred it with a wooden spoon.

The cottage looked as quaint and humble as I'd expect a troll's cottage to look. It reminded me of the one where the seven dwarves lived with Snow White. The floors were dirt, packed down into a smooth black from wear.

The table sitting in the center of the kitchen was made of thick, scarred wood. A broom sat propped in one corner, and a flower box sat below each of the small round windows. Like the flowers in the garden at home, these bloomed bright purple and pink, even though it was way past the season for them.

"Will you be staying for supper?" she asked, sprinkling something into the pot on the stove.

"What?" I asked, surprised by her invitation.

"I need to know." She turned to face me, wiping her hands on her dress to clear them of spices. "I'll have to make rolls if I'm feeding another mouth."

"Oh, no, I'm okay." I shook my head, realizing it wasn't an invitation. She was afraid that I would impose myself on her meal and her family, and my stomach twisted sourly. "Thank you, though."

"What is it that you want, then?" She put her hands on her hips, and her eyes were as dark and hard as Finn's when he was upset.

"What? You . . ." I floundered, surprised by the directness of her question. "You invited me in."

"You were lurking around. I know you want something." She grabbed a rag from the metal basin that served as a sink and began washing the table off, even though it didn't appear dirty. "I'd rather you come out and be done with it."

"Do you know who I am?" I asked softly.

I didn't want to tout any superiority, but I didn't understand why she was reacting this way. Especially if she knew that I was the Princess, I didn't know why she'd be so curt.

"Of course I know who you are," she said. "And I assume you know who I am."

"Who are you?" I asked, even though I knew.

"I'm Annali Holmes, lowly servant of the Queen." She stopped wiping the table so she could glare at me. "I'm Finn's mother. And if you came to see him, he isn't here."

My heart would've dropped if I wasn't so confused by the way she was treating me. I felt like she was accusing me of something, and I didn't even know what.

"I—I didn't—" I stuttered. "I went for a walk. I needed fresh air. I didn't mean anything."

"You never do," Annali said with a tight smile.

"You've only just met me."

She nodded. "Maybe so. But I knew your mother, quite well." She turned away, putting a hand on the back of one of the dining room chairs. "And I know my son."

I understood too late where her anger came from. Her husband and my mother had been involved in an affair years ago. Annali had known about it, so of course she'd taken issue with me. I don't know why I hadn't realized it sooner.

Here I was, messing up her son's life, after my mother had almost ruined her life. I swallowed hard and realized I shouldn't have come here. I didn't need to bother Finn or hurt his family any more than I already had.

"Mom!" a girl called from another room, and Annali instantly composed herself, forcing a smile.

A girl of about twelve came into the kitchen carrying a battered schoolbook. She wore layers consisting of a worn dress and wool sweater, looking tattered and cold despite the warmth of the house. Her hair was the same dark mess my hair had always been, and she had a smudge of dirt on her cheek.

As soon as she saw me, her jaw dropped and her eyes widened.

"It's the Princess!" the girl gasped.

"Yes, Ember, I know who it is," Annali said with as much kindness as she could muster.

"Sorry. I've forgotten my manners." Ember tossed the textbook on the table and did a quick, low curtsy.

"Ember, you don't need to do that, not in our own home," Annali chastised her tiredly.

"She's right. I feel silly when people do that," I said.

Annali shot me a look from the corner of her eye, and for some reason, I think agreeing with her made her hate me more. Like I was undercutting her parenting.

"Oh, my gosh, Princess!" Ember squealed and ran around the table to greet me. "I can't believe you're in my house! What are you doing here? Is it about my brother? He's out with my father, but he'll be back soon. You should stay for supper. All my friends at school will be so jealous. Oh, my gosh! You're even prettier than Finn said you were!"

"Ember!" Annali snapped when it appeared that Ember wouldn't stop.

I blushed and looked away, unsure of how to respond to her. I understood in theory why it might be exciting to meet a Princess, but I couldn't see anything exciting about meeting me.

"Sorry," Ember apologized, but it didn't dampen her delight at all. "I've been begging Finn to let me meet you, and he—"

"Ember, you need to do your schoolwork." Annali wouldn't look at either of us.

"I came out because I didn't understand it." Ember pointed to her textbook.

"Well, work on something else, then," Annali told her.

"But Mom!" Ember whined.

"Ember, now," Annali said firmly, in a tone I recognized from years of Maggie and Matt scolding me.

Ember sighed and picked up her textbook before trudging to her room. She muttered something about life not being fair, but Annali ignored it.

"Your daughter is delightful," I said once Ember had gone.

"Don't talk to me about my children," Annali snapped.

"I'm sorry." I rubbed at my arms, not knowing what to do. I didn't even know why I was here. "Why did you invite me in if you don't want me around?"

"Like I have a choice." She rolled her eyes and went over to the stove. "You came here for my son, and I know I can't stop you."

"I didn't . . ." I trailed off. "I wanted to talk to Finn, not take him away from you." I sighed. "I just wanted to say good-bye."

"Are you going somewhere?" Annali asked, her back to me as she stirred the stew.

"No. No, I can't go anywhere, even if I had somewhere else I wanted to be." I pulled at the sleeves of my shirt and stared down at the floor. "I really didn't mean to upset you. I don't even know why I came here. I knew I shouldn't."

"You really didn't come here to take him away?" Annali turned around to face me, narrowing her eyes.

"He left," I said. "I can't force him to return . . . I wouldn't want to, even if I could." I shook my head. "I'm sorry I bothered you."

"You really aren't anything like your mother." Annali sounded surprised by that, and I looked up at her. "Finn said you weren't, but I didn't believe him."

"Thank you," I said. "I mean . . . I don't want to be like her."

I heard men's voices coming up the road. The cottage walls were startlingly thin, and I looked out the small window next to the door. The glass was warped and blurred, but I could see two dark figures walking toward the house.

"They're home." Annali sighed.

My heart hammered in my chest, and I had to squeeze my hands together to keep them from trembling. I still had no idea what I was doing here, and with Finn rapidly approaching the door, I wished I hadn't come at all. I couldn't think of anything to say to him. There was plenty I actually wanted to say, but this was entirely the wrong place and time.

The door to the cottage pushed open, bringing along a cold wind, and I wanted to escape into it. But a man blocked my path, looking about as shocked and sick as I felt. He stopped right in the doorway, so Finn couldn't get past him, and for a minute he simply stared at me.

His eyes were lighter than Finn's and his skin tanner, but I saw enough of Finn in him to know that he was his father. And yet there was something almost pretty about him, his skin softer and cheekbones higher. Finn was far more rugged and strong, and I preferred that.

"Princess," he said after a lengthy silence.

"Yes, Thomas," Annali said without even trying to hide the irritation in her voice. "It's the Princess, now step inside before you let all the warm air out."

"My apologies." Thomas bowed before me, then stepped aside so Finn could come in.

Finn didn't bow, and he didn't say anything. His expression remained blank, and his eyes were too dark to read. He folded his arms across his chest, and he wouldn't take his eyes off me, so I looked away. The air seemed too thick to breathe, and I did not want to be here.

"To what do we owe the pleasure?" Thomas asked when nobody said anything. He'd gone over to Annali, looping his arm around his wife's shoulders. She rolled her eyes when he did it, but she didn't push his arm away.

"Getting fresh air," I mumbled. My mouth felt numb, and I had to force myself to speak.

"Shouldn't you be getting back?" Annali suggested.

"Yes." I nodded quickly, grateful for an escape from this.

"I'll walk you," Finn said, speaking for the first time.

"Finn, I don't think that's necessary," Annali said.

"I have to be sure she gets home," Finn said. He opened the door, letting in the frosty air that seemed like a wonderful reprieve from the suddenly stifling kitchen. "Are you ready, Princess?"

"Yes." I nodded and stepped toward the door. I waved vaguely at Annali and Thomas, unwilling to actually look at them. "It was lovely meeting you. Tell Ember I said good-bye."

"You're welcome here anytime, Princess," Thomas said, and I could actually hear Annali hitting him in the arm as I walked out of the cottage.

I took a deep breath and walked up the gravel road. The stones dug into my bare feet, but I liked it better that way. It distracted me from the awkward tension hanging between Finn and me.

"You don't have to walk with me," I said quietly as we reached the top of the gravel road. From there, the road turned into smooth tar leading back to the palace.

"Yes, I do," Finn replied coolly. "It's my duty."

"Not anymore."

"It's still my duty to carry out the Queen's wishes, and keeping the Princess safe is her highest wish," he said in a way that was almost taunting.

"I'm perfectly safe without you." I walked faster.

"Does anybody even know that you left the palace?" Finn asked, giving me a sidelong glance as he matched my pace, and I shook my head. "How did you even know where I lived?" I didn't answer because I didn't want Duncan to get in trouble, but Finn figured it out on his own. "Duncan? Excellent."

"Duncan's doing a perfectly adequate job!" I snapped. "And you must think so, otherwise you wouldn't have left me in his care."

"I have no control over whose care you're left under," Finn said. "You know that. I don't know why you're angry with me for that."

"I'm not!" I walked even faster, so I was almost jogging. That didn't bode well for me, because I stepped on a sharp rock. "Dammit!"

"Are you okay?" Finn asked, stopping to see what was the matter.

"Yeah, I just stepped on a rock." I rubbed my foot. It didn't appear to be bleeding, and I attempted to walk on it. It stung a little, but I'd survive. "Why couldn't we take your car?"

"I don't have a car." Finn shoved his hands in his pockets and slowed down.

I hobbled a little, and he didn't offer to help me. Not that I would've accepted his offer, but that was beside the point.

"What do you call that Cadillac you always drive?" I asked.

"Elora's," he said. "She lends me the car for work, the same way she lends all the trackers cars. But we don't own them. I don't actually *own* anything."

"What about your clothes?" I asked, mostly just to irritate him. I assumed he actually owned them, but I wanted to argue with him about something.

"Did you see that house back there, Wendy?" Finn stopped and pointed to his house. We'd gone too far to see it anymore, but I looked at the trees blocking my view. "That's the house I grew up in, the house I live in, the house I will probably die in. That's what I have. That is *all* I have."

"I don't have anything that's really mine either," I said, and he laughed darkly.

"You still don't get it, Wendy." He rested his eyes on me, and his mouth twitched into a bitter smile. "I'm just a tracker. You have to stop this. You have to go be a Princess, do what's best for you, and let me go do my job."

"I really didn't mean to bother you, and you don't need to walk me home." I turned and walked again, more quickly than my foot would've liked.

"I'm making sure you get there safely," Finn said, following a step behind.

"If you're just doing your job, then go do it!" I stopped and whirled on him. "But I'm not your job anymore, right?"

"No, you're not!" Finn shouted and stepped closer to me. "Why did you come to my house today? What did you think that would accomplish?"

"I don't know!" I yelled. "But you didn't even say good-bye!"

"How does saying good-bye help anything?" He shook his head. "It doesn't."

"Yes, it does!" I insisted. "You can't just leave me!"

"I have to!" His dark eyes blazed, making my stomach flip. "You *have* to be the Princess, and I can't ruin that. I won't."

"I understand, but . . ." Tears welled in my eyes, and I swallowed hard. "You can't keep going like you do. You have to at least say good-bye."

Finn stepped closer to me. His eyes smoldered in a way that only he could manage, and the chill in the air seemed to disappear entirely. I leaned in to him, even though I was afraid he'd be able to feel the way my heart hammered in my chest.

I stared up at him, praying he would touch me, but he didn't. He didn't move at all.

"Good-bye, Wendy," Finn said, so quietly I could barely hear him.

"Princess!" Duncan shouted.

I pulled my gaze away from Finn to see Duncan standing a little ways down the road, waving his arms like a maniac. The palace was right around the corner, and I hadn't realized how close we were. When I looked at Finn, he'd already taken several steps away from me, toward his house.

"He can take you the rest of the way home." Finn gestured to Duncan and took another step back. I didn't say anything, so he stopped. "Aren't you going to say good-bye?"

"No." I shook my head.

"Princess!" Duncan shouted again, and I heard him racing

toward us. "Princess, Matt noticed you were missing, and he wanted to alert the guards. I have to bring you back before he does."

"I'm coming." I turned toward Duncan, putting my back to Finn.

I walked with Duncan to the palace, not even looking back at Finn once. I was quite proud of myself. I hadn't yelled at him for not telling me about my father, but I did say some of the things I wanted to say.

"I'm lucky that Matt was the one who saw you were gone, and not Elora," Duncan said as we rounded the bend to the palace. The asphalt road gave way to a cobblestone driveway that felt much better on my feet.

"Duncan, is that how you live?" I asked.

"What do you mean?"

"Like Finn's house." I pointed toward it with my thumb. "Do you live in a cottage like that? I mean, when you're not busy tracking."

"Yeah, pretty much." Duncan nodded. "I think mine's a little bit nicer, but I live with my uncle, and he was a really good tracker before he retired. Now he's a teacher at the mänks school, and that's still not so bad."

"Do you live around here?" I asked.

"Yeah." He pointed up the hill, north of the palace. "It's pretty well hidden in the bluff, but it's right up that way." He looked at me. "Why? Did you wanna go visit?"

"Not right now. Thanks for the invitation, though," I said. "I was just curious. Is that how all the trackers live?"

"Like me and Finn?" Duncan was thoughtful for a moment, then nodded. "Yeah, pretty much. All the trackers that stay around, anyway."

Duncan walked ahead and opened the front doors, but I stopped and stared up at the palace, where intertwined vines grew over a massive white exterior. When the sunlight hit it, it glittered beautifully, but it was almost blindingly white.

"Princess?" Duncan waited at the open doors for me. "Is everything all right?"

"Would you die to save me?" I asked him bluntly.

"What?"

"If I was in danger, would you be willing to die to protect me?" I asked. "Have other trackers done that before?"

"Yes, of course." Duncan nodded. "Many other trackers have given their lives in the name of the kingdom, and I'd be honored to do the same."

"Don't." I walked up to him. "If it ever comes down to a situation between me and you, save yourself. I'm not worth dying for."

"Princess, I—"

"None of us are," I said, looking at him seriously. "Not the Queen or any of the Markis or Marksinna. That's a direct order from the Princess, and you have to follow it. Save yourself."

"I don't understand." Duncan's whole face scrunched in confusion. "But . . . if it's as you wish, Princess."

"It is. Thank you." I smiled at him and walked into the palace.

THIRTEEN

captive

The debris had been cleared from the ballroom, much to Tove's chagrin, but the skylights were still covered with tarps. Tove had liked having all the junk around because it gave me something to practice on, but he decided that the tarps would be easier anyway.

Duncan had stayed away today. I think his brain was getting frazzled from me playing around with it. Since he sometimes got hit with stray brain waves when I tried too hard, we all thought it'd be best if he hung around somewhere else for a while.

I'd been trying for hours to get one of the tarps to move, and all I'd managed was a ripple across it. Even that was questionable. Tove said it was probably me, but I suspected it was a strong gust of wind blowing across it.

My head was actually starting to hurt, and I felt like a jackass, holding my arms up in the air, pushing at nothing.

"Nothing's happening." I sighed and dropped my arms.

"Try harder," Tove replied. He lay on the floor near me, his arms folded neatly beneath his head.

"I can't try any harder." I sat down on the floor with an unlady-like thud, but I knew Tove wouldn't care. I had a feeling he barely even noticed I was a girl. "I'm not trying to whine here, but are you sure I can even do this?"

"Pretty sure."

"Well, what if I give myself an aneurysm trying to do something I can't even do?" I asked.

"You won't," he said simply. He lifted an arm up, and holding his palm out, he made the tarp above him lift up and strain against the bungee cords holding it down. It settled down, and he looked over at me. "Do that."

"Can I take a break?" I asked, almost pleading with him. My brow had started to sweat, and stray curls were sticking to my temples.

"If you must." He lowered his arm and folded it behind his head again. "If you're really having a hard time with this, maybe you need to work up to it more. Tomorrow you can practice on Duncan again."

"No, I don't wanna practice on him." I pulled my knee up to my chest and rested my cheek against it. "I don't want to break him."

"What about that Rhys?" Tove asked. "Can you practice on him?"

"No. He's completely out of the question." I picked at a spot on the marble floor and thought for a minute. "I don't want to practice on people."

"It's the only way you'll get good at it," Tove said.

"I know, but . . ." I sighed. "Maybe I don't want to be good at it. I mean, controlling it, yes, I want to be good at that. But I don't want to be able to use mind control on anyone. Even bad people. It doesn't feel right to me."

"I understand that." He sat up, crossing his legs underneath him as he turned to face me. "But learning to harness your power isn't a bad thing."

"I'm stronger than Duncan, right?"

"Yes, of course." Tove nodded.

"Then why is Duncan guarding *me*?" I asked. "If I'm more powerful."

"Because he's more expendable," Tove replied simply. I must've looked appalled, because Tove hurried to explain. "That's the way the Queen sees it. The way Trylle society sees it. And . . . if I'm being really honest, I agree with them."

"You can't really believe that my life has more value simply because I'm a Princess?" I asked. "The trackers are living in squalor, and we expect them to die for us."

"They're not living in squalor, but you're right. The system is totally messed up," Tove said. "Trackers are born into a lifetime of debt simply because they're born here, and not left somewhere out in the world collecting an inheritance. They are indentured servants, which is just a polite name for slaves. And that is not right at all."

It wasn't until Tove said it that I realized that's exactly what it was. The trackers were little more than slaves. I felt sick.

"But you do need guards," Tove went on. "Every leader in the free world has bodyguards of some kind. Even pop stars have them. It's not a horrible thing."

"Yes, but in the free world, the bodyguards are hired. They choose it," I said. "They're not forced."

"You think Duncan was forced? Or Finn?" Tove asked. "They both volunteered for this. Everyone did. Protecting you is a great honor. Besides that, living in the palace is a sweet deal."

"I don't want anyone getting hurt over me," I said and looked directly at him.

"Good." His mouth curled up into a smirk. "Then learn to defend yourself. Move the tarp."

I stood up, preparing to conquer the tarp once and for all, but a blaring siren interrupted everything.

"You hear that, right?" Tove asked, cocking his head at me.

"Yeah, of course!" I shouted to be heard over it.

"Making sure it wasn't just me," Tove said.

That made me wonder what it sounded like inside his head. I knew he heard things everybody else didn't hear, but if that included things like blaring sirens, I understood why he always seemed so distracted.

"What is that?" I asked.

"Fire alarm, maybe?" Tove shrugged and stood up. "Let's go check it out."

I put my hands over my ears and followed him out of the ballroom. We'd barely made it out into the hallway when the alarm stopped blaring, but my ears kept ringing. We were in the south wing, where business was conducted, and a few of the Queen's associates were out in the hall, looking around.

"Why is that blasted thing going off?" Elora shouted from the front hall. Her words echoed from inside my head too, and I hated how she did that mind-speak thing when she was angry.

I couldn't hear the answer to her question, but there was definitely a commotion going on. Grunting, yelling, slamming, fighting. Something was going down in the rotunda. Tove kept walking without hesitation, so I picked up my pace.

"Where did you find him?" Elora asked, but this time I couldn't hear her inside my head. But we were close enough to the front hall that she sounded quite loud.

"He was hanging around the perimeter," Duncan said, and I hurried at the sound of his voice. I wasn't sure what he'd gotten himself into, but it couldn't be good. "He'd knocked out one of the guards when I saw him."

When I reached the front hall, Elora was standing halfway down the curved staircase. She had on a long dressing gown, so I assumed she'd been lying down with another one of her migraines when the alarm went off. Rubbing her temple, she surveyed the room with her usual disdain.

The front doors were still wide open, letting an early snowfall blow in. A group of guards were in a struggle in the center of the rotunda, and the wind gusted in, shaking the chandelier above them. Duncan stood off to the side, much to my relief, because the fight did not seem to be going well.

At least five or six guards were trying to tackle someone in the middle. A couple of the guards were really huge muscular dudes too, and they couldn't seem to get a handle on this guy. I couldn't get a good look at him because he kept slipping between them.

"Enough!" Elora shouted, and a pain pierced my skull.

Tove put both his hands to his head, pressing against it hard, and continued to do so even after the pain in my head stopped.

The guards backed off as Elora commanded, leaving ample room for the guy in the center, and I finally saw what all the fuss was about. His back was to me, but he was the only troll I'd seen with hair that light.

"Loki?" I said, more surprised than anything, and he turned to me.

"Princess." He gave me a lopsided smirk, and his eyes sparkled.

"You know him?" Elora asked, her words dripping with venom.

"Yeah. I mean, no," I said.

"Come, now, Princess, we're old friends." Loki winked at me. He turned to Elora, attempting to give her his most winning smile, and spread his arms wide. "We're all friends here, aren't we, Your Highness?"

Elora narrowed her eyes at him, and Loki suddenly collapsed to his knees. He made a horrible guttural sound and clenched his stomach.

"Stop!" I yelled and ran toward him. At the same time, the front door slammed shut and the chandelier above shook.

Elora took her eyes off him to glare at me, but fortunately, she didn't cause me to writhe in pain. I stopped before I reached Loki. He'd doubled over, his forehead resting against the marble floor. I could hear him gasping for breath, and he turned his head away from me so I couldn't see how much pain he was in.

"Why on earth would I stop?" Elora asked. She had one hand on the banister, and her knuckles grew white as her grip tightened. "This troll was trying to break in. Isn't that right, Duncan?"

"Yes." Duncan sounded uncertain, and his eyes flitted over to me for a second. "I believe he was, at least. He looked . . . suspicious."

"Suspicious behavior doesn't give you carte blanche to torture someone!" I yelled at her, and her expression only got stonier. I knew I wasn't helping the situation, but I couldn't contain myself.

"He's Vittra, is he not?" Elora asked.

"Yeah, he is, but . . ." I licked my lips and looked over at Loki. He'd sat up a bit and composed himself some, but his face was still drawn. "He was good to me when I was there. He didn't hurt me, and he actually helped me. So . . . we should at the very least show him the same respect here."

"Is that true?" Elora asked him.

"Yes, it is." He sat on his heels so he could stare up at her. "I've found that I get what I want more often with basic decency than unnecessary cruelty."

"What's your name?" Elora asked, unmoved by his statement.

"Loki Staad." He held his chin up high when he said that, as if he was proud.

"I knew your father." Elora's lips moved into a thin smile, but it wasn't a pleasant one. It was the kind someone would have after stealing candy from a small child. "I hated him."

"That surprises me, Your Majesty." Loki smiled broadly at her, erasing any sign that he'd been in agony moments ago. "My father was a stone-cold jerk. That sounds like your taste exactly."

"It's funny, because I was going to say you remind me so much of him." Elora's icy smile remained frozen in place as she descended the rest of the stairs, and Loki did an admirable job of not letting his falter. "You think you can use your charm to get out of anything, but I don't find you charming at all."

"That's a shame," Loki said. "Because, with all due respect, Your Highness, I could rock your world."

Elora laughed, but it sounded more like a cackle when it echoed off the walls. I wanted to yell at Loki, to tell him to stop baiting her, and I wished I could do that mind-speak Elora did all the time.

Right now I had to make sure that Elora didn't kill Loki. He'd helped me in Ondarike, risking his own life. We'd only spoken a little, but he'd put himself in jeopardy for me.

Before we left the Vittra palace, there had been a moment when I'd almost asked him to join us. I hadn't, and I wasn't sure if I'd made the right decision or not. There was something about Loki that I couldn't explain, a connection I shouldn't feel.

Oddly, the thing that struck me the most about what Loki had done when he'd let us escape was that he'd disobeyed orders. He'd been put in charge of keeping guard over me, with insubordination punishable by death.

Yet Loki had chosen me over duty, defying his monarch and his kingdom. That was something that Finn wouldn't even do.

Elora stopped in front of him. Loki remained on his knees, looking up at her, and I wished he'd get rid of that stupid grin on his face. It only antagonized her.

"You are a small, insignificant creature," Elora said, staring down at him. "I can and will destroy you the moment I see fit."

"I know." Loki nodded.

Her dark eyes were locked on his, and she stared at him for some time before I realized she was doing something to him. Saying something or controlling him somehow. He wasn't writhing in pain, but his grin had fallen away.

With a heavy sigh, she looked away from him and motioned to the guards.

"Take him away," Elora said.

Two of the larger guards came up behind Loki and grabbed him by his arms, pulling him to his feet. Loki was out of it after whatever Elora had done to him, and he couldn't seem to stand.

"Where are they taking him?" I asked Elora as the guards

dragged him away. Loki's head lolled back and forth, but he was still awake and alive.

"It's none of your concern where they take him or what happens to him," Elora hissed at me.

She cast a glance around the room, and the other guards dispersed to do their job. Duncan lingered, waiting for me, and Tove stood a few feet back. Tove would never be intimidated by my mother, and I appreciated that about him.

"Someday, I will be Queen, and I should know what is done with prisoners," I said, reaching for the sanest argument I had. She looked away from me and didn't say anything for a moment. "Elora. Where did they take him?"

"Servants' quarters, for now," Elora told me.

She glanced over at Tove, and I had a feeling if he wasn't here, this whole conversation would go much differently. Tove's mother Aurora wanted to overthrow my mother, and Elora didn't want Tove or Aurora to see any sign of weakness or unrest. And as much as I disagreed with her methods, I saw the need to respect her wishes here.

"Why? Won't he just leave?" I asked.

"No, he can't. I saw to it that if he tries to leave, he'll collapse in agony," Elora said. "We need to build a proper prison, but the Chancellor always vetoes it. So I'm left holding him myself." She sighed and rubbed her temple again. "We'll have a meeting to see what should be done with him."

"What will be done with him?" I asked.

"You will attend the meeting to see what being a Queen entails, but you will not speak up in his defense." Her eyes met mine, hard and glowing, and in my mind, she said, *You cannot defend*

him. It will be an act of treason, and your minor defense of him now
could get you exiled if Tove reports this to his mother.

She appeared even wearier than she had before. Her skin was
normally porcelain-smooth, but a few wrinkles had sprouted up
around her eyes. She held one hand to her stomach for a moment,
as if to catch her breath.

"I need to lie down," Elora said, and she held out her arm.
"Duncan, please escort me to my chambers."

"Yes, Your Majesty." Duncan hurried over to help her, but as
he dashed past me, he shot me an apologetic smile.

I just shook my head. I don't know what else he could've
done. The Vittra had tried to kill me, Finn, Tove, my brother,
pretty much every person I cared about, and Loki was one of
them. I shouldn't be defending the Vittra at all, but Loki was
different.

While I agreed that him turning up here did seem suspicious,
he'd done nothing to justify torture. I wasn't for letting him run
wild, but I was willing to give him the benefit of the doubt. I wanted
to find out what he was doing here before I locked him up and
threw away the key.

When Elora left, I took a deep breath and shook my head. I
knew I'd gotten myself a top spot on her shitlist, and that couldn't
help matters at all.

"That was good," Tove said, and I'd almost forgotten he was
there. I turned to see him grinning at me with an odd look of pride.

"What are you talking about?" I asked. "I made everything
worse. Elora's mad at me, so she'll take it out on Loki. And I don't
even know why he's here or why he came alone. I'm trying to rescue him, and I'm not even sure what his motives are."

"No, that went really bad," Tove agreed. "But I was talking about the door and the chandelier."

"What?" I asked.

"When Elora was tormenting him, you made the door slam and the chandelier shake." Tove gestured to both of them as if that would mean something to me.

"That was the wind or something."

"No, you did that," Tove assured me. "It was involuntary, but you did it. And that's progress."

"So anytime I want to shut a door, I just have to get Elora to torture somebody," I said. "Sounds easy enough."

"Knowing your mother, it would be easy." He grinned.

We went back to train more, but I was distracted and couldn't make anything move for the remainder of the day. After Tove had gone, I headed up to my room. I thought I'd check on Matt first, since the alarm going off had to have freaked him out, and Rhys was at school. I knocked on Matt's door, and when he didn't answer, I ventured inside, but he wasn't there.

With the Vittra breaking in, I felt a little freaked about not knowing where Matt was. Before I decided on an all-out search of the premises, I went to my room to grab a sweater, and I found a note from Matt pinned to the door.

Gone over to Willa's. Be back later.
—Matt

Great. I ripped the note down and went into my room. But I'd told him I'd be training all day, so he didn't need to wait around for me. I could have really used some time to talk to him, since everything felt like absolute chaos, and he was hanging out with

Torn

Willa, which didn't even make sense. I couldn't imagine what the two of them would be doing, spending all that time together. They should be hating each other.

I flopped on my bed and fell asleep pretty quickly. I didn't realize I'd been that tired, but I guess using my abilities took a lot out of me.

FOURTEEN

stockholm syndrome

I'd gotten used to the defense meetings after the big Vittra break-in during my christening ceremony.

We met in the War Room in the south wing. The walls were plastered with maps. Red and green patches speckled them, indicating other tribes of trolls.

A huge mahogany table stood at one end, a drawing board behind it. Elora and Aurora, Tove's mother, stood at the far side of the table. For some reason, they always led the defense meetings together. Aurora didn't trust Elora to run the kingdom, but I still didn't know why Elora tolerated Aurora taking any amount of control.

Chairs littered the rest of the room, most of them mismatched because they'd been pulled from other rooms to fill the space. Our mothers commanded the meetings, so Tove and I were always the first people in attendance. It worked to our advantage, and we hid in the back.

The usual twenty or so attendees were here: Garrett Strom, Willa's father and my mother's possible boyfriend; the Chancellor, a pasty, overweight man who stared at me in a way that made my skin crawl; Noah Kroner, Tove's ever-silent father; and a few other Markis, Marksinna, and trackers.

Soon the room started filling up more than normal. People I'd never seen before filtered in, including a lot more trackers. None of the trackers took a seat, because that would have been impolite with limited seating. Duncan stood behind me, despite the fact that I told him to sit down three times.

Willa burst in a few minutes before the meeting was set to start, and she pushed her way through the crowded room. Her bracelets jangled as she stepped over a tracker, smiling brightly at me before flopping into the chair next to mine.

"Sorry I'm late." Willa readjusted her skirt, pulling it down so it hit her knees. She brushed her hair from her eyes and smiled at us. "Did I miss anything?"

"Nothing's happened yet," I said.

"There are a lot of people here, aren't there?" Willa glanced around the room. Her father looked at us, and she waved at him.

"Sure are," I agreed.

The chair directly in front of me was empty, so Tove slid it back and forth with his abilities.

Crowds tended to overwhelm him. It was too much noise inside his head. When he drained some of his power by moving objects, it weakened his capacity to hear things and helped silence the static.

"Is it really a big deal, then?" Willa asked me and lowered her voice. "I heard you knew the Vittra that they caught."

"I don't know him." I shifted in my chair. "I saw him when I was with the Vittra. It's not a big deal."

"Did you subdue him?" Willa asked, looking up at Duncan.

She was asking him directly, and not asking me if my tracker had done something. She—Willa—was treating people with basic human dignity, and it freaked me out.

Duncan puffed up with pride, then seemed to remember that I'd defended Loki. His expression shifted to shame, and he lowered his eyes. "I saw him knock another guard out, and I called for backup. That was all."

"How come he didn't knock you out?" I asked.

I hadn't had a chance to talk to Duncan much since yesterday. I'd been wondering how they'd been able to capture Loki, when he could've rendered them unconscious with a single look.

"He didn't think he had to." Duncan looked proud again, and I let him. "My appearance deceived him, and the other guards tackled him."

"What was he doing when you found him?" Willa asked.

"I couldn't tell exactly." Duncan shook his head. "I think he was peeking through a window."

"He was probably looking for Wendy," Tove said offhandedly, and the chair in front of me slid so far back, it almost hit my shins. "Sorry."

"Careful," I said, pulling my legs up to be safe.

I wrapped my arms around my knees, and Elora glared at me. I didn't move, and I heard Elora's voice in my head: *That is not how a Princess sits.* I was wearing pants, so I decided to ignore her, and I looked over at Tove.

"Why do you think he was looking for me?" I asked. Loki had let me go once. I didn't know why he'd tried to get me now.

"He wants you," Tove said simply.

"You are the Princess," Willa pointed out, as if I'd forgotten.

"On the subject of which, do you want to have a girls' night tonight?"

"What do you mean?" I asked.

"I feel like I haven't seen you much lately, and I thought it'd be fun if we did our nails and watched movies," Willa said. "You've been under so much stress lately, you need to kick back."

"It would help your training if you shut off your mind sometimes," Tove said.

"That sounds really great, Willa, but I was thinking of seeing if Matt wanted to do something," I said. "This all has to be so confusing, and I haven't been able to spend much time with him."

"Oh, Matt's busy." Willa readjusted the clasp on her bracelet. "He's doing something with Rhys tonight. Some brother bonding thing, I guess."

I watched Tove move the chair back and forth, and I tried not to feel anything about what Willa said. Matt and Rhys needed to spend time together, and I had been busy a lot. It was good for them. It was good for me.

Somebody sat down in the chair in front of me, and Tove let out a dramatic sigh. Elora glared at him, but his own mother didn't. That had never made sense to me either.

Aurora was always looking down on Elora and me, but Tove acted out way more than I did. Tove did whatever he wanted, whenever he wanted. I at least tried to have some decorum.

"It is really packed," Willa said again as more Trylle filed in.

It was down to standing room only, so even some of the Markis and Marksinna didn't get chairs. Elora cleared her throat, preparing to start the meeting, when two more trackers snuck into the room.

I could barely see them as they came in, but I recognized them instantly. Finn and his father, Thomas. They found a spot at the edge of the room. Finn crossed his arms over his chest and Thomas leaned on the bookcase behind him.

"Good. They're calling out the big guns," Tove whispered.

"What?" I pulled my gaze away from Finn.

"Finn and Thomas." Tove nodded at them. "They're the best. No offense, Duncan."

"None taken," Duncan said, and I think he meant it.

"We need to get this meeting under way," Elora said loudly, to be heard over the buzz of the crowd.

It took a minute, but the room fell silent. Elora's eyes traveled over the audience, purposely keeping them off Thomas, the same way Finn kept his eyes off me.

"Thank you," Aurora said with a saccharine smile and stepped closer to my mother.

"As you all know, we've had an intruder in the palace," Elora said calmly. "Thanks to our alarm system and the quick thinking of our trackers, he was caught before he could do any damage."

"Is it true that it's the Markis Staad?" Marksinna Laris asked. She was a nervous Trylle who once made a comment about how she loved that I let my hair go untamed, and how she'd never be brave enough to do something that unrefined.

"Yes, it does appear to be the Markis Staad," Elora said.

"Markis?" I whispered. Willa gave me a questioning look, and I shook my head.

Loki Staad was a Markis? I'd assumed that Loki was a tracker, like Duncan and Finn. The Markis and Marksinna were the royals of the community, and they were protected. Or at the very least, they didn't do their own dirty work. Willa was a Marksinna, and she was one of the more levelheaded, unspoiled ones I'd met.

"What does he want?" somebody else asked.

"It doesn't matter what he wants." The Chancellor got up, his face drenched with sweat from the exertion of standing. "We need to send the Vittra a message. We will not be bullied. We must execute him!"

"You can't kill him!" I shouted, and Elora shot me a look that made my ears ring. Everyone in the room turned to look at me, including Finn, and my own conviction even surprised me. "It's not humane."

"We're not barbarians." The Chancellor dabbed at his brow and gave me a condescending smile. "We'll make his death as painless and benevolent as possible."

"The Markis didn't do anything." I stood up, unwilling to sit and let them propose murder. "You can't kill someone without just cause."

"Princess, it's for your own protection," the Chancellor said, sounding baffled by my response. "He's repeatedly tried to kidnap and harm you. That's a crime against our people. Execution is the *only* course of action that makes sense."

"It's not the only course," Elora said carefully. "But it is something we will consider."

"You cannot be serious," I said. "*I'm* the one he kidnapped, and I'm saying he doesn't deserve that."

"Your concerns will be taken under advisement, Princess," Aurora said, that same too-sweet smile plastered on her face.

The crowd erupted with low murmurs. I'm sure I heard the word "treason," but I couldn't tell from where. Someone in front of me muttered something about Stockholm syndrome, followed by a chuckle.

"Hey, she's the Princess," Willa snapped at them. "Show a little respect."

"We can barter with them," Finn said, raising his voice to be heard over the rumblings.

"Pardon?" Aurora raised an eyebrow, and Elora all but rolled her eyes at him.

"We have the Markis Staad," Finn went on. "He's the highest Vittra royal after the King. If we kill him, we have nothing. They'll come after the Princess with even more fervor because we took out their only hope of an heir."

"You're proposing that we work with the Vittra?" Elora asked.

"We don't negotiate with terrorists!" a Markis shouted, and Elora held up her hand to silence him.

"We haven't been negotiating, and look at where it's gotten us," Finn said and gestured toward the ballroom. "The Vittra have broken into the palace twice in the last month. We lost more Trylle in that last battle than we have in almost twenty years."

I sat down again, watching Finn argue his point. He had a way of commanding the room, even if he wouldn't look at me. Moreover, everything he said was right.

"This is the biggest bargaining chip we've ever had," Finn said. "We can use Markis Staad to get them to back off. They don't want to lose him."

"He's not the biggest bargaining chip," Marksinna Laris interrupted. "The Princess is." Everyone's eyes turned to me. "The Vittra have never come after us like this before. All they want is the Princess, and in a way, they have a right to her. If we give the Vittra what they want, they'll leave us alone."

"We're not giving them the Princess." Garrett Strom stood up and held his hands out. "She is *our* Princess. Not only is she the most powerful heir we've ever had, but she's one of us. We won't give the Vittra one of our own people."

"But this is all about her!" Marksinna Laris got up, her voice getting shriller. "This is all happening because of the bad treaty the Queen made twenty years ago, and we're all paying the price!"

"Do you remember what it was like twenty years ago?" Garrett asked. "If she hadn't made that treaty, the Vittra would've slaughtered us."

"Enough!" Elora shouted, and her voice echoed through my head, through all our heads. "I called this meeting so we could discuss the options together, but if you are not capable of a proper discourse, then I will end it. I do not need your permission to conduct my business. I am your Queen, and my decisions are final."

For the first time ever, I understood why Elora could be so hard. The people in this room were openly discussing sacrificing her only child, and thought nothing of it.

"For now, I will keep the Markis Staad at the palace until I decide what to do with him," Elora said. "If I decide to execute him or barter for him, it will be my decision, and I will let you know." She smoothed out nonexistent creases in her skirt. "That is all."

"We need to reinstate Finn," Tove said before the crowd had a chance to disperse.

"What?" I whispered. "No, Tove, I don't think—"

"All trackers need to be on hand right now," Tove said, ignoring me. "All the storks in the field should be called back to roost. Both Finn and Thomas need to be at the palace. I can stay here and help, but I don't think that's enough."

Amanda Hocking

"Tove can stay at the palace," Aurora offered up too quickly. "If that would help."

"We have additional trackers on staff," Elora told him, but I saw her looking at Thomas from the corner of her eye. "A new alarm system is in place, and the Princess is never left unguarded."

"They sent a Markis after her," Tove reminded her. "Thomas and Finn are the best we have. They've both been your own personal guards for the better part of two decades."

Elora seemed to consider this for a moment.

She nodded. "Both of you, report for duty tomorrow morning."

"Yes, Your Grace," Thomas said, bowing.

Finn said nothing, but he gave Tove a wary glance before departing. The rest of the crowd began to dissipate after that, but I remained sitting in the corner with Tove, Willa, and Duncan.

Garrett, Noah, the Chancellor, and two other Marksinna lingered to talk to Elora and Aurora. I could feel Elora seething, and I knew I should get out of the room before she had a chance to chew me out. But I needed a moment.

"Why did you do that?" I asked Tove.

Tove shrugged. "It's the best way to keep you safe."

"So?" I asked in a hushed whisper, since a few people still milling about could overhear. "Why is it so important to keep me safe? Maybe the Vittra should have me. Marksinna Laris is right. If all these people are getting hurt over me, then maybe I should go—"

"Laris is a stupid, uppity bitch," Willa cut in before I could finish that thought. "And nobody's gonna sacrifice you because things are tough. That's insane, Wendy."

"The royals are crazy and paranoid. What's new?" Tove leaned forward, resting his elbows on his knees. "You're going to be good for the people. But you have to live long enough to do it."

"That's comforting." I leaned back in the seat.

"I'll head home and pack," Tove said, standing up.

"You really think you need to stay here to watch out for me?" I asked.

"Probably not," Tove admitted. "But it's better than staying at home, and it'll be easier for me to help you with your training."

"Fair enough," I said.

"So." Willa turned to me after Tove walked away. "You *need* to have a girls' night. Especially since the house is going to be crawling with boys from now on."

I would've agreed to anything if it got me out of the War Room before Elora had a chance to lecture me, but a girls' night actually didn't sound that bad. Willa looped her arm through mine as we left the room.

We camped out in my room all night. I thought Willa would want to play dress-up or something silly, but we both wore comfy pajamas and lounged around.

After the meeting, I'd asked about the history between the Vittra and Trylle, and Willa had found a book in her father's things. She let me read through it, and answered my questions as often as she could. In exchange, I had to do karaoke with her and let her give me a pedicure.

I didn't make it through as much of the book as I would have liked, and I didn't find out all that much. Vittra attacked, Trylle retaliated. Sometimes the body count was quite substantial, other times it was only minor property damage.

I ended up staying up way too late with Willa, and by the end of the night, the book had been forgotten. We resorted to singing along with Cyndi Lauper and dancing.

Willa spent the night, and she was a massive bed hog, so I slept terribly. I stumbled out of the bedroom in the morning, feeling like a train wreck. I wanted to go downstairs, eat something, drink some water, and then not move again for another three or four hours.

Duncan wasn't loitering outside my door when I left my room, and I thought it was good for him that he finally got a chance to sleep in.

I made it a few steps down the hall when I realized why he'd slept in.

Finn walked toward me, his hands clasped behind his back, and I groaned inwardly. He was already dressed, his pants freshly pressed and his hair slicked back. My hair was insane, and I had to look awful.

"Good morning, Princess," Finn said when he reached me.

"Yeah, or something like that," I said.

Finn nodded once, and he walked past me. I looked around, expecting to see another person summoning him, but there wasn't anyone else.

"What are you doing?" I asked.

"My job, Princess." He glanced back over his shoulder. "I'm walking the halls to watch for intruders."

"So you're not even gonna talk to me?"

"That's not part of my job," Finn said and kept walking.

"Excellent," I said with a sigh.

Stupidly, some part of me had been excited about the prospect of Finn being reinstated. But I should've known better. Just because he'd be around all the time didn't mean anything would change between us. It would only make the whole situation more awkward and painful.

FIFTEEN

capulets & montagues

"Why are you here?" I demanded, and Loki only raised an eyebrow in response.

His room was in the old servants' quarters, and it wasn't quite the cell I'd expected. Duncan had explained that the palace had once been overflowing with live-in help, but the last few decades had seen a drastic reduction in both the mänsklig and the Trylle who stayed around. Meaning there were fewer people to staff the palace.

Even though we didn't have a dungeon, I'd thought Loki would be kept someplace similar to where the Vittra had put me. But this was just a room, similar to the one Finn stayed in when he lived here, except this one had no windows. It was small, with an adjoining bathroom and a twin bed.

To top it off, Loki's bedroom door was wide open. A tracker stood guard a little ways down the hall, but he wasn't even at the door. I had convinced Duncan to distract him because I wanted to talk to Loki alone for a minute, and it hadn't been that hard for Duncan to steer the guard away.

Loki lay on top of the blankets on the bed, his hands folded behind his head and his legs crossed at the ankles. A plate of food sat on the end table, untouched.

"Princess, I didn't know you'd be visiting, or I'd have straightened up the place." Loki smirked and gestured vaguely around his room. There was hardly anything in it, so it wasn't messy at all.

"Why are you here, Loki?" I repeated. I stood just outside the door, my arms crossed over my chest.

"I don't think the Queen would like it much if I left." He sat up, swinging his long legs over the edge of the bed.

"Why don't you leave?" I asked, and he laughed.

"I can't very well do that, now, can I?" Loki stood up and sauntered toward me.

Some rational part of me thought I should step back, but I refused to. I didn't want him to see any weakness, so I raised my chin high, and he stopped at the doorway.

"I don't see anything stopping you."

"Yes, but your mother works best in ways you cannot see," he said. "If I were to leave the room, I'd become so violently ill, I'd be unable to walk."

"How do you know for sure?"

"Because I tried to leave." Loki smiled. "I wasn't going to let a thing like bodily harm stop me from escaping, but I underestimated the Queen. She's very, very good with persuasion."

"How does that work? She used persuasion and told you what would happen if you left the room?" I asked. "And now you can't leave?"

"I don't know exactly how persuasion works." Loki turned away from me, growing bored with the conversation. "It's never been my thing."

"What is your thing?" I asked.

"This and that." Loki shrugged and sat back down on the bed.

"Why did you come here?" I asked. "What were you hoping to gain?"

"Isn't it obvious?" He grinned, that same mischievous way he always did. "I came here for you, Princess."

"By yourself?" I arched an eyebrow. "The last time Vittra came for me here, they sent a fleet, and we still defeated them. What were you thinking, coming here on your own?"

"I thought I wouldn't get caught." He shrugged again, totally nonplussed by the whole thing, as if being held captive were no big deal.

"That's completely idiotic!" I yelled at him, exasperated by his lack of concern over the situation. "You know they want to execute you?"

"So I've heard." Loki sighed, staring down at the floor for a moment. Something occurred to him, though, because he quickly brightened and stood up. "I heard you're campaigning on my behalf." He walked over to me. "That wouldn't be because you'd miss me too much if I were gone, would it?"

"Don't be absurd," I scoffed. "I don't condone murder, even for people like you."

"People like me, eh?" He cocked an eyebrow. "You mean devilishly handsome, debonair young men who come to sweep rebellious princesses off their feet?"

"You came to kidnap me, not sweep me off my feet," I said, but he waved his hand at the idea.

"Semantics."

"But I don't understand why you're a kidnapper," I said. "You're a Markis."

"I am the closest the Vittra have to a Prince," he admitted with a wry smile.

"Then why the hell are you here?" I asked. "The Queen would never let me go on a rescue mission."

"She let that other Markis go after you," Loki pointed out, referring to Tove. "The one that threw me against the wall."

"That's different." I shook my head. "He's strong, and he didn't come alone." I narrowed my eyes at Loki. "Did you come alone?"

"Yes, of course I did. Nobody else would be stupid enough to join me after what happened the last time we paid you a visit."

"That really doesn't explain why you're here," I said. "Why would you volunteer for this, knowing how dangerous it is? *Do* you know how dangerous it is? When I said they wanted to execute you, you laughed it off, but they really mean to do it, Loki."

"I missed you too much, Princess, and I couldn't stop myself from coming." He tried to say it with his usual gusto, but honesty tinged his smile.

"Don't make jokes." I rolled my eyes.

"That was the answer you were looking for, wasn't it? That I chose to come back for you?" Loki leaned against the doorframe, just inside the room, and sighed. "My dear Princess, you think too highly of yourself. I *didn't* volunteer."

"I didn't think that." I bristled and my cheeks reddened slightly. "If you didn't volunteer, then why did they send you?"

"I let you get away." He stared off down the hallway, where Duncan had distracted the tracker. "The King sent me to correct my error."

"Why were you in charge of guarding me in Ondarike? Why you? Why not a tracker or something?"

"We don't have many trackers because we don't have changelings." Loki looked at me. "The hobgoblins do a lot of our dirty work, but you could overpower them without even trying. The Vittra that came after you last time are only slightly more powerful than mänsklig, which is how you managed to defeat them. I'm the strongest, so the King sent me after you."

"Who are you?" I asked, and he opened his mouth, probably to say something witty and sarcastic, so I held up my hand to stop him. "My mother said she knew your father. You're close to the Vittra King and Queen."

"I'm not close to the King." Loki shook his head. "Nobody is close to the King. But I do have history with the Queen. His wife, Sara, was once my betrothed."

"What?" My jaw dropped. "She's . . . she's much older than you."

"Ten years older." Loki nodded. "But that's how arranged marriages work a lot of the time, especially when there are so few of the marrying kind in our community. Unfortunately, before I came of age, the King decided he wanted to wed her."

"Were you in love with her?" I asked, surprised to find myself caring at all.

"It was an arranged marriage!" Loki laughed. "I was nine when Sara married the King. I got over it. Sara thought of me like a little brother, and she still does."

"And what about your father? Elora said she knew him."

"I'm sure she did." He ran a hand through his hair and shifted his weight. "She lived with the Vittra for a while. First, right after they were married, they lived here in Förening, but once Elora became pregnant, Oren insisted she move to his house."

"And she did?" I asked, surprised that Elora had been coerced into anything.

"She didn't have a choice, I suppose. When the King wants something, he can be very . . ." Loki trailed off. "I was in their wedding. Did you know that?"

When he looked at me, he smiled at the memory, and his cocky demeanor slipped. There was something disarmingly honest about his smile, missing his usual snark, and when he looked like that, he was almost impossibly handsome. He was truly one of the best-looking guys I'd ever laid eyes on, and for a moment I felt too flustered to say anything.

"You mean my mother and my father's?" I asked when I found my words.

"Yes." He nodded. "I was very young, maybe two or three, and I don't remember it much, except that my mother took me, and she let me stay up all night dancing. I walked down the aisle and threw petals, which is a very unmasculine thing to do, but there were no other children of royal blood to be in the wedding."

"Where were the children?"

"The Vittra didn't have any, and the Trylle were all gone as changelings," Loki explained.

"You remember Elora and Oren's wedding? And you were only a toddler?" I asked.

He smirked. "Well, it was the wedding of the century. Everyone was there. It was quite the spectacle."

I realized that he was constantly using sarcasm and humor to keep me at a distance, much the same way that Finn protected himself with a hard exterior. A moment ago, as he remembered his mother, I'd seen a glimmer of something real, the same glimmer I'd seen in Ondarike when he'd empathized with me about being a prisoner.

"Do you know why they got married?"

"Oren and Elora?" His eyebrows furrowed. "Don't you know?"

"I know that Oren wanted an heir to the throne and Vittra can't have kids, and Elora wanted to unite the tribes," I said. "But why? Why was it so important that the Vittra and Trylle unite?"

"Well, because we've been warring for centuries." Loki shrugged. "Since the beginning of time, maybe."

"Why?" I repeated. "I've been reading the history books, and I can't find a clear reason why. Why do we hate each other so much?"

"I don't know." He shook his head helplessly. "Why did the Capulets hate the Montagues?"

"Lord Montague stole Capulet's wife from him," I answered. "It was a love triangle thing."

"What?" Loki asked. "I don't remember Shakespeare saying that."

"I read it in a book somewhere." I waved Loki off. "It doesn't matter. My point is—there's always a reason."

"I'm sure there is one," Loki agreed.

For a moment, he let his gaze linger on me, his caramel eyes almost seeming to stare right through me. I became acutely aware of how close he was to me, and that we were hidden away in the privacy of his room.

Lowering my eyes, I took a step back from him and demanded that my heart stop racing.

"Now the principals have become too different," Loki said at last. "The Vittra want more, and the Trylle want to hang on to their crumbling empire for dear life."

"If anyone has a crumbling empire, it's the Vittra," I countered. "At least we can procreate here."

"Ooh, low blow, Princess." Loki put his hand to his chest with false hurt.

"It's the truth, isn't it?"

"So it is." He dropped his hand and returned to his usual sly grin. "So, Princess, what's your plan for getting me out of here alive?"

"I don't have any plan," I said. "That's what I've been trying to tell you. They want to kill you, and I don't know how to stop them."

"Princess!" Duncan called from the end of the hall.

I looked back to see him standing in front of the irritated tracker. I didn't know what Duncan had said to hold him off from guarding Loki, but Duncan had clearly exhausted that avenue.

"I have to go," I told Loki.

"Your tracker is summoning you?" Loki glanced down the hall. Duncan gave me a sheepish smile as the guard walked toward us to resume his post.

"Something like that. But listen, you need to be good. Do what they say. Don't cause any trouble," I said, and Loki gave me an exaggerated innocent look, like, *What, me?* "It's the only chance I have to convince them not to execute you."

"If it's as you wish, Princess." Loki bowed before turning his back to me and walking to his bed.

The guard returned, giving me a deeper bow than Loki had, and I smiled at him before hurrying down the hall. I'd wanted to talk to Loki a bit more, although I wasn't sure that it would've accomplished anything. Because the guard was my subordinate, I could've pushed the issue, but I didn't want it going around the palace that I was spending time with Loki. As it was, I had taken a risk that I shouldn't have.

"Sorry," Duncan said when I reached him. "I tried to stall him, but he was afraid of getting in trouble or something. Which is silly, because you're the Princess and his boss, but—"

"It's fine, Duncan." I smiled and brushed him off. "You did a good job."

"Thanks." He paused for a moment, looking startled by my minuscule bit of praise.

"Do you know where I can find Elora?" I asked and kept walking.

"Um, I believe she's in meetings all day." Duncan checked his watch as he fell into step next to me. "She should be with the Chancellor right now, going over the security precautions in case Loki isn't a solitary incident."

I wasn't completely sure why Loki had come here, but I didn't think it was to hurt me or the people of Förening. He'd seemed upset in Ondarike that Kyra had gotten violent with me, and he hadn't even really hurt any of the guards when they captured him here in the palace. If Kyra or other Vittra had come with him, they'd almost certainly fight harder and probably attack me in the process.

Had Loki come here to protect me? Was this his way of letting me escape from the Vittra again?

"I'm pretty sure Loki is an isolated threat, and he's not even really a threat," I said. "I don't think the Vittra have the numbers to launch a counterattack."

"Is that what he told you?"

I nodded. "In so many words, yes."

"And you trust him?" Duncan asked. His tone carried no hint of sarcasm or irritation, and I had a feeling that he trusted my instincts. If I approved of Loki, then Duncan would too.

"I do." I furrowed my brow, a little surprised to find that I meant it. "I think he helped me escape in Ondarike."

"I understand." He nodded, my reasoning enough for him.

"I need to talk to Elora. Alone," I said as we reached the stairs. "Does she have an opening in her schedule?"

"I'm really not sure," Duncan said. When I started climbing the stairs, Duncan fell a step behind, following me up. "I'd have to check with her adviser, but if you really need to speak to her, I can stress the importance so she can squeeze something in."

"I really need to speak with her," I said. "If you talk to her or her adviser, and she doesn't have time to fit me in, find out any time that she's alone. I'll corner her in the bathroom if I have to."

"All right." Duncan nodded. "Do you want to me to run and do that now?"

"That would be fantastic. Thank you."

"No problem." He smiled broadly, always so happy to be of service, and dashed back the way we'd come to find Elora.

I continued back to my room to think. Between the kidnapping, my parentage, Tove's training, and now my attempts to save Loki, my head was spinning. Not to mention that my own people were so eager to throw me under the bus at the defense meeting yesterday.

I wondered if this was the place for me. I really didn't care to rule a kingdom, so in a way, it didn't matter what crown I ended up wearing. Sure, Oren seemed evil, but Elora wasn't far off from that herself.

If I left with the Vittra, they would leave the Trylle alone. Maybe that would be the best move I could ever make as Princess.

"Wendy!" Matt shouted, drawing me from my thoughts. I'd

been passing his room on the way to my own, and he had his door open.

"Matt," I replied lamely as he rushed out of his room to meet me. He was in such a hurry that he carried the book he'd been reading with him. "Sorry I haven't seen you much lately. I've been busy around here."

"No, I understand," he said, but I wasn't sure he did. He held the book to his chest and crossed his arms in front of it. "How are you? Is everything still okay? Nobody's really telling me anything, and with the attack the other day—"

"It wasn't an attack." I shook my head. "It's just Loki, and he's—"

"Is that the guy that kidnapped you?" Matt asked, his voice hard.

"Yeah, but . . ." I tried to think of some excuse to rationalize a kidnapping, but I knew Matt wouldn't buy any of it, so I stopped. "He's only one guy. He can't do that much. They have him locked up, and everything's fine. It's safe."

"How is it safe if there's still people breaking in?" Matt countered. "The reason we're staying here is because it's the best place for you, but if they can't keep you safe—"

"It's safe," I insisted, cutting him off. "This place is crawling with guards. We're better off here than we would be out in the real world."

I didn't know if that was true exactly, but I didn't want Matt going off to find out for himself. Oren knew how protective I was over Matt now, and he was definitely the type of guy who would use that against me if he had the chance. Matt's best bet was staying here, under the watchful eye of the Trylle.

"I still don't completely understand what's happening here or who these people are," Matt said finally. "I have to trust you on this, and I need to know that you're safe."

"I'm safe. Honest. You don't need to worry about me anymore." I gave him a sad smile, realizing that was true. "But how have you been? Have you been finding stuff to keep you busy?"

"Yeah, I've been spending some time with Rhys, which has been nice," Matt said. "He's a good kid. A little . . . weird, but good."

"I told you."

"You did." He smiled.

"And I see you found something to read." I pointed to the book he held.

"Yeah, Willa found this for me, actually." Matt uncrossed his arms so he could show me the book. It was hand-bound in faded leather. "It's all the blueprints and designs for the palaces over the years."

"Oh, yeah?" I took it from him so I could leaf through the yellowed pages. They showed the ornate designs of all the lush homes the royalty had lived in.

"I told Willa I was an architect, and she tracked down this book for me." Matt moved closer to me so he could admire the drawings with me. "Her dad had it, I guess."

I instantly felt stupid. Matt's only real passion in life was architecture, and we lived in a luxurious palace perched on the edge of a bluff. Of course he would love this, and I couldn't believe it hadn't occurred to me sooner.

Matt started pointing things out in the drawings, telling me how ingenious they were. I nodded and sounded amazed when it seemed appropriate.

I talked to Matt a bit longer, then headed down to my room to take a break. No sooner had I flopped down on my bed than I heard a knock at the door. Sighing, I got out of bed and threw it open.

Then I saw Finn, standing in my bedroom doorway, his eyes the same shade of night they always were.

"Princess, I need you," he said simply.

métier

B eg pardon?" I said when I found my voice.

"The Queen has found time to see you," Finn said. "But you need to hurry."

With that, he turned to walk down the hall. I stepped out and shut my bedroom door behind me. When Finn heard it, he slowed a bit, so I assumed I was supposed to catch up to him.

"Where is she?" I asked. I didn't hurry to catch him, so he glanced at me. "Where am I meeting Elora?"

"I'll take you to her," Finn replied.

"You don't need to. I can find her myself."

"You're not to be left alone." He paused until I reached him, then we continued side by side.

"This place is swarming with guards. I think I can manage walking down the hall to see Elora," I told him.

"Perhaps."

I hated that I had to walk down the halls with him and pretend like I didn't care about him. The silence felt too awkward between us, so I struggled to fill it.

"So . . . what's it like working with your father?" I asked.

"It's acceptable," Finn said, but I heard the tightness in his voice.

"'Acceptable'?" I glanced over at him, searching for any sign that would give away how he really felt, but his face was a mask. His dark eyes stared straight ahead, and his lips were pressed into a thin line.

"Yes. That's an apt way to describe it."

"Are you close to your father?" I asked, and when he didn't answer, I went on. "You seemed close to your mother. At least, she cares a great deal for you."

"It's hard to be close to someone who you don't know," he said carefully. "My father was gone most of my childhood. When he started being around more, I had to leave for work."

"It's good that you get to be around each other now," I said. "You can spend some time together."

"I could give you the same advice in regard to the Queen." He gave me a sidelong glance, something teasing in his eyes that played against the ice in his words.

"Your father seems much easier to know than my mother," I countered. "He seems at least vaguely human."

"You know that's an insult here," Finn reminded me. "Being human is something we strive against."

"Yeah, I can tell," I muttered.

"I'm sorry for the way things went at the defense meeting." He'd lowered his voice, speaking in that soft, conspiratorial way he did when it was only the two of us.

"It's not your fault. In fact, you came to my aid. I owe you a debt of gratitude."

"I don't agree with the things they said in there." Finn slowed to a stop in front of a heavy mahogany door. "The way they blamed you and your mother for what's happened here. But I don't want you to hold it against them. They're just afraid."

"I know." I stood next to him, taking a deep breath. "Can I ask you something, honestly?"

"Of course," he said, but he sounded hesitant.

"Do you think it would be better for me to go with the Vittra?" I asked. His eyes widened, and I hurried on before he could answer. "I'm not asking if it's best for me, and I want you to put your feelings aside, whatever those may be. Would it be in the best interest of the Trylle, of all the people living here in Förening, if I went with the Vittra?"

"The fact that you are willing to sacrifice yourself for the people is exactly why they need you here." His eyes stared deeply into mine. "You need to be here. We all need you."

Swallowing hard, I lowered my eyes. My cheeks felt flushed, and I hated that simply talking to Finn could do this to me.

"Elora's inside waiting," he said quietly.

"Thank you." I nodded, and without looking at him, I opened the door and slipped inside her office.

I'd never been in the Queen's private study before, but it was about the same as her other offices. Lots of bookshelves, a giant oak desk, and a velvet chaise lounge poised in front of the windows. A painting of Elora hung on one wall, and from the looks of the brushstrokes, I'd guess it was a self-portrait.

Elora sat at her desk, a stack of papers spread out before her. She had an ivory dip pen in her hand, complete with an inkwell to dip it in, and she held it perilously over the papers, as if afraid of what she might sign.

She hadn't lifted her head yet, and her black hair hung around her face like a curtain, so I wasn't sure if she knew I was there.

"Elora, I need to talk to you." I walked toward her desk.

"So I've been told. Spit it out. I don't have much time today." She looked up at me, and I almost gasped.

I'd never seen her look haggard before. Her normally flawless skin appeared to have aged and wrinkled overnight. She had defined creases on her forehead that hadn't been there yesterday. Her dark eyes had gone slightly milky, like early cataracts. A streak of white hair ran down the center of her part, and I don't know why I hadn't noticed it when I first came in.

"Princess, really." Elora sighed, sounding irritated. "What do you want?"

"I wanted to talk to you about Lo—uh, the Vittra Markis," I stumbled.

"I think you've already said quite enough on that." She shook her head, and a drop of ink slipped off the pen onto the desk.

"I don't think you should execute him," I said, my voice growing stronger.

"You made your feelings perfectly clear, Princess."

"It doesn't make sense, policywise," I went on, refusing to let this go. "Killing him will only incite more Vittra attacks."

"The Vittra aren't going to stop whether we execute the Markis or not."

"Exactly!" I said. "We don't need to antagonize them. Too many people have died over this already. We don't need to add anyone else to the death toll."

"I can't keep him prisoner for much longer," Elora said. Then, in a rare moment of honesty, her façade slipped for a minute, and

I saw how truly exhausted she was. "What I'm using to hold him is . . . it's draining me."

"I'm sorry," I said simply, unsure how to respond to her admittance of frailty.

"It should please Your Young Majesty to know that I'm right now searching for a solution," Elora said, sounding particularly bitter when she referred to me as *Majesty*.

"What are you planning to do?" I asked.

"I'm looking over past treaties." She tapped at the papers in front of her. "I'm trying to come up with an exchange agreement, so we can give back the Markis and buy ourselves some peace. I don't know that Oren will ever stop coming after you, but we need some time before he launches another attack."

"Oh." I was momentarily disarmed. I hadn't expected her to do anything to help me, or Loki. "What makes you think that Oren can mount another attack? The Vittra seem too damaged to fight right now."

"You know nothing about the Vittra or your father," Elora said, simultaneously weary and condescending.

"And whose fault is that?" I asked. "If I'm left in the dark about things, it's because you're the one who left me there. You expect me to rule this place, yet you refuse to tell me anything about it."

"I don't have time, Princess!" Elora snapped. When she looked at me, I could've sworn I saw tears in her eyes, but they disappeared before I could be certain. "I want so much to tell you everything, but I don't have time! You're on a need-to-know basis. I wish that it could be different, but this is the world that we live in."

"What do you mean?" I asked. "Why don't you have time?"

"I don't even have time for this discussion." Elora shook her head and waved me off. "You have much you need to do, and I have a meeting in ten minutes. If you want me to save your precious Markis, I suggest you get on your way and let me do my job."

I lingered in front of her desk for a moment longer before I realized I had nothing more to say to her. For once, Elora was on my side, and she didn't plan to execute Loki. It would actually be better if I left before I ended up saying something that would change her mind.

I expected to find Finn waiting in the hall to take me to my room, but instead I saw Tove. He leaned against the wall, absently rolling an orange between his hands.

"What are you doing here?" I asked.

"It's nice to see you too," Tove said dryly.

"No, I mean, I wasn't expecting you."

"I was coming to see you anyway, so I let Finn go." Tove smirked and shook his head.

"Am I supposed to train today?" I asked. I enjoyed training with Tove, but he'd thought it best that I take a day or two off so I didn't get burned out.

"No." Tove tossed the orange up in the air as we started walking away from Elora's study. "I'm staying here now, and I thought I should check up on you."

"Oh, right." I'd forgotten that Tove would be living here for a while, helping to ensure the palace was safe. "Why should you check up on me?"

"I don't know." He shrugged. "You just seem . . ."

"Is my aura off-colored today?" I asked, giving him a sidelong glance.

"Yeah, actually." He nodded. "Lately it's been a sickly brown, almost a sulfur-yellow."

"I don't know what color sulfur is, and even if I did, I don't know what that means," I said. "You talk of auras, but you never explain them."

"Yours is usually orange." He held the fruit up as if to illustrate, then began tossing it from hand to hand. "It's inspiring and compassionate. You get a purple halo when you're around people you care about. That's a protective and loving aura."

"Okay?" I raised an eyebrow.

"At the meeting yesterday, when you stood up and you were fighting for something you believed in, your aura glowed gold." Tove stopped walking, lost in thought. "It was dazzling."

"What does gold mean?" I asked.

"I don't know exactly." He shook his head. "I've never seen it quite like that. Your mother's tends to be gray tinged with red, but when she's in full Queen mode, she gets flecks of gold."

"So gold means . . . what? I'm a leader?" I asked skeptically.

"Maybe." He shrugged again and started walking.

Tove walked downstairs, and even though I'd wanted solitude, I went with him. He proceeded to explain all he knew about auras and what each color meant.

The purpose of an aura still eluded me. Tove said it gave him clarity into another person's character and that person's intentions. Sometimes if the aura was really powerful, he could feel it. Yesterday at the meeting, mine had felt warm, like basking in the summer sun.

He stopped at the sitting room and flopped down in a chair by the fireplace. He began peeling the orange and tossing its skin into the unlit hearth. I sat on the couch nearest him and stared out the window.

Autumn was beginning to give way to an early winter, and heavy sleet beat down outside. As it fell against the glass, it sounded like it was raining pennies.

"How much do you know about the Vittra?" I asked.

"Hmm?" Tove took a bite of the orange, and he glanced at me, wiping the juice from his chin.

I rephrased the question. "Do you know much about the Vittra?"

"Some." He held out an orange slice to me. "Want some?"

"No, thanks." I shook my head. "How much is 'some'?"

"I meant like a slice or two, but you can have the rest if you really want." He extended the orange to me, but I politely waved him off.

"No, I meant tell me what you know about the Vittra," I said.

"That's too vague." Tove took another bite, then grimaced and tossed the remainder of it into the fireplace. He rubbed his hands on his pants, drying the juice from them, and looked about the room.

He seemed distracted today, and I wondered if the palace was too much for him. Too many people with too many thoughts trapped in one space. He normally only visited for a few hours at a time.

"Do you know why the Vittra and the Trylle are fighting?" I asked.

"No." He shook his head. "I think it's about a girl, though."

"Really?" I asked.

"Isn't it always?" He sighed and got up. He went over to the mantel and pushed around the few ivory and wood figurines that rested on it. Sometimes he used his fingers, sometimes he used his mind to move them. "I heard once that Helen of Troy was Trylle."

"I thought Helen of Troy was a myth," I said.

"And so are trolls." He picked up a figurine depicting an ivory swan intertwined with wooden ivy, and he touched it delicately, as if afraid of damaging the intricate design. "Who's to say what's real or not?"

"Then, what? Troy and Vittra are the same thing? Or what are you saying here?"

"I don't know." Tove shrugged and put the figurine back on the mantel. "I don't put much stock in Greek mythology."

"Great." I leaned on the couch. "What *do* you know?"

"I know that their King is your father." He paced the room, looking around at everything while looking at nothing. "And he's ruthless, so he won't stop until he gets you."

"You knew he was my father?" I asked, gaping at him. "Why didn't you tell me?"

"It wasn't my place." He looked out the window at the sleet. He went right up to it and pressed his palm to the glass, so it left a steamy print from the warmth of his skin.

"You should've told me," I insisted.

"They won't kill him," Tove said absently. He leaned forward, breathing on the glass and fogging it up.

"Who?" I asked.

"Loki. The Markis." He traced a design in the fog, then rubbed it away with his elbow.

"Elora says she's going to try to—"

"No, they *can't* kill him," Tove assured me and turned to face me. "Your mother is the only one powerful enough to hold him, aside from me and you."

"Wait, wait." I held up my hand. "What do you mean, nobody's strong enough to hold him? I saw the guards contain him in the hall when he was captured. Duncan even helped bring him down."

"No, Vittra work differently from us." Tove shook his head and sat down on the opposite end of the couch. "Our abilities lie in here." He tapped the side of his head. "We can move objects with our minds or control the wind."

"Loki can knock people out with his mind, and the Vittra Queen can heal them," I said.

"The Vittra Queen has Trylle blood in her, back a generation or two in order for her to be Queen. Loki has our blood, actually. His father used to be Trylle."

"Now he's Vittra?" I asked, remembering what Elora had said about knowing Loki's father.

"He was for a while. Now he's dead," Tove said matter-of-factly.

"What? Why?" I asked.

"Treason." Tove leaned forward, and using his mind, he lifted a vase up off a nearby table. I wanted to snap at him and tell him to pay attention, but I knew that was actually what he was trying to do.

"We killed him?" I asked.

"No. I believe he tried to defect back to Förening." He bit his lip, concentrating as the vase floated in the air. "The Vittra killed him."

"Oh, my gosh." I leaned back on the couch. "Why would Loki support the Vittra still?"

"I don't know Loki, nor did I know his father." The vase floated down, landing gently on the table. "I can't tell you their reasoning for anything."

"How do you know this stuff?" I asked.

"You would know it too, if it weren't for the state of things." Tove exhaled deeply, seeming calmer after moving the vase. "It's part of the training you'd be undergoing now, learning our history.

But because of the attacks, it's more important that you be prepared for battle."

"How do Vittra powers differ?" I asked, returning to the topic.

"Strength." He flexed his arm to demonstrate. "Physically, they're unmatched. Even their minds are more impenetrable, which makes it harder for people like you and Elora to control them. It even makes it more difficult for me to move them. And like us, the more powerful the Vittra, the higher the ranking, so a Markis like Loki is awfully strong."

"But you threw Loki like he was nothing at the Vittra palace," I reminded him.

"I've been thinking about that." His brow furrowed in confusion. "I think he let me."

"What do you mean? Why?"

"I don't know." Tove shook his head. "Loki let me subdue him then, and he let them capture him here. Elora's power over him is real, but the other guards . . ." He shook his head. "They don't stand a chance against him."

"Why would he do that?" I asked.

"I have no idea," Tove admitted. "But he's much stronger than all of us. Elora wouldn't be able to hold him long enough for them to kill him."

"Could you?" I asked tentatively.

"I believe so." He nodded. "I mean, I'm capable, but I wouldn't do it."

"Why not?" I asked.

"I don't think we should. He hasn't done anything to hurt us, not really, and I want to see what he's up to." He shrugged, then glanced over at me. "And you don't want me to."

"You would go against Elora's wishes if I asked you to?" I asked, and he nodded. "Why? Why would you do something for me and not her?"

"My loyalty lies with you, Princess." Tove smiled. "I trust you, and other Trylle will learn to trust you, once they see what you can do."

"What can I do?" I asked, feeling oddly touched by Tove's admission.

"Lead us to peace," he said, with so much conviction, I didn't want to argue with him.

SEVENTEEN

numb

After hearing what Tove had to say about Loki, I wanted to talk to him. He hadn't been very forthcoming with me, but I had to know why he'd come here. What did he hope to gain from breaking into the Trylle palace alone?

But, much to my disappointment, Loki's guards had gotten stricter.

Word of my talk with him had gotten out, and the guards decided they needed to work twice as hard to keep me away from him. Duncan had gotten his butt chewed for letting me see Loki at all, and when he finally returned to fulfill his duty as bodyguard, he refused to let me go near the prisoner.

I could've used persuasion on Duncan, but I'd already screwed with his brain enough while practicing on him. I'd also sworn off using persuasion on anyone, though I hadn't told Tove about it.

Besides, it would be good for me to actually use my day off to relax. Tomorrow, I'd go back to training, and I could try to see Loki after that. I was sure I could find a way around the guards without using persuasion on anybody.

I didn't spend much time by myself, though. Duncan escorted me to my room, and I'd barely been in it for five minutes when Rhys got home from school. He made a pizza and invited me over to his room for bad movies and relaxation with him, Matt, and Willa.

Since I felt like I hadn't been spending enough time with any of them, I agreed and made Duncan tag along. I sat on the couch and made sure to keep a safe distance from Rhys, but I didn't have to try that hard because Matt was chaperoning.

Although Matt seemed to be letting his big-brother duties slide. He seemed preoccupied with Willa, teasing her and laughing with her. She surprised me more than anybody, though. She actually ate the pizza. Even I wouldn't eat pizza, but Willa ate it with a smile.

Unlike the last time I watched movies in Rhys's room, I made sure to leave before I fell asleep. I excused myself while everybody was in the middle of watching *The Evil Dead*.

On my way to my room, I saw Finn making his rounds. I said hello to him, but he wouldn't even nod or acknowledge my presence. Duncan apologized on Finn's behalf, which only made me angrier. Finn shouldn't need other trackers to make me feel better.

The next morning, Tove woke me bright and early. With him living in the palace, he no longer had to commute here. It felt way too early to get up, but Tove's insomnia had gotten worse since moving to the palace, so I didn't complain.

After I got ready, we spent a long day training. We went to the kitchen, which was ordinarily deserted, but with all the guards and people in the palace, the cook was on full time. Much to the chef's dismay, Tove had me practicing on moving pots and pans.

I was hoping for something like *The Sword in the Stone*, with all the dancing dishes, but it didn't work out that way. I did get a couple cast-iron pans to float, and I nearly took off Duncan's head when I flung a saucepan across the room using only my mind.

Part of me was ecstatic that I'd finally gotten stuff to move. Tove thought it had something to do with me slamming the door when Elora was hurting Loki. It had unlocked whatever had been preventing me from harnessing my potential.

The part of me that was thrilled was eventually drowned out by the part of me that was exhausted. By the time we finished, I'd never felt so drained in all my life. Duncan offered to help me up the stairs to my room, and while I could've used it, I refused to let him. I had to learn to master this stuff on my own.

I didn't want people like Duncan and Finn, and even Tove, risking their lives to protect me. Or even if they weren't risking their lives, I didn't want to *need* them. I was stronger than the rest of them, and I had to take care of myself.

I knew I couldn't master everything overnight, but I'd work as hard as I needed to until I was as strong as everyone believed I could be.

After a long stretch of training, I took a short break, and then we had a defense meeting. Tove, Duncan, and I went, along with a few select guards, and Elora. Both Finn and his father Thomas were already in the room when we arrived. I said hello to them, and while Thomas responded, Finn ignored me. Again.

The meeting didn't amount to much. Elora filled us in on what was happening. No more Vittra had broken in. Loki hadn't escaped. She went over the guard shifts with the trackers. I wanted to ask about her plan to barter with the Vittra over Loki, but Elora shot me a warning gaze, and I knew now wasn't the time to bring it up.

When the meeting ended, I wanted to head to my room, take a

long hot shower, and go to sleep. Just before I hopped in the shower, I realized I was out of body wash and went to the hall closet for more.

My brain felt numb and seemed to be short-circuiting. For some reason, I could barely feel my extremities, like my fingers and toes. A migraine pulsed at the base of my skull, and the vision in my left eye was a little blurry.

Training today had been harder on me than I had allowed myself to admit. Tove offered several times to take a break, but I'd refused, and it was catching up with me now.

I think that's why I lost it when Finn walked past me again without saying hello. I'd walked down the hall, wrapped in my robe, to get the body wash, and Finn happened to be making his rounds once again. He walked by, I said hello, and he wouldn't even nod or smile at me.

And that was it. That was the final straw.

"What the hell, Finn?" I shouted, whirling on him. He stopped, but only because I'd startled him. He looked at me, blinking and slack-jawed. I don't think I'd ever seen him look so caught off-guard before. "Of course you won't say anything. Just stare blankly at me like you always do."

"I–I—" Finn stammered, and I shook my head.

"No, really, Finn." I held up my hand to stop him. "If you can't be bothered to even acknowledge my existence, you shouldn't start now."

"Wendy." He sighed, sounding exasperated. "I'm simply doing my job—"

"Whatever." I rolled my eyes. "Where exactly in your job description does it say be a dick to the Princess and ignore her? Is that in there somewhere?"

"I am merely doing my best to protect you, and you know it."

"I get that we can't be together. And it's not like I'm so weak-willed that the simple act of saying hello to me will cause me to jump your bones in the hall." I slammed the closet door. "There is absolutely no reason for you to be so rude to me."

"I'm not." Finn's expression softened, looking pained and confused. "I . . ." He lowered his gaze to the floor. "I don't know how I'm supposed to act around you."

"Why would you think that ignoring me would be the best way to go?" I asked, and to my own surprise, tears brimmed in my eyes.

"This is why I didn't want to be here." He shook his head. "I begged the Queen to let me go—"

"You begged her?" I asked, and that was too much.

Finn did not beg. He had too much pride and honor to beg for anything. And yet he'd wanted to be away from me so badly, he'd resorted to begging.

"Yes!" He gestured to me. "Look at you! Look at what I'm doing to you!"

"So you know that you're doing it?" I asked. "You know and you're doing it anyway?"

"I have so few options, Wendy!" Finn shouted. "What do you want me to do? Tell me what it is you think I should do."

"I don't want anything from you anymore," I admitted, and I walked away.

"Wendy!" Finn called after me, but I shook my head and kept going.

"I'm too tired for this, Finn," I muttered and went into my room. As soon as I closed the door, I leaned against it and started to cry. I don't even really know why, though. It wasn't that I missed Finn. It was as if I couldn't control my emotions. They just poured out of me in epic sobs.

I collapsed in bed and decided the only cure for this was sleeping.

EIGHTEEN

secrets

It took Duncan twenty minutes to wake me up the next morning, or so he told me later. He tried knocking first, but I didn't hear that at all. When he moved on to shaking me, it still didn't wake me. He'd been convinced I was dead until Tove showed up and splashed cold water in my face.

"What the hell?" I shouted, sitting up.

Water dripped down my face, and I blinked it away to see both Tove and Duncan holding their heads. My heart pounded in my chest, and I pushed my hair out of my eyes.

"You did it again, Princess," Tove said, rubbing his temple.

"What?" I asked. "What's going on?"

"That brain-slap thing you do." Tove grimaced, but Duncan had already dropped his hand. "We scared you into waking up, so you lashed out in your sleep. But it's fading now."

"Sorry." I got out of bed in my drenched pajamas. "That doesn't explain the water, though."

"You wouldn't wake up." Duncan explained what had happened with wide, nervous eyes. "I was afraid you were dead."

"I told you she wasn't dead." Tove cast a pointed look at him and stretched his jaw wide, working out the aches from the slap I'd accidentally given him.

"Are you okay?" Duncan moved closer to me, inspecting for injuries.

"Yeah, I'm fine." I nodded. "Other than being wet. And I'm still tired."

"We'll skip training today," Tove informed me.

"What?" I turned sharply to him. "Why? I'm just starting to get stuff down."

"I know, but it's too draining," Tove said. "You'll pull a muscle or something. We can practice more tomorrow."

I tried to protest, but it was only halfhearted, and Tove wouldn't hear of it anyway. Even after a good night's sleep, I still felt drained and exhausted. One whole side of my head felt strangely numb, like half of my brain had fallen asleep. That wasn't true, obviously, since I wasn't having a stroke, but I did need a break.

Tove left to do whatever it was that Tove did with his free time, and Duncan promised me a relaxing day, whether I liked it or not.

First order of business was changing out of my wet clothes and taking a shower. After I came out of the bathroom, I found Duncan planted on my unmade bed. He started listing all the low-key, quiet things we could do that day, but none of them sounded like fun.

"Would you say talking with friends is relaxing?" I asked, running a towel over my wet curls. Since my head hurt, I wanted to leave my hair down for a change.

"Yeah," Duncan said hesitantly.

"Great. Then I know what I can do." I tossed the towel on a nearby chair, and Duncan moved to the edge of the bed.

"What?" Duncan narrowed his eyes at me. I hadn't sounded excited about any of his ideas, so he clearly didn't trust whatever I wanted to do.

"I'm going to talk to a friend," I said.

"What friend?" Duncan got off the bed and followed close behind me as I opened my bedroom door.

"Just a friend." I shrugged and went out into the hall.

"You don't have that many friends," Duncan pointed out, and I pretended to be offended. "Sorry."

"It's okay. It's true," I said as we walked past Rhys's and Matt's rooms.

"Oh, no." Duncan shook his head as he caught on. "Princess, you're supposed to be relaxing. And that Vittra Markis is certainly not a friend."

"He's not exactly an enemy either, and I only want to talk to him."

"Princess." He sighed. "This is a bad idea."

"Your concerns have been noted, Duncan. And I don't mean to pull rank on you here, but I am the Princess. You can't really stop me."

"You're not supposed to be talking to him at all, you know," Duncan said, falling in step behind me. "The Queen talked to the guards after your last visit."

"If you don't approve, you don't have to come with," I pointed out.

"Of course I'm going to come with." He bristled and quickened his pace. "I'm not about to let you talk to him alone."

"Thanks for your concern, but I'll be all right." I looked over at him. "I don't want to get you in any trouble or anything. If you need to stay, that's okay."

"No, it's not okay." He gave me a hard look. "It is my job to protect you, Princess. Not the other way around. You need to stop getting so caught up in my safety."

We reached the staircase at the same time a booming knock came from the front door. Nobody ever knocked. They always rang the doorbell, which sounded like very loud wind chimes.

Stranger still, Elora came into the rotunda and walked toward the door, the long black train of her dress dragging on the marble floor behind her.

We were still on the second floor, and Elora was directly below us. I ducked down behind the banister before she saw me, and Duncan did the same. Through the wooden lattice, I saw Elora clearly.

She was by herself, and before she opened the front door, she paused and glanced behind her. Her face was smoother and younger than when I had seen her the other day, but her hair had two additional streaks of bright white running through it.

"Why is she answering the door?" Duncan whispered. "And she's without a guard."

"Shh!" I waved a hand to shush him.

With the coast appearing clear, Elora opened the front door. A gust of icy wind blew inside the hall, and Elora had to grip the door tightly to keep it from slamming back.

A woman slid inside as Elora pushed the door back, fighting it with as much grace as she could muster. A dark green cloak hung over the woman's head, shielding her face from us. Her burgundy dress appeared to be satin, and the hem pooled around her feet, looking tattered and wet from the elements.

"So good of you to make it in this weather." Elora gave her a smile, the tight condescending one.

She smoothed her hair, making it lie so it covered up the white streaks better. The woman said nothing, and Elora gestured to the second floor, which didn't make sense. The south wing on the main floor was where all business was conducted. Elora was directing the guest to her private quarters.

"Come," Elora said as she and the woman started walking. "We have much to discuss."

I grabbed Duncan's arm and dashed across the hall before Elora began ascending the stairs. The only thing at the top of the stairs was a small broom closet, and I opened the door as silently as it would let me.

Once inside, I shut the door almost all the way, leaving a small gap for me to peer through. Duncan was pressed against my back, trying to peek out the crack too, and I elbowed him in the stomach so I could have some room to breathe.

"Ouch!" Duncan winced.

Quiet! I snapped.

"You don't need to shout," Duncan whispered.

"I di—" I was about to tell him I hadn't shouted when I realized I hadn't said anything at all. I'd merely thought it, and he'd heard me. I'd done the mind-speak trick that Elora always did.

Duncan, can you hear me? I asked in my head, trying it out, but he didn't say anything. He just stood on his tiptoes and looked over my head.

I would've tried again but I heard Elora reaching the top of the stairs, and I turned my attention to her. Elora stood between her guest and the broom closet, so I couldn't see the other woman's face. Besides that, she still had that green cloak up.

I waited a few beats after they passed before pushing the door open. I leaned out, looking down the hall at their diminishing figures. They walked past the tracker standing watch outside of Loki's cell, but that was the only guard on the second floor.

The main floor was crawling with guards. I usually had one or two in my vicinity, but otherwise, the second floor was empty.

"Why would Elora bring someone up here?" Duncan asked, stepping out from behind me to watch them.

"I don't know." I shook my head. "Do you know where they're going?"

"No, the Queen doesn't invite me into her personal space," Duncan said.

"Yeah, me neither."

I decided that I needed to trail the Queen and find out why she was being so secretive. I slunk along the wall, staying as close to it as I could. Duncan came with, and we looked like a couple of *Looney Tunes* characters trying to hide behind skinny trees and small rocks.

Elora pushed open the massive doors at the end of the hall, and I froze. That was her bedroom, or at least that's what I'd been told. I'd never actually been there before. I pressed myself as flat as I could against the wall, and when Elora turned to shut the doors behind her, she didn't look up.

"What the hell is she doing?" I asked.

"I could ask you the same thing," Loki said, catching me off guard.

His room was only a few doors down from where Duncan and I attempted to hide. Loki leaned on the doorframe, as far out as he dared go anymore, and his guard glared at him when Loki spoke to me.

With all my attention on Elora, I'd forgotten Loki was up here. I stepped away from the wall and stood up straighter, smoothing out my damp curls as best I could.

"That's really none of your concern." I walked closer to him slowly and with purpose, and he smirked at me.

"It's all the same to me, but you and your friend there"—Loki nodded to Duncan—"look like a couple of Acme Spy School dropouts."

"I'm glad it's all the same to you." I crossed my arms over my chest.

"But I am curious." Loki's forehead crinkled with genuine interest. "Why are you stalking your own mother?"

"Princess, you needn't answer his questions," the guard said, giving Loki a sidelong glance. "I can shut the door, and you can be on your way."

"No, I'm quite all right." I gave him a polite smile before turning a severe gaze on Loki. "Did you see who my mother was with?"

"No." Loki's smile grew broader. "And I'm guessing neither did you."

"Princess, this really doesn't seem all that relaxing," Duncan interjected.

"Duncan, I'm fine."

"But Princess—"

Duncan! My mind-speak kicked in again, surprising me, and I hurried to use it while I still could. I turned to face him. *I'm fine. Now please escort this guard somewhere else.*

"Fine." Duncan sighed. He turned to the guard. "The Princess needs a moment alone."

"But I have strict orders—"

"She's the Princess," Duncan said. "Do you really wanna argue with her?"

Both Duncan and the guard seemed reluctant to go. As they walked away, Duncan stared at me, and the guard continued to sputter about how much trouble he'd be in if the Queen found out.

"I see you learned a new trick." Loki grinned at me.

"I've got more tricks than you'll ever know," I said, and Loki arched an approving eyebrow.

"If you want to show me a few tricks, my door is always open." He gestured to his room and moved to the side, in case I wanted to step in.

I don't know exactly what I was thinking, but I took him up on the offer. I went inside his room, narrowly brushing past him as I did. I sat down on his bed, since he didn't have any chairs, but I sat up as straight as possible. I didn't want to look comfortable or give him the wrong impression.

"Make yourself at home, Princess," Loki teased.

"I am at home," I reminded him. "This is my house."

"For now," Loki agreed and sat down on the bed. He made sure to sit close to me, and I scooted away, leaving two feet of space between us. "I see how it is."

"Tove told me about you," I said. "I know how powerful you are."

"And yet you come into my room, alone?" Loki asked. He leaned back, propping himself up with his arms and watching me.

"You know how powerful I am," I countered.

"Touché."

"The King assigned you to guard me because of how strong you are," I said. "You let me go."

"Is that a question?" Loki looked away and picked a piece of lint off his black shirt.

"No. I know that you did." I kept looking at him, hoping it would make him give something away, but his expression only grew sullen and bored. "I want to know why you let me go."

"Princess, when you came into my room, I thought you wanted to play, not talk politics." He pouted and rolled onto his side, so he could stare up at me despondently.

"Loki, I'm being serious," I scoffed.

"So am I." Loki sat up straight again, using the opportunity to move closer to me. One of his hands rested right behind me, so his arm brushed against my back.

"Why won't you tell me why you let me go?" I asked, forcing my voice to stay even as I looked into his eyes.

"Why do you want to know so badly?" he asked, his voice deep and serious.

"Because." I swallowed. "I need to know if you're playing some kind of game."

"And what if I am?" He kept his eyes locked on mine, but he raised his chin, defiant. "Will you have them kill me?"

"No, of course not," I said.

He tilted his head, examining me, then realization dawned. "You're actually appalled by the idea."

"Yes, I am. Now will you tell me why you let me go?"

"Probably for the same reason you don't want to kill me."

"I don't understand."

I wanted to shake my head, but I was too afraid to break eye contact with him. I wasn't using persuasion on him or anything, but I was keeping his attention, and if I lost that, he might stop talking.

"I think you do, Princess." He swallowed hard and took a deep breath before speaking again. "I know what it's like to be a prisoner, and I thought it would be nice to see somebody escape for a change."

"I believe that," I admitted. "But why come after me again? Why let me go just to track me down?"

"I already told you. King's orders."

"He sent you here alone?"

"Not exactly." Loki shrugged, but never looked away from me. His eyes were almost piercing through me. "I asked to go alone. I told him you trusted me, and I could get you to leave with me."

My heart skipped a beat, and I knew I should be nervous or upset with him, but I wasn't. "Do you really believe that?"

"I don't know. But I hadn't planned on trying. I just knew that if Oren sent others along with me, they wouldn't stop until they got you, and that didn't seem fair."

"So you're not going to try to drag me back to Ondarike?" I asked.

He narrowed his eyes a little, as if really considering it. "No. It'd be far too much trouble."

"Too much trouble?" I said doubtfully. "Couldn't you just knock me out again and throw me over your shoulder? Or at least you could've when you first got here, before you let yourself become a prisoner."

"I didn't *let* myself." He laughed. "Sure, I didn't fight as hard as I could, but there wasn't a point. I didn't really want to take you away. I just wanted it to look like I did, so the King wouldn't have any reason to kill me."

I tilted my head, studying him. "So you're only here to save your own neck?"

"It seems that way, doesn't it?"

"Have you done something to me?" I asked.

I felt a little light-headed, and my pulse was racing. His caramel eyes almost seemed to hypnotize me, and my stomach fluttered. The only time I'd felt something like this before had been around Finn, and I didn't want to believe that I might feel something like that for Loki, that I might be attracted to him. So I hoped that Loki had put me under some kind of spell, maybe the same way that he'd rendered me unconscious before.

"Like what?" Loki raised a curious eyebrow.

"I don't know. Like that knockout trick you did on me before."

"No, I haven't." He let out a long sigh, almost sounding regretful. "And I doubt that I ever will again."

"Why not?" I asked.

The corner of one side of his mouth curled a bit, and he leaned in closer to me. For a moment I was afraid he might kiss me, and as my heart hammered in my chest, I realized that I was more afraid that he wouldn't.

His eyes were still locked on mine, but I pulled my gaze away, searching his face. His tanned skin was smooth and flawless, his jaw strong and yet somehow delicate. Loki was quite stunning in his own right, and I think I'd been trying to ignore that since I met him.

Just before his lips touched mine, he stopped short. I could actually feel the warmth of his breath on my cheek.

"I want to know that when you're with me, you're here because you want to be, not because you're forced." He paused. "And right now you're not moving."

"I—I—" I tried to stutter out some kind of response, and I looked away and jumped up off the bed.

"Now who's the one playing games?" Loki sighed. He leaned back on the bed and watched me.

I took a deep breath and crossed my arms over my chest.

"Wendy!" Duncan shouted from down the hall, and I turned to see Finn standing in the doorway, glowering at both Loki and me.

"Princess, you need to leave his room immediately," Finn said. His voice sounded even, but I could hear the rage seething beneath.

"What is that about, by the way?" Loki asked, giving me a confused look. "Why are these trackers telling you what to do all the time? You're almost Queen. You have dominion over everything."

"I suggest you keep your mouth shut before I shut it for you, Vittra." Finn glared at Loki, and his eyes burned. Loki, for his part, didn't appear even mildly threatened, and he yawned.

"Finn—" I sighed, but I left the room anyway. I couldn't talk to Loki in front of Finn, and I didn't want to fight with Finn in front of Loki.

"Not now, Princess," Finn said through gritted teeth.

As soon as I came out of the room, Finn grabbed the door and slammed it shut. I faced him, preparing to yell at him for overreacting, but he grabbed my arm and started yanking me down the hall.

"Knock it off, Finn!" I tried to pull my arm from him, but physically he was still stronger than me. "Loki is right. You are my tracker. You need to stop dragging me around and telling me what to do."

"Loki?" Finn stopped so he could glare suspiciously at me. "You're on a first-name basis with the Vittra prisoner who kidnapped you? And you're lecturing *me* on propriety?"

"I'm not lecturing you on anything!" I shouted, and I finally got my arm free from him. "But if I were to lecture you, it would be about how you're being such a jerk."

"Hey, maybe you should just calm—" Duncan tried to interject. He'd been standing a few feet away from us, looking sheepish and worried.

"Duncan, don't you dare tell me how to do my job!" Finn

stabbed a finger at him. "You are the most useless, incompetent tracker I have ever met, and first chance I get, I'm going to recommend that the Queen dismiss you. And trust me, I'm doing you a favor. She should have you banished!"

Duncan's entire face crumpled, and for a horrible moment I was certain he would cry. Instead, he just gaped at us, then lowered his eyes and nodded.

"*Finn!*" I yelled, wanting to slap him. "Duncan did nothing wrong!" Duncan turned to walk away, and I tried to stop him. "Duncan, no. You don't need to go anywhere."

He kept walking, and I didn't go after him. Maybe I should have, but I wanted to yell at Finn some more.

"He repeatedly left you alone with the Vittra!" Finn shouted. "I know you have a death wish, but it's Duncan's job to prevent you from acting on it."

"I am finding out more about the Vittra so I can stop this ridiculous fighting!" I shot back. "So I've been interviewing a prisoner. It's not that unusual, and I've been perfectly safe."

"Oh, yeah, 'interviewing,'" Finn scoffed. "You were flirting with him."

"Flirting?" I repeated and rolled my eyes. "You're being a dick because you think I was flirting? I wasn't, but even if I was, that doesn't give you the right to treat me or Duncan or anybody this way."

"I'm not being a dick," Finn insisted. "I am doing my job, and fraternizing with the enemy is looked down on, Princess. If he doesn't hurt you, the Vittra or Trylle will."

"We were only talking, Finn!"

"I saw you, Wendy," Finn snapped. "You were flirting. You even wore your hair down when you snuck off to see him."

"My hair?" I touched it. "I wore it down because I had a headache from training, and I wasn't sneaking. I was . . . No, you know what? I don't have to explain anything to you. I didn't do anything wrong, and I don't have to answer to you."

"Princess—"

"No, I don't want to hear it!" I shook my head. "I really don't want to do this right now. Just go away, Finn!"

I turned my back on him so I could catch my breath. I could feel him, standing behind me, but eventually he walked away. I wrapped my arms around myself to keep from shaking. I couldn't remember the last time I'd been this angry, and I couldn't believe the way Finn had talked to Duncan and me.

Elora's bedroom door creaked open at the end of the hall, pulling me from my thoughts. I looked up to see her opening the massive doors, but I didn't even bother to hide.

The woman with the cloak stepped out, and she had her hood pushed down so I could see her face. She smiled at Elora, that same dazzling, saccharine smile she always had. When she saw me, the smile never changed.

It was Aurora, and I had no idea why she'd be sneaking around with my mother.

NINETEEN

arrangements

It took some convincing, but I finally managed to talk Duncan into staying. I'd found him practicing his resignation speech. He was terrified of letting the Queen or me down, but once I got him to see that he wasn't, he agreed not to leave.

I spent the rest of the day going along with every one of his suggestions, including that I relax quietly. Which meant, even though my mind raced a mile a minute, I had to lie still in bed and watch a marathon of *Who's the Boss?* on the Hallmark Channel with Duncan.

But the break was good for me. When I got up the next day, I still didn't feel like I had all my energy back, but I looked refreshed enough for Tove to resume training.

During our session, I told Tove about how I'd done mind-speak on Duncan, but it only worked when I was irritated. Using that logic, Tove spent most of the morning trying to irritate me into using it. Sometimes it worked, but most of the time I just got pointlessly annoyed.

We were getting ready to break for lunch when Thomas came

down. Since coming back to the palace, he'd been guarding Elora, and she had sent him to retrieve me.

"So . . ." I began, filling the silence with small talk as we walked to her drawing room. "How is being back in the palace?"

I looked up at him. His brown hair had been slicked down, making him look more like Finn, but there was something much softer about his features. The oddest thing crossed my mind just then, ~~that he looked~~ like a kept man.

"It looked different when I lived here," Thomas replied in the same cool way Finn always answered my questions.

"Did it?" I asked.

"The Queen likes to redecorate," Thomas said.

"She never seemed much like a decorator to me," I said honestly.

"People aren't always what they seem."

I didn't have a response to that, so we walked the rest of the way to the parlor in silence. Thomas held open the door for me, and when I entered the room, I found Elora lying on a chaise lounge.

"Thank you, Thomas." Elora smiled at him, and it might have been the most sincere I'd ever seen her look.

Thomas bowed before leaving, but he didn't say anything. I found something almost sad in that. Or would've, if I'd approved of my mother having an affair with a married man.

"You needed to see me?" I asked Elora and sat down on the couch nearest to her.

"Yes. I'd hoped to meet you in my study, but . . ." She shook her head and trailed off, as if I'd know what that meant. She looked worn, but not as bad as I'd seen her the other day. She seemed to be on the mend.

"Have you made any progress with the Vittra?" I asked.

"Yes, actually." Elora had been lying back, but she moved so she was sitting up a bit. "I've been in contact with the Vittra Queen. She's quite fond of the Markis Staad for reasons that remain a complete mystery to me, but she's willing to do an exchange for him."

"That's great news," I said, but my cheer felt a bit forced. I was happy that Loki wouldn't be executed, but I was surprised to find that I felt a bit sad to see him go.

"Yes, it is," Elora agreed, but she didn't sound happy. She only sounded tired and melancholy.

"Is something the matter?" I asked gently, and she shook her head.

"No, actually, everything's . . . as it should be." She smoothed out her dress and forced a thin smile. "The Vittra agreed to no more attacks until after the coronation."

"The coronation?" I asked.

"The coronation where you become Queen," Elora elaborated.

"I'm not going to be Queen for a while, am I?" I asked, feeling nervous at the prospect. Even with as much training as I'd done lately, I still felt completely unprepared to rule. "Like a long while, right?"

"Not for a while, no." Elora smiled wanly. "But time has a way of creeping up on you."

"Well, I'm in no rush." I leaned back on the couch. "You can keep the crown as long as you'd like."

"I will." Elora actually laughed at that, but it sounded hollow and sad.

"Wait. I don't understand. The King agreed to peace until *after* I'm Queen?" I asked. "Won't that be too late to kidnap me?"

"Oren's always believed he can take anything he wants," Elora said. "But he wants valuable things, and you're far more valuable as a Queen. I imagine that he thinks you'll be an even greater ally then."

"Why would I be his ally?" I asked.

"You are his daughter," she said, almost regretfully. "He sees no reason that you won't come around to his way of thinking." She looked up at me, her dark eyes distant. "You must protect yourself, Princess. Rely on the people around you, and defend yourself by any means you can."

"I'm trying," I reassured her. "Tove and I have been training all morning, and he says I'm doing quite well."

"Tove is very powerful." Elora nodded in agreement. "That's why it's essential to keep him close to you."

"Well, he's staying down the hall from me," I said.

"He is powerful," Elora reiterated. "But he's not strong enough to lead."

"I don't know." I shrugged. "He has good insight."

"He's scatterbrained and often irrational." She stared off at nothing for a moment. "But he is loyal, and he will stand by your side."

"Yeah . . ." I didn't understand what she was getting at. "Tove's a great guy."

"I am relieved to hear you say that." Elora exhaled and rubbed her temple. "I didn't have it in me to fight with you today."

"Fight with me about what?" I asked.

"Tove." She looked at me like it should be obvious. "I didn't tell you?"

"Tell me what?" I leaned forward, totally confused.

"I thought I just told you. A moment ago." Her brow furrowed, showing even more wrinkles. "It's all going so fast."

"What is?" I stood up, feeling real concern for her. "What are you talking about?"

"You only just got here, and I thought I'd have more time." She shook her head. "Well, anyway, it's all been arranged."

"What?" I repeated.

"Your marriage." Elora looked up at me, wondering why I didn't understand what she meant already. "You and Tove are to be married as soon as you turn eighteen."

"Whoa." I held up my hands and took a step back, as if that would defend me somehow. "What?"

"It's the only way." Elora lowered her eyes and shook her head, as if she'd done everything she could to prevent it. And considering how much she loathed Aurora, she probably had done everything she could. "To protect the kingdom and to protect the crown."

"What?" I repeated. "But I turn eighteen in three months."

"At least Aurora will be planning it all," Elora said wearily. "She'll have the wedding of the century ready by then."

"No, Elora." I waved my hands. "I can't marry Tove!"

"Why ever not?" She batted her dark lashes at me.

"Because I don't love him!"

"Love is a fairy tale that mänks tell their children so they'll have grandchildren," Elora said, brushing me off. "Love has nothing to do with marriage."

"I . . . You can't really expect me . . ." I sighed and shook my head. "I can't."

"You must." Elora stood up, pushing herself up with her arm. She steadied herself on the chaise for a moment, as if she might fall. When she was certain she was steady, she stepped toward me. "Princess, it is the only way."

"The only way to what?" I asked. "No. I'd rather not be Queen than marry someone I don't love."

"Don't say that!" Elora snapped, and the familiar venom returned to her words. "A Princess must *never* say that!"

"Well . . . I can't do it! I refuse to marry him! Or anyone, unless I want to!"

"Princess, listen to me." Elora gripped my arms and looked directly in my eyes. "The Trylle already think you should be shipped to the Vittra because of who your father is, and that is all the ammo Aurora needs to get you overthrown."

"I don't care about the crown," I insisted. "I never did."

"Once you're overthrown, you'll be exiled to live with the Vittra, and I know that you don't think the Markis Staad seems that bad," Elora went on. "Maybe he isn't. But the King is. I lived with him for three years, but when you were born, I left him, knowing what that would mean for our kingdom. But I had to leave him, that's how bad a man he is."

"I won't go back to the Vittra," I said. "I'll move to Canada or Europe or something."

"He will find you," Elora said. "And even if he doesn't, if you left, it would be the end of our people. Tove is powerful, but he is not strong enough to run a kingdom or stand up to Oren. The Vittra would attack and destroy the Trylle. He would kill everyone, especially the ones you love."

"You don't know that." I backed away so she wasn't touching me.

"Princess, yes, I do." Her eyes locked with mine, her sincerity unmistakable.

"You saw it?" I asked and looked around the room for a painting. One that would show me the devastation that she'd seen.

"I saw that they need you," Elora said. "They need you to survive."

I'd never seen her look desperate before, and it scared the hell out of me. I liked Tove, but not romantically, and I didn't want to marry someone I didn't love. Especially when I might love someone else.

But Elora was pleading with me to do this. She believed everything she was saying, and I hated to admit it, but she had a compelling argument.

"Elora . . ." My mouth felt dry, and it was hard to swallow. "I don't know what to say."

"Marry him, Princess," Elora commanded. "He'll protect you."

"I can't marry someone so he'll be my bodyguard," I told her quietly. "Tove deserves to be happy. And I would like a chance at it too."

"Princess, I'm not . . ." She squeezed her eyes shut and pressed her fingers to her temple. "Princess."

"I'm sorry. I'm not trying to argue with you," I said.

"No, Princess, I . . ." She reached out, grabbing the back of the couch to catch herself.

"Elora?" I rushed over to her and put my hand on her back. "Elora, what's wrong?"

Blood seeped from her nose, but it was no simple nosebleed. It was like an artery had opened up. Her eyes rolled back in her head, and her body went limp. She collapsed, and I barely caught her in my arms.

"Help me!" I shouted. "Somebody! *Help!*"

TWENTY

dynasty

Thomas rushed in first. I'd already lowered Elora to the floor, where she twitched like she was having a small seizure.

I'd crouched down next to her, but Thomas pushed me out of the way to tend to her. I leaned against the couch while he attempted to revive her, praying my mother would be okay.

"Wendy," Finn said.

I hadn't even heard him come in. I looked up at him with tears blurring my vision, and he held out his hand to me. I took it, and let him pull me to my feet.

"Get Aurora Kroner," Thomas told Finn. *"Now."*

"Yes, sir." Finn nodded.

He still had my hand, and he pulled me out of the room. He walked fast because time was of the essence. My legs felt numb and rubbery, but I pushed them to hurry.

"Go find Tove or Willa. Even Duncan," Finn said when we reached the main hall. "I'll come and get you later."

"What's wrong with Elora?" I asked.

"I don't have time, Wendy." Finn shook his head, his eyes pained. "I'll get you when there's anything to tell you."

"Go," I said, nodding to hurry him along.

Finn raced out the front door, leaving me in the hall, alone and scared.

Duncan found me exactly as Finn had left me. He'd heard about Elora's collapse from the other trackers, who'd gone into lockdown mode. I heard them bustling about the palace, but that was secondary. My mother might be dying.

Duncan suggested we go up to my room, but I didn't want to be that far away. I needed to be close in case something happened. We sat in the living room, and he tried to comfort me, but it was futile.

Finn came back a few minutes later with Aurora, and they rushed down the hall. Her dress billowed out behind her, and her hair had come loose from its bun, blowing back as she ran.

Garrett and Willa came shortly after. Garrett went down to check on Elora's progress while Willa sat with me. She put her arm around my shoulders and kept reminding me how strong Elora was. Nothing could stop her.

"But . . . what if she dies?" I asked, staring blankly at the unlit fireplace in front of me.

The living room had a horrible chill from the icy wind beating against the windows. Duncan knelt in front of the fireplace. He had been trying to light a fire for the past few minutes.

"She won't die." Willa squeezed me tighter.

"No, Willa, I'm being honest," I said. "What happens if the Queen dies?"

"She's not going to die." Willa forced a smile. "We don't need to worry about that right now."

"I've almost got this fire lit," Duncan lied to change the subject.

"It's gas, Duncan," Willa told him. "You just turn a knob."

"Oh." Duncan did as she said, and a bright flame roared up through the fireplace.

Staring down at Elora's blood that had gotten on my shirt, I was surprised to find how scared I felt. I didn't want her to die.

She always seemed so strong, so composed, and it made me wonder how much pain she was in. We'd met in the drawing room today, and she'd wanted to meet me in the study. She wasn't well enough to move, I realized. She shouldn't have been standing or exerting herself at all, let alone arguing with me. I'd made her already frail condition even worse.

Why hadn't she told me about how debilitated she was? But I already knew the answer. Her sense of duty came before everything else.

"Princess," Finn said, pulling me from my thoughts. He stood at the entrance to the living room, his face drawn.

"Is she okay?" I jumped up at the sight of him, pulling away from Willa.

"She's asked to see you." Finn pointed toward her drawing room and wouldn't meet my eyes.

"So she's awake? She's alive? Is she okay? Does she know what happened? Did Aurora fix her?" I asked. My questions came out too rapidly for him to answer, but I couldn't seem to slow myself.

"She'd rather tell you everything herself," Finn said simply.

"That sounds like her." I nodded. She was awake and wanted to see me. That had to be a good sign.

Willa and Duncan gave me reassuring smiles, but they couldn't mask their anxiety. I told them I'd be back soon, and that I was sure everything would be fine. I didn't know if that was true or not, but I had to ease their fears somehow.

I walked with Finn down the corridor to the parlor. Finn kept his pace slow and deliberate. I wanted to run to Elora, but I forced myself to stay with him. I wrapped my arms around myself and rubbed my hands along them.

"Is she angry with me?" I asked him.

"The Queen?" Finn seemed surprised. "No. Of course not. Why would she be?"

"I was arguing with her when she . . . If I hadn't been antagonizing her, she might not have gotten so . . . sick."

"No, you didn't do this." He shook his head. "In fact, it's good that you were with her. You got her help right away."

"What do you mean?" I asked.

"You called for help using your thoughts." He tapped his forehead. "We were too far away, and we wouldn't have known if you hadn't done that. Elora might be in a lot worse shape if you hadn't been there."

"What's wrong with her?" I asked him directly. "Do you know?"

"She'll need to tell you."

I thought about pushing Finn for more information, but we were almost to her. Besides, it didn't feel right to argue with him now.

His whole demeanor had changed, seeming softer and more somber. He'd let some of his guard down around me again, and while I wasn't in the mood to take advantage of that, I did enjoy the familiar feel of being with him without a giant wall between us. I missed him.

Aurora came out of the parlor just before we reached it. Her normally flawless skin had gone gray. Her dark eyes were glossed over, and her hair hung in unruly waves around her face. She leaned up against the wall, supporting herself, and struggled to catch her breath.

"Marksinna?" Finn quickly went to her, putting his arm around her to steady her. "Are you all right?"

"I'm only tired," Aurora said as Finn helped her to a chair in the hallway. She moved like an old woman, and her bones creaked as she eased herself down in the chair. "Will you get my son? I need to lie down, and I want him to help me home."

"Yes, of course," Finn said, and he gave me an apologetic look. "Princess, will you be all right seeing the Queen alone?"

"Yes." I nodded. "Go get Tove. I'll be fine."

Finn hurried away to retrieve Tove for his mother, and I went on to the room. I felt guilty for leaving Aurora alone in the hallway looking so completely drained, but I had my own mother to attend to.

The door to the parlor was still open, and I stayed in the hall for a moment, watching.

Elora lay on her chaise lounge, the way she had when I arrived, but she had a black fur blanket over her. Her raven hair had gone even whiter, so it now appeared to be white streaked with black and not the other way around. Her eyes were closed, and the blood had been wiped from her face.

Garrett had pulled up a chair so he sat right next to her head. He held one of her hands in both of his, and gazed at her with worry and adoration. His tousled hair was even more unkempt than normal, and some of her blood stained his shirt.

On the other side of the chaise lounge, Thomas stood keeping watch. He had the same stoic stance all the trackers did when they were on guard duty, but his eyes rested heavily on Elora. They weren't filled with the same intensity as Garrett's, but something glimmered in them, some faint remembrance of whatever had transpired between Thomas and Elora years ago.

When she opened her eyes, it was Thomas that Elora looked up at. Garrett's jaw flexed as he clenched his teeth, but he said nothing. He didn't even drop her hand.

"Elora?" I said timidly and stepped inside the room.

"Princess." Her voice sounded weak, and she made a poor attempt at a smile.

"You wanted to see me?" I asked.

"Yes." She tried to sit up, but Garrett gently placed his hand on her shoulder.

"Elora, you need to rest," Garrett told her.

"I am fine." She waved him off but lowered herself back down. "I need to speak privately with my daughter. Can you both leave us for a moment?"

"Yes, Your Majesty." Thomas bowed. "But for your sake, please take it easy."

"Of course, Thomas." She offered him a tired smile, and he bowed again before leaving.

"I'll be right down the hall if you need me," Garrett said, but he seemed hesitant to stand. He wouldn't even walk toward the door until Elora glared at him. "If you need anything, call for me. Or send the Princess. Okay?"

"If it will get you to leave quicker, I will agree to anything." Elora sighed.

Garrett paused as he passed me, and he looked like he wanted to say something, probably remind me to take it easy. Elora said his name, and he hurried along. He closed the door behind him, and I took his seat next to Elora.

"How are you feeling?" I asked.

"I've been better, obviously." She readjusted the blanket over her, getting more comfortable on the chaise. "But I will live to fight another day, and that's what matters."

"What happened?" I asked. "Why did you just collapse?"

"How old do you think I am?" Elora asked, turning so her eyes met mine. A few days ago they'd been almost black, but now they had the gray haze of cataracts.

Her age was a hard question to answer. When I'd first met her, I'd have pegged her for fifty-something. A very beautiful fifty, but even then, she'd had an aged quality under her stunning features.

Now, lying on the chaise, frail and tired, Elora looked even more advanced in age than that. She looked like an old woman, but I didn't want to say that to her, of course.

"Um . . . forty, maybe?"

"You're kind, and a bad liar." She pushed herself up, so she was sitting up a bit. "That's something you'll need to work on. The horrible reality is that being a leader involves a lot of lying."

"I'll practice my poker face later," I said. "You look good, though, if that's what you're asking. Just tired and run-down."

"I am tired and run-down," Elora admitted wearily. "And I'm only thirty-nine."

"Thirty-nine what?" I asked, confused, and she propped her head on her hand so she could look at me.

"Thirty-nine years old," she said, smiling wider. "You seem shocked. I don't blame you. Although I'm surprised you didn't catch on sooner. I told you that I married your father when I was very young. I had you when I was twenty-one."

"But . . ." I stammered. "Is that what's wrong with you? Are you aging too fast?"

"Not exactly." She pursed her lips. "It's the price we pay for our abilities. When we use them, they drain us and age us."

"All the stuff you do—like the mind-speak and holding Loki prisoner—that's killing you?" I asked.

She nodded. "I'm afraid so."

"Then why do it?" I wanted to shout at her, but I kept my voice as even as I could. "I can understand defending yourself, but calling Finn with mind-speak? Why would you do something if it's killing you?"

"The mind-speak doesn't use as much." Elora waved it off. "The things that are really draining I only do when I have to, like housing a prisoner. But what uses it the most is the precognitive painting, and that I can't control."

I glanced at several paintings Elora had leaned up against the windows. Across the hall, she had a locked room filled with these paintings.

"What do you mean, you can't control it?" I asked. "Just don't do it."

"I can't see the visions, but they fill my head." She gestured to her forehead. "It's an agonizing blackness that takes over until I paint and get them out. I can't stop them from coming, and it's too painful to ignore them. I would go insane if I tried to keep them all inside."

"But it's killing you." I slumped in the chair. "Why even teach other Trylle how to use their abilities, if it means they'll grow weak and old?"

"That's the price." She sighed. "We go mad if we don't use them, we age if we do. The more powerful we are, the more cursed we are."

"What do you mean?" I asked. "I'll go crazy if I stop?"

"I don't really know what will happen to you." Elora rested her chin on her hand, eyeing me. "You're your father's daughter too."

"What?" I shook my head. "You mean because I have Vittra blood too?"

"Precisely."

"Tove told me about them. He said they're very strong, but I'm not strong." I remembered all the fights I'd been in throughout my illustrious school career, and how I'd taken a beating as often as I'd given one. "I'm not like that."

"Some are physically strong, yes," Elora clarified. "That Loki Staad, I believe, is very strong. If I recall correctly, he could lift a grand piano by the time he could walk."

"Yeah, I can't do that."

"Oren isn't that way. He is . . ." She trailed off, thinking. "You met him. How old do you think he is?"

"I don't know." I shrugged. "A few years younger than you, maybe."

"When I married him, he was seventy-six, and that was twenty years ago," Elora said.

"Whoa. What?" I stood up. "You're telling me that he's nearly a hundred? He's over twice your age? So you look older, and he looks younger? How?"

"He's something like immortal."

"He's immortal?" I gaped at her.

"No, Princess, I said he's something *like* immortal," Elora said carefully. "Oren ages, but at a much slower rate, and he heals very quickly. It's hard for him to be hurt. He's one of the last pure-blooded Vittra to be born."

"That's what makes me so special, and that's why you weren't worried when I told you that my host mother almost killed me." I rested my hands on the back of the chair, supporting myself with it. "You think I'm like him."

"The hope is that you're like us both," Elora said. "You'll have the Trylle abilities to move and control things, and the Vittra abilities to heal and be strong enough to handle them."

"Holy hell." My hands trembled, and I sat down. "Now I know how a racehorse feels. I wasn't conceived. I was bred."

Elora bristled a bit at the accusation. "That's not exactly how it was."

"Really?" I looked over at her. "That's why you married my father, wasn't it? So you could make me—your perfect little biological weapon. Once you did, you left him and tried to keep me all for yourself. That's what this whole feud is about now, isn't it? Who can control me?"

"No, that's not right." Elora shook her head. "I married your father because I was eighteen and my parents told me to. Oren seemed kind at first, and everyone told me it was the only way we could stop the fighting. I could stop the bloodshed if I would only marry him, so I agreed to it."

"What bloodshed?" I asked. "What were the Trylle and the Vittra fighting over?"

"The Vittra are dying. Their abilities are fading, they're running out of money, and Oren's always believed that he's entitled to anything he wants." Elora took a breath. "What he wanted was everything we had. Our wealth, our population.

"But what he wanted most was *my* power," she went on. "My mother's, originally. When she refused his advances, he waged endless battles against us. We used to be a great people with cities all over the world, but now he's left us with a few isolated pockets."

"And you married that? A man who killed your people because your mother wouldn't have him?" I asked.

"They didn't explain it all to me when we became engaged, but Oren agreed to peace in exchange for my hand in marriage," Elora said. "My parents believed they didn't have a choice, and Oren turned on the charm. He might not have telekinesis, but Oren can be very persuasive when he wants."

"So you married him and united the people. What went wrong?" I asked.

"Some of the cities revolted, refusing to mix with the Vittra," Elora said. "My parents were still King and Queen, and they wanted to reason with them. They sent Oren and me as ambassadors, to sway them to our way of thinking.

"In the very first city, people questioned us. Him in particular," Elora continued. "He managed to charm them, and using some of my own persuasion, we convinced even the most ardent doubter to join the Vittra alliance. Later, this would prove to be a fatal mistake.

"I never loved Oren, but in the beginning of our marriage, I cared for him. I thought I might one day grow to love him. What I didn't realize was how hard he had to work to be that way, and as we went on our tour, his mask began to slip.

"We stopped in a village in Canada, and we had a town hall meeting with all the Trylle, the way we had in the other cities." Elora paused, staring out the window at the icy weather. "Everyone was there. Even the mänsklig children, all the trackers and their families.

"Someone asked Oren what he hoped to gain from all this, and for some reason, it was more than Oren could bear." She let out a deep breath and lowered her eyes. "He began yelling and attacking them, and the villagers began fighting back. So . . . Oren killed them all. We were the only two survivors.

"He spun the story, and I went along with it because I didn't know what else to do. My parents had convinced me that we needed him for peace. Oren was my husband, and I had been complicit in the murders of our own people because I didn't stand up to him. If I had, I would've been killed too, but that didn't change the fact that I did nothing to save them."

"I'm sorry," I said, unsure how else to respond to her confession.

"Oren was labeled a war hero, and I . . ." She trailed off, picking absently at the fur that covered her.

"Why did you stay with him?" I asked.

"You mean after I realized that I'd married a monster?" Elora asked with a sad smile. "I didn't used to be the way I am now. I was much more trusting, much more willing to hope and believe, and follow. That is one thing I can thank your father for. He made me realize that I had to be a leader."

"What made you finally leave?" I asked.

"Oren made an effort after we got back. He tried to be kind, or as kind as he could manage. He didn't beat me or call me names. He would be patronizing to my every thought or word, but we had peace. No war. No deaths. A bad marriage seemed worth it to me. I could handle that if no one else had to die.

"Then I became pregnant with you, and it all changed." Elora rearranged herself on the chaise. "What I didn't realize then was that you were all he ever wanted. A perfect heir to his throne. We tried for nearly three years before I conceived, and the wait had worn on him as it was.

"As soon as he found out he was having a child, it was like a switch flipped inside him." Elora snapped her fingers. "He was even more domineering. He never let me leave the room. He didn't even want me to leave the bed, in case it would risk losing you.

"My mother and I began looking into families for you to go to. I knew I had to leave you as a changeling, not because it was what we did, but because I couldn't let Oren raise you." She shook her head. "Oren did not want that. He wanted you all for himself.

"So when my father, the King, decreed that you must be a changeling, the way all heirs to the throne had been, Oren took me, and we left. We lived in Ondarike, where he had me locked up as a prisoner.

"Two weeks before you were due, my mother and father broke me out of his palace. My father was killed in the fight, along with many other brave Trylle. My mother took me away to a family she'd been secretly researching—the Everlys. It was a hasty switch, but they seemed to have everything you would need.

"After I had you, I . . ." She stopped, completely lost in thought.

"You what?" I prompted when she didn't say anything.

"It was the best thing for you," she said. "I know you had problems with your host family, but I didn't have time to pick or be choosy. I just needed you hidden from Oren."

"Thank you," I said lamely.

"As soon as you were born, I left. Your grandmother held you, but I didn't have the chance. We had to run to keep the Vittra off your scent. We went to a safe house, a chalet in Canada. When Oren had lived here, we hadn't trusted him enough to tell him of all our secret places." She closed her eyes and took a breath. "But he found us in the chalet.

"That Markis you're so fond of?" Elora gestured in the direction of Loki's room. "It was his father that led Oren to us. He's the one who got everyone killed.

"Oren killed my mother in front of me, and he vowed to get you as soon as you returned." Elora swallowed. "He let me live because he wanted me to see him follow through on his promise. He wanted me to know that he'd won."

TWENTY-ONE

confessions

I wanted to ask Elora more questions, but she already looked so worn. She would never admit to being exhausted, but it was painfully clear that she should've been sleeping instead of speaking to me in the first place.

We talked for a bit more, and then I excused myself. I paused when I reached the door and looked back. Elora had already sunk down on the chaise, and she held her hands over her eyes.

Garrett waited outside the door, pacing the hall. Thomas stood a few yards down, giving him space, and Aurora and Finn were long gone.

"How is she?" Garrett asked.

"She's . . . good, I think." I really wasn't sure how Elora was doing. "She's resting, and that's what counts."

"Good." Garrett nodded. He stared at the closed drawing room door for a moment, then turned his concern to me. "Your talk went well, then?"

"Yeah." I rubbed the back of my neck. I didn't know what to make of it all.

Elora had been so cold to me since I'd met her, to the point where I'd been certain she hated me, but now I wasn't so sure. I had no idea how she must feel about me.

Elora hadn't been much older than me when she married a man over three times her age, a man she didn't even know. He turned out to be ruthless and cruel, but she sacrificed her happiness and well-being for her kingdom.

Then, to defend her unborn child, to save me, she risked everything. Both her parents lost their lives in a matter of months, killed by her own husband, for a child she couldn't even be around.

I wondered if she hated me, if she blamed me for her parents' deaths, for all the trouble Oren had caused her since I'd been born.

I didn't know how close Elora had been with her parents, but before the christening ceremony, she suggested that I take the name Ella, after her mother.

And Elora had spared Loki. His father had gotten her mother killed and nearly cost both Elora and me our lives, yet when given the chance for vengeance, Elora hadn't taken any on Loki. I was starting to think I had misjudged her completely.

Elora's insistence on perfection and on me being Queen became much clearer. So much had been lost for me, to ensure that I would someday take the Trylle throne.

My stomach twisted with shame as I realized how ungrateful I must have seemed to her. After everything she and her family and the entire Trylle population had done for me, I had given them so little in return.

When I looked up into Garrett's worried eyes, I realized something else. His wife—Willa's mother—had died long before Willa had come home. I wondered if she had died in one of the battles my father had waged against the Trylle. If Garrett had lost someone he loved because of me.

"I'm sorry," I told him with tears stinging my eyes.

"What on earth for?" Garrett moved toward me, surprised by my display of emotion, and put his hand on my arm.

"Elora told me everything." I swallowed the lump in my throat. "Everything that happened with Oren. And I'm sorry."

"Why are you sorry?" Garrett asked. "All of that was before you were even born."

"I know, but I feel like . . . I should've been better. That I *should* be better," I corrected myself. "After everything you went through, you deserve a great Queen."

"That we do," Garrett admitted with a small smile. "And you know that, so we should be on the right track." He lowered his head to meet my eyes. "I'm certain you'll be a great Queen someday."

I wasn't sure if I believed him, but I knew that I had to do everything I could to make that happen. I would not let my kingdom down. I couldn't.

Garrett needed to tend to Elora, so I left him to it. Thomas stayed outside the door, still standing guard but giving them alone time.

Duncan, Willa, and Matt were waiting for me by the stairs. As soon as I saw Matt's face, I couldn't hold it together any longer. Tears spilled down my cheeks, and Matt wrapped his arms around me.

Once I calmed down, we went up to my room. Duncan got us all hot tea, and I made him sit down and pour himself a cup. I hated when he acted like a servant. Willa curled up next to me on the bed, comforting in a way that made me miss my aunt Maggie.

"So she's dying?" Matt asked. He leaned against my desk, rolling the empty teacup between his hands.

I wasn't sure how much Duncan or Willa knew about my parentage or about how the Trylle abilities hurt us. I didn't want to tell them too much, especially Matt, and make them worry. So I left out all the major plot points, and only let them know that Elora was sick.

"I think so," I said. She hadn't said that exactly, but she had aged so rapidly. She looked to be in her seventies now, and that was after Aurora Kroner had healed her.

"That really sucks," Duncan said, sitting on the chest at the foot of my bed.

"You were talking to her and she just collapsed?" Willa asked. She rested her elbow on the pillow next to mine and propped her head up so she could look at me.

"Yeah." I nodded. "The worst part is I was arguing with her right before it happened."

"Aw, sweetie." Willa reached out and touched my arm. "You know it wasn't your fault, right?"

"Did she say what she's dying from?" Matt asked. The crease on his forehead deepened; he knew I had left something out.

"You know Elora." I shrugged. "She's vague on details."

"That's true," Matt said with a sigh, and that answer seemed to satisfy him. "I just don't like mysterious illnesses."

"Well, nobody does, Matt," Willa said with a teasing lilt to her voice.

"What were you and the Queen arguing about?" Duncan asked. He was changing the subject, which I would've been grateful for, until I remembered the answer to his question.

I was supposed to marry Tove Kroner.

"Oh, hell." I leaned my head back so it thudded against the headboard.

"What was that for?" Willa asked.

"Nothing." I shook my head. "It was just a stupid disagreement. That's all."

"Stupid?" Matt came over and sat on the bed by my feet. "Stupid how?"

"You know, normal stuff," I floundered. "Elora wanted me to be a better Princess. More punctual and stuff like that."

"You do need to be more punctual," Matt agreed. "Maggie was always on you about that."

Another reminder of Maggie stung my heart. I hadn't spoken to her since we'd returned to Förening. Matt had a few times, but I'd been avoiding her calls. I had been busy lately, but the real reason I put off talking to her was because hearing her voice would only make me miss her too much.

"How is Maggie?" I asked, ignoring the ache in my chest.

"She's good," Matt said. "She's staying in New York with friends, and she's really confused about everything that's going on. I keep telling her that everything's fine, that we're safe, and she needs to lay low."

"Good."

"You need to talk to her, though." Matt gave me a hard look. "I can't keep being the go-between."

"I know." I picked at chipped paint on my teacup and lowered my eyes. "I don't know how to answer her questions. Like, where we are and when we're coming back and when I'll see her again."

"I don't know how to answer them either, but I make do," Matt said.

"Wendy's had a long day," Willa said, coming to my rescue. "I don't think now is the time to lecture her on things she should be doing."

"You're right." Matt gave her a small smile before looking at me apologetically. "I'm sorry. I didn't mean to get on your case, Wendy."

"No, it's fine," I said. "You're just doing your job."

"I don't really know what my job is anymore," Matt said wearily.

Someone knocked at the door, and Duncan jumped up to get it.

"Duncan, stop it." I sighed. "You're not the butler."

"Maybe not, but you're still the Princess," Duncan said, and he opened my bedroom door.

"I hope I'm not disturbing anything," Finn said, looking past Duncan at me.

As soon as his dark eyes landed on mine, my breath caught in my throat. He stood at the door, his black hair mussed a bit. His vest was still neatly pressed but it was marred with a dark stain from Elora's blood.

"No, not at all," I said, sitting up farther.

"Actually, we were—" Matt began, his voice hard.

"Actually, we were leaving," Willa cut him off. She scooted off the bed, and Matt shot her a look, which she only smiled at. "We were just saying that we had something to do in your room. Weren't we, Matt?"

"Fine," Matt grumbled and stood up. Finn moved aside so Matt and Willa could walk out of the room, and Matt gave him a warning glare. "But we'll just be right across the hall."

Willa grabbed Matt's hand to keep him moving. Finn, as usual, seemed oblivious to Matt's threats, which only made Matt angrier.

"Come on, Duncan," Willa said as she pulled Matt from my room.

"What?" Duncan asked, then caught on. "Oh. Right. I'll be . . . um . . . outside."

Duncan closed the door behind him, leaving me alone with Finn. I sat up straight and moved to the edge of the bed so my legs dangled over. Finn stayed by the door and didn't say anything.

"Did you need something?" I asked carefully.

"I wanted to see how you were doing." He looked at me in that way that went straight through me, and I lowered my gaze.

"I'm good, considering."

"Did the Queen explain things to you?" Finn asked.

"I don't know." I shook my head. "I don't know if I'll ever really understand this world."

"She told you she's dying?" Finn asked, and hearing him say it made it worse.

"Yeah," I said thickly. "She told me. And she finally told me what makes me so special. That I'm the perfect blend of Trylle and Vittra. I'm the ultimate bloodline."

"And you didn't believe me when I said you were special." That was Finn's attempt at a joke, and he smiled ever so slightly.

"I guess you were right." I pulled down my hair, which had gotten messy from lying on it, and ran my fingers through it.

"How are you taking that?" Finn asked, coming closer to the foot of my bed. He stopped by the bedpost and absently touched my satin bedding.

"Being the chosen one for both sides in an epic troll battle?"

"If anybody can handle it, you can," he reassured me.

I looked up at him, and his eyes betrayed some of the warmth he felt for me. I wanted to throw myself into his arms and feel them wrap around me, protecting me like granite. To kiss his temples and cheeks, to feel his stubble rubbing against my skin.

Despite how badly I wanted that—I wanted it so much I ached—I knew that I had to become a great Princess, which meant that I had to use some restraint. Even if the restraint killed me.

"Elora wants me to marry Tove," I blurted out. I hadn't meant to tell him that way, but I knew it would ruin the moment. Break the spell we were under before I acted on it.

"So she told you?" Finn said with a heavy sigh.

"What?" I blinked at him, startled by his response. "What do you mean, she told me? You knew? How long did you know?"

"I'm not sure, exactly." He shook his head. "I've known for a long while, before I met you or Tove."

"What?" I gaped at him, unable to find the words that matched the confusion and anger inside me.

"The marriage had been arranged for some time, the Markis Kroner and the Princess Dahl," Finn explained calmly. "I believe it was only finalized a few days ago, but it was what Aurora Kroner had always wanted. The Queen knew it was her best chance to secure the throne and keep you safe."

"You knew?" I repeated, unable to get past that part. "You knew that she wanted me to marry somebody else, and you never told me?"

He appeared confused by my reaction. "It wasn't my place."

"Maybe it wasn't your place as a tracker, but as the guy making out with me in this bed, yeah, I think it was your place to tell me that I'm supposed to marry someone else."

"Wendy, I repeatedly told you we couldn't be together—"

"Saying we shouldn't be together isn't the same thing, and you know it!" I snapped. "How could you not tell me, Finn? He's your friend. He's *my* friend, and you never thought to tell me?"

"No, I didn't want to interfere with the way you thought of him."

"Interfere with what?" I asked.

"I was afraid you might hate him to spite your mother, and I didn't want that. I wanted you to be happy with him," Finn said. "While you wouldn't be marrying for love, you are friends. You could have a happy life together."

"You . . . what?" My heart felt like it had been ripped in half. For a moment, I didn't speak. I couldn't make my mouth work. "You expect me to marry him."

"Yes, of course," Finn said, almost wearily.

"You're not even gonna try to . . ." I swallowed back tears and looked away from him. "When Elora told me, I fought with her. I fought for you."

"I am sorry, Wendy." His voice had gotten low and thick. He stepped closer and raised his hand as if he meant to touch me, but dropped it instead. "But you will be happy with Tove. He can protect you."

"I wish everyone would stop talking about him that way!" I sat back on the bed, exasperated. "Tove is a person! This is *his* life! Doesn't he deserve better than being somebody's watchdog?"

"I can imagine worse things in life than being married to you," Finn said quietly.

"Don't." I shook my head. "Don't joke. Don't be nice." I glared up at him. "You kept this from me. But worse still, you didn't fight for me."

"You know why I can't, Wendy." His dark eyes smoldered, and

his fists clenched at his side. "Now you know who you are and what you mean to the kingdom. I can't fight for something that isn't mine. Especially not when you mean so much to our people."

"You're right, Finn, I'm not yours." I nodded, looking down at the floor. "I'm not anybody's. I have a choice in all of this, and so do you. But you have no right to take my choice away from me, to tell me who I should marry."

"I didn't arrange this marriage," Finn said incredulously.

"But you think I should marry him, and you've done nothing to stop it." I shrugged. "You might as well have arranged it yourself."

I wiped at my eyes, and he didn't say anything. I lay down on my bed and rolled over so my back was to him. After a few minutes, I heard him walk away and the door shut behind him.

accord

S ara Elsing, Queen of the Vittra, was set to arrive at three the next afternoon to collect Loki Staad, so the morning was filled with a series of defense meetings. I attended with Tove, Aurora Kroner, Garrett Strom, the Chancellor, and a select few trackers, like Finn and his father.

Elora was noticeably absent. She didn't have the strength for it, and she wouldn't be able to regain her strength until after Loki left.

When we stopped for lunch, Tove invited me to join him, but I declined. I liked Tove as much as I always had, but I felt weird around him knowing that we were expected to marry.

Also, I wanted to get in a moment alone with Loki before he left. It might be the last chance I ever got to speak with him.

This time, I didn't use Duncan to do my dirty work. I sent the guards away myself. They protested, but with an icy glare I reminded them I was the Princess. I didn't care if anyone talked about it. Loki was leaving anyway. There would be nothing left to gossip about.

"Ooo, I love it when you're feisty," Loki said after I made the guards leave. He leaned on the footboard of the bed, his usual cocky grin plastered on his face.

"I'm not being feisty," I said. "I wanted to talk to you."

"You've come to say good-bye, I take it?" He arched an eyebrow. "You'll miss me terribly, I know, but if you want to avoid all that, you can always come with me."

"That's quite all right, thank you."

"Really?" Loki wrinkled his nose. "You can't actually be excited about the upcoming nuptials."

"What are you talking about?" I asked, tensing up.

"I heard you're engaged to that stodgy Markis." Loki waved his hand vaguely and stood up. "Which I think is ridiculous. He's boring and bland and you don't love him at all."

"How do you know about that?" I stood up straighter, preparing to defend myself.

"The guards around here are horrible gossips, and I hear everything." He grinned and sauntered toward me. "And I have two eyes. I've seen that little melodrama play out between you and that other tracker. Fish? Flounder? What's his name?"

"Finn," I said pointedly.

"Yes, him." Loki rested his shoulder against the door. "Can I give you a piece of advice?"

"By all means. I'd love to hear advice from a prisoner."

"Excellent." Loki leaned forward, as close to me as he could before he'd be racked with pain from attempting to leave the room. "Don't marry someone you don't love."

"What do you know of love or marriage?" I asked. "You were all set to marry a woman ten years older than you before the King stole her away."

"I wouldn't have married her anyway." Loki shrugged. "Not if I didn't love her."

"Now you've got integrity?" I scoffed. "You kidnapped me, and your father was a traitor."

"I've never said a nice word about my father," Loki said quickly. "And I've never done anything bad to you."

"You still kidnapped me!" I said dubiously.

"Did I?" Loki cocked his head. "Because I remember Kyra kidnapping you, and me preventing her from pummeling you to death. Then, when you were coughing up blood, I sent for the Queen to help you. When you escaped, I didn't stop you. And since I came here, I've done nothing to you. I've even been good because you told me to be. So what terrible crimes have I committed against you, Princess?"

"I—I—" I stammered. "I never said you did anything terrible."

"Then why don't you trust me, Wendy?"

He'd never called me by my name before, and the underlying affection underneath it startled me. Even his eyes, which still held their usual veil of playfulness, had something deeper brewing underneath. When he wasn't trying so hard to be devilishly handsome, he actually was.

The growing connection I felt with him unnerved me, but I didn't want him to see that. More than that, it didn't matter what feelings I might be having for him. He was leaving today, and I would probably never see him again.

"I do trust you," I admitted. "I do trust you. I just don't know why I do, and I don't know why you've been helping me."

"You want the truth?" He smiled at me, and there was something sincere and sweet underlying. "You piqued my curiosity."

Amanda Hocking

"You risked your life for me because you were curious?" I asked doubtfully.

"As soon as you came to, your only concern was for helping your friends, and you never stopped," Loki said. "You were kind. And I haven't seen that much kindness in my life."

He looked away from me then, staring at an empty spot down the hall. I think he was trying to hide the sadness in his eyes, but I saw it just the same—a strange loneliness that looked out of place on his strong features.

Loki shook his head, trying to shake off whatever he'd been feeling, and gave me a crooked smile that looked surprisingly dismal. "I thought for once that acting decent ought to be rewarded. That's why I let you go, and that's why I didn't bring you back to the King."

"If it's so horrible there, why don't you stay with us?" I asked without thinking.

"No." He shook his head and lowered his eyes. "Tempting though the offer may be, your people wouldn't allow it, and my people . . . well, let's just say they wouldn't react well if I didn't come home. And whether I like it or not, it is my home."

"I know that feeling all too well." I sighed. Though Förening was starting to feel more like home, I wasn't sure that it ever would completely.

"See? I told you, Princess." Loki's smile returned more easily. "You and I aren't all that different."

"You say that like it means something."

"Doesn't it?"

"No, not really. You're leaving today, going home to my enemies." I let out a deep breath, feeling an ache inside my chest. "If

I'm lucky, I'll never see you again. Because if I do, that means we're at war, and I'd have to hurt you."

"Oh, Wendy, that's perhaps the saddest thing I've ever heard," Loki said, and he looked like he meant it. "But life doesn't have to be all doom and gloom. Don't you ever see the silver lining?"

"Not today." I shook my head. I heard Garrett summon me from down the hall, which meant that lunch was over and the meetings were about to start up. "I have to get back. I'll see you when we make the exchange with the Vittra Queen."

"Good luck." Loki nodded.

I turned to walk away, and I hadn't made it very far when I heard Loki calling after me.

"Wendy!" Loki leaned out into the hall, so far it made him grimace with pain. "If you're right, and the next time we see each other is when our kingdoms are at war, you and I never will be. I'll never fight you. That I can promise you."

The meetings continued on, each one with the same grueling pace. The participants kept repeating the same information. What to do if the Vittra reneged on the deal. What to do if the Vittra attacked. What to do if the Vittra tried to kidnap me.

And it all boiled down to one answer—fight back. Tove and I would use our abilities, the trackers would use their strength and skill, and the Chancellor would cower in the corner.

Our last step before the Vittra Queen officially arrived was to sign the treaty. It'd already been sent over to the Vittra first, so Oren's name was scribbled across the bottom in blood red. Garrett had to take it up to Elora in her room, and she added her own signature. Once he came back down with it, all we had to do was wait in the War Room for Sara to arrive.

At two-thirty, Elora released Loki, and he promised to be on his best behavior. Just the same, Thomas and Finn treated him like they thought he was a bomb about to explode.

Since we were meeting the dignitary of an enemy nation, I thought I'd better look the part of the Princess, especially since Elora was unable to join us. I dressed in a dark violet gown, and I'd enlisted Willa to help me with my hair.

"If I'd known you'd look so beautiful, I would've gotten dressed up," Loki teased when Finn and Thomas brought him into the War Room. Finn shoved him into a seat unnecessarily hard, but Loki didn't protest.

"Don't get familiar with the Princess," Duncan told him, giving him a stony look.

"My apologies," Loki said. "I wouldn't want to get familiar with anyone."

Loki looked about the room. Duncan, Finn, Thomas, Tove, the Chancellor, and I were the ones set to meet Sara. The rest of the house was on standby, should we need them, but we didn't want to look like we were ambushing Sara when she arrived.

"Did you change your mind and decide to execute me?" Loki asked, looking us over. "Because you all look like you're going to a funeral."

"Not now," I said, fidgeting with my bracelet and watching the clock.

"Then when, Princess?" Loki asked. "Because we only have about fifteen minutes until I leave."

I rolled my eyes and ignored him.

By the time the doorbell chimed, I'd taken to pacing the room. I nearly jumped when I heard it. The exchange was supposed to be clean and simple, but I wasn't sure what to expect. My father had lied and betrayed the Trylle before.

"Here we go," I said and took a deep breath.

I carried the treaty in my hands, a tube of paper rolled up and tied with a red ribbon, and I led the way down the corridor to the front hall. Duncan followed directly behind me on my left side, and Tove was at my right. Finn and Thomas each took one of Loki's arms, in case he decided to struggle or fight, and the Chancellor brought up the rear.

Two other guards had let the Queen in, and they waited with her. She stood in the center of the rotunda, flakes of snow sticking to her crimson cloak. She'd pushed the hood down, and her cheeks were rosy from the cold. She'd arrived alone, except for Ludlow, the small hobgoblin I'd seen in the Vittra palace.

"Princess." Sara smiled warmly when she saw me. She did a small curtsy, and I returned it, making sure to keep it equally small.

"Queen. I trust you traveled well," I said.

"Yes, though the roads were a bit icy." She gestured to the doors behind her with velvet-gloved hands. "I hope we didn't keep you waiting."

"No, you arrived on time," I assured her.

"She's here now," Loki said, but I didn't look back to see if he was pulling at Finn and Thomas. "Can you let me go?"

"Not until the agreement is finalized," Finn said through gritted teeth.

"My Queen, can we settle this, please?" Loki called to her, sounding irritated. "This tracker is getting handsy."

"The Markis hasn't been too much trouble?" Sara asked, her cheeks reddening with embarrassment.

"Not too much," I replied with a thin smile. "When we return him to you, you agree to peace until my coronation. Is that correct?"

"Yes." Sara nodded. "The Vittra will not attack you as long as Elora is Queen. But as soon as you become Queen, the cease-fire is over."

I handed the treaty over to her. I'd expected her to unroll it and double-check it for accuracy, but she simply nodded again, apparently deciding to trust us.

"Now they can let me go?" Loki asked.

"Yes," I said.

I heard a skirmish behind me, and then Loki walked past me, smoothing out his shirt. Sara gave him a disapproving look, and he took his place at her side.

"It's all settled, then?" Loki asked.

"It appears that way," Sara said. "Princess, you know you are always welcome at our palace."

"I do," I admitted.

"The King wanted me to extend an invitation to you," Sara said. "If you return to the Vittra to take your rightful place at his side, he will offer amnesty to Förening and everyone who lives here."

I faltered for a moment, unsure how to respond. I didn't want to go there, and I certainly didn't trust the King, but it was hard to pass up. It would protect everybody I cared about, including Matt and Finn.

I glanced at Loki, expecting him to be grinning or teasing me to join him, but instead, his cocky smile had faltered. He swallowed, and his caramel eyes were almost frightened.

"Princess." Tove touched my arm, just above my elbow. "We

have other business to attend to this afternoon. Perhaps we should see our guests out."

"Yes, of course." I smiled thinly. "If you'll forgive me, I do have things I need to do."

"Of course." Sara smiled. "We don't need to take up any more of your time."

"It's just as well." Loki looked relieved and smiled at me. "Ondarike is no place for a Princess."

"Markis," Sara said coolly.

She did another curtsy, which I reciprocated, then turned away. Ludlow the hobgoblin never said anything, but he gathered up her train so it wouldn't drag on the ground. As they walked to the door, Loki started to say something, but Sara silenced him.

He glanced over his shoulder once, his eyes meeting mine, and I was surprised to find how much my heart ached at seeing him go. We hadn't spent that much time together, but I'd felt oddly connected almost since the moment I met him.

Then he was gone out the door, and out of my life, and I actually wanted to cry.

Once they were gone, I let out a deep breath.

"That wasn't so bad," I said. It wasn't bad at all, really. The nerve-racking buildup had been the worst part.

The Chancellor was sweating like a pig, but this was nothing new. I smiled gratefully at Tove. It had been nice having him at my side. Backup and support were never a bad thing.

"Those little hobgoblins freak me out." Duncan shuddered at the thought of Ludlow. "I don't know how they can live with them."

"I'm sure they think the same thing about you," Finn muttered.

"I think we all know what we have to do," the Chancellor said, wringing his pudgy hands together.

"What?" I asked, since I had no idea what we had to do.

"We need to attack them while the truce is still in play," the Chancellor said. Sweat dripped down into his beady eyes, and his white suit had wet circles all over it.

"The whole point of the truce is that we have peace," I said. "If we attack them, we negate that, and we're back at war."

"We need to get a drop on them when they're not expecting it," the Chancellor insisted, his jowls shaking. "This is our only chance to have the upper hand!"

I shook my head. "No, this is our chance to rebuild after the last attack and find ways to handle this conflict peaceably. We need to work on uniting the Trylle and being as strong as we can be. Or coming up with something we can offer the Vittra to get them off our back."

"Well, we know what we can offer them." The Chancellor eyed me.

"We're not negotiating with them," Finn interjected.

The Chancellor glared at him. "Of course, *you're* not negotiating with anybody for anything."

"We can't cross negotiations out," Tove said, and before Finn could protest, he went on. "Obviously, we're not giving them the Princess, but we can't rule out other options. Enough people have died already. And after fighting for all this time, nobody has won. I think we need to try something different."

"Exactly," I agreed. "We should use this time to figure out what that might be."

"You want to find something new to barter with?" the Chancellor scoffed. "We can't trust the Vittra King!"

"Just because he plays dirty doesn't mean we have to," I said.

"And the only reason we won this last fight is because it happened on our turf and they left their strongest players at home," Tove said. "If we meet them at their house, they have the advantage. They would crush us the way they have every other time. We need to learn from our mistakes."

"Fine!" The Chancellor threw up his hands. "Do what you want! But the blood will be on your hands, not mine."

The Chancellor stalked off, defeated. I smiled up at Tove.

"Thanks for backing me up," I said.

Tove shrugged. "It's what I do."

proposal

After Sara and Loki left, I went up to report to Elora how I'd done. Garrett was sitting with her in the drawing room, where Elora was lying down. Her skin color had brightened, but she was still out of it.

I kept my explanation brief, but they both seemed proud of me. It had been my first official duty as a Princess, and I'd passed. Elora actually said I did well. When I left, I felt surprisingly good.

I met Tove on my way back from the room. He came from the kitchen, and he had a handful of grapes. He offered me one, but I didn't feel much like eating, so I shook my head.

"Do you feel like a real Princess yet?" Tove asked me as he munched on a grape.

"I don't know." I pulled off the heavy diamond necklace I'd worn to look the part. "But I don't know if I ever will. I think I'll always feel like an imposter."

"Well, you definitely look like a real Princess."

"Thanks." I turned to him and smiled. "And you did really well today. You were focused and very regal."

"Thanks." He tossed a grape in his mouth and grinned. "I spent a lot of time rearranging my furniture before the meeting started. It seemed to help."

"It did."

We walked in silence for a bit, him eating his fruit and me fiddling with the necklace. The silence between us didn't feel awkward, though, and I thought about how nice it was. Being able to be with someone without it feeling forced or weird or agonizingly restrained.

I also started to understand what Elora and Finn meant. Tove was strong and intelligent and kind, but his abilities made him too frazzled to be a leader. He did an amazing job of backing me up and supporting me, and I knew that no matter what, he'd be at my side.

"So." Tove swallowed the last grape and stopped. He stared down at the floor and tucked his tangled hair behind his ears. "I'm sure that the Queen has told you of the arrangement that she and my mother made." He paused. "You know, about us getting married."

"Yeah." I nodded, feeling strangely nervous to hear him bring it up.

"I don't agree with them sneaking around and plotting things, like we're pawns in a game and not people." Tove chewed the inside of his cheek and looked down the hallway. "It's not right, and I told Aurora that. She needs to stop treating me like a . . . I don't know. A pawn."

"Yeah," I agreed, and I kept nodding.

"She thinks she can control me all the time, and I know your mother tries to do the same stuff with you." He sighed. "It's like they had all these ideas of who we would be before we got here, and they refuse to adjust them even when they see we're not what they expected."

"Yeah, that's true," I said.

"I know about your past." He glanced over at me, resting his eyes on me only for a second. "Aurora told me about your father and how you're at risk of losing the crown because of him, because of your parents' mistakes. That's stupid because I know how powerful you are and how much you care about people."

"Thank you?" I said uncertainly.

"You need to be Queen. Everyone who knows anything knows that, but most people don't know anything, and that is a problem." He scratched at the back of his head and shifted his weight. "I would never take that away from you. No matter what happens, I'd never take the crown from you, and I'd defend you against anybody who tried."

I didn't say anything to that. I'd never heard Tove talk so much before, and I didn't know what he was getting at.

"I know that you're in love with . . . well, not me," he said carefully. "And I'm not in love with you either. But I do respect you, and I like you."

"I respect and like you too," I said, and he gave me a small smile.

"But it's a number of things, and it's none of them." He let out a deep breath. "That didn't make sense. I mean, it's because you need somebody to help you keep the throne, and somebody on your side, and I can do that. But . . . it's just because I think . . . I want to."

"What?" I asked, and he actually looked at me, letting his mossy eyes stare into mine.

"Will you . . . I mean, do you want to get married?" Tove asked. "To me?"

"I, um . . ." I didn't know what to say.

"If you don't want to, nothing has to change between us," Tove said hurriedly. "I asked because it sounds like a good idea to me."

"Yeah," I said, and I didn't know what I would say until it was coming out of my mouth. "I mean, yes. I do. I will. I would . . . I'll marry you."

"Yeah?" Tove smiled.

"Yes." I swallowed hard and tried to smile back.

"Good." He exhaled and looked back down the hall. "This is good, right?"

"Yeah, I think so," I said, and I meant it.

"Yeah." He nodded. "I sorta feel like throwing up now, though."

"I think that's normal."

"Good." He nodded again and looked at me. "Well, I'll let you go . . . do whatever you need to do. And I'll go do what I do."

"Okay." I nodded.

"All right." He randomly patted me on the shoulder, then nodded again, and walked away.

I had no idea what I'd just agreed to. I wasn't in love with Tove, and I really didn't think he was in love with me.

Tove and I understood and respected each other, and that was something. But more important, it was what the kingdom needed. Elora was convinced that marrying Tove was the best thing for me and for the Trylle.

I had to do what was best for our people, and if that meant marrying Tove, then so be it. There were a lot worse people I could end up married to.

I changed out of my gown, then I took Duncan with me to the library. He helped me find some good history texts about the Trylle, and I began reading through them. Finn had had me skim some things before my christening ceremony, but if I planned to rule these people, I needed to understand who they were.

I spent the rest of the evening in the library, getting as much information as I could. Duncan ended up passed out and curled up in one of the chairs. It was late when I woke him up to walk me to my room. I wasn't sure how much protection groggy Duncan really offered, but I doubted I needed it anyway.

The next morning, Tove and I went to the atrium to do some training, and I enjoyed getting back in a routine. Duncan went along, and if things seemed awkward between Tove and me, Duncan didn't say anything. It did feel weird being newly engaged, but Tove did a good job of keeping me on task.

I was getting a better mastery of my abilities, and they were becoming stronger. I lifted the throne off the floor, with Duncan sitting in it, and it didn't require as much concentration as it had before. Right behind my eyes pain throbbed dully, but I ignored it.

When Tove moved a chair, levitating it in a circle to demonstrate what he wanted me to do, I couldn't help but think of Elora. How weak and frail she looked from being drained by her powers.

I knew that we needed to use our powers to keep from going crazy, and with Tove especially, draining his abilities was the only thing that kept him sane. But it made me nervous. I didn't want him to end up like my mother, dying of old age before he was even forty.

When we'd finished practicing, I felt tired, but in a pleasant way. I was becoming stronger and more self-reliant, and I liked that.

Elora was still in her drawing room, recuperating, so I went down to see her. She'd gotten off the chaise, which was a good sign, but she'd taken to painting again.

She sat on a stool facing the windows, an easel in front of her. The shawl wrapped around her had slipped off one shoulder, but she didn't seem to notice. Her long hair hung down her back, shimmering silver now more than black.

"Are you sure you should be doing that?" I asked as I came into her room.

"I've had a terrible migraine for days, and I need to get rid of it." She made a sweeping stroke across the canvas.

I walked up behind her so I could get a better look at it, but so far it was only dark blue sky. Elora stopped painting and set her brush down on the easel.

"Is there something you needed from me, Princess?" Elora swiveled around to face me, and I was relieved to see that the milkiness had vanished from her eyes.

"No." I shook my head. "I just wanted to see how you're doing."

"Better," she said with a heavy sigh. "I will never be quite the same again, but I'm better."

"Better is something."

"Yes, I suppose it is." She turned to the window and the overcast day.

The sleet and wind had finally let up, but the skies remained gray and murky. The maples and elms had given up most of their leaves and stood dead and barren for winter. The evergreens that populated the bluff looked brittle after the beating they'd taken lately, and ice clung to their branches, weighing them down.

"Tove asked me to marry him," I told her, and she whipped her head to face me. "And I agreed."

"You've accepted the arrangement?" Elora raised her eyebrow, in wonder and approval.

"Yes." I nodded. "It's . . . it's what's best for the kingdom, so that's what I must do." I nodded again, to convince myself. "And Tove is a good guy. He'll make a good husband."

Immediately after I'd said it I realized that I had no idea what would make a good husband. I'd spent almost no time around married couples, and I'd never had a boyfriend. I didn't know what category Finn and I fell into, but it couldn't count for much.

Elora was still watching me, so I gulped and forced a smile. Now wasn't the time to worry about what I'd agreed to. I had time to learn what it meant to be a wife before we were wed.

"Yes, I am certain he will," Elora murmured and turned to her painting.

"Are you really?" I asked.

"Yes," she said, with her back still to me. "I won't do to you what was done to me. If I thought you needed to do something terrible, that it was in the best interest of the Trylle, I would still ask it of you. It would still be your duty, but I would tell you exactly what you were doing. I'd never let you go in blind."

"Thank you," I said, meaning it. "Do you regret marrying my father?"

"I try not to have any regrets," Elora said wearily and picked up her paintbrush. "It's unbecoming of a Queen to have misgivings."

"How come you never married again?" I asked.

"Who would I marry?"

I nearly said Thomas, but that would only enrage her. She couldn't have married him. He was a tracker, and he was already married. But that wasn't where her anger would come from. I was sure she'd be incensed that I had learned of the affair.

"Garrett?" I asked, and Elora made a noise that sounded like a laugh. "He loves you, and he's a distinguished Markis. He's eligible."

"He's not that distinguished," she said. "He is kind, yes, but marriage isn't about that. I told you before, Princess, that love has nothing to do with marriage. It's an alignment between two parties, and I have not had any reason to align myself with anyone else."

"You don't want to marry for the sake of doing it?" I asked. "Don't you ever get lonely?"

"A Queen is many things, but alone is never one of them." She held the brush, poised right above the canvas as if she meant to paint, but she didn't. "I don't need love or a man to complete me, and someday you'll find that's true for yourself. Suitors will come and go, but you will remain."

I stared out the window, unsure of what to say to that. There was something noble and dignified in that idea, but something about it felt a bit tragic. Believing that I would end up alone, that I would die alone, was never comforting.

"Besides that, I didn't want Willa in line for the crown," Elora said and began painting again. "That is what would've happened if I'd married Garrett. She would've become a Princess, a viable option for the throne, and I could never have that."

"Willa wouldn't be a bad Queen," I said, and I was astonished to find that I actually did think that.

Willa had really grown on me since I'd been here, and I think she'd grown up as well. She had kindness and insight I'd initially thought her incapable of.

"Nevertheless, she won't be Queen. You will."

"Not for a long time, hopefully." I sighed.

"You need to be ready, Princess." She looked over her shoulder at me. "You must be prepared for it."

"I am trying," I assured her. "I've been training and going to all the meetings. I've even been studying in the library. But I still don't feel like I'll be ready to be a real Queen for years."

"You don't have years," Elora told me.

"What do you mean?" I asked. "When will I be Queen? How long do I have?"

"Do you see that painting?" Elora gestured to a canvas I'd seen in her room before, resting against a shelf.

A close-up of me looking much as I did now, except wearing a white gown. On my head, I had an ornate platinum crown filled with diamonds.

"So?" I asked. "I'll be Queen someday. We both know that."

"No, look at that picture." She pointed at it with the handle of her brush. "Look at your face. How old are you?"

"I'm . . ." I squinted and crouched in front of it. I couldn't be sure exactly, but I didn't look a day older than I did now. "I don't know." I stood up. "I could be twenty-five, for all I know."

"Perhaps," Elora allowed, "but that's not the feeling I get."

"What is the feeling you get?" I asked. She turned her back to me, not giving anything away. "How do I become Queen anyway?"

"You become Queen when the reigning monarchs are deceased," Elora said matter-of-factly.

"You mean I'll be Queen after you die?" I asked, and my heart thudded in my chest.

"Yes."

"So you think . . ." I had to take a fortifying breath before I could continue. "You're dying soon."

"Yes." She painted on, as if I'd just asked her about the weather instead of her impending death.

"But . . ." I shook my head. "I'm not ready. You haven't taught me everything I need to know!"

"That is why I have been pushing you, Princess. I knew we didn't have much time, and I needed to be hard on you. I had to be sure you could do this."

"And now you're sure?" I asked.

"Yes." She faced me again. "Don't panic, Princess. You must never panic, no matter what obstacle you face."

"I'm not panicking," I lied. My heart wanted to race out of my chest, and I felt light-headed. I sat on the couch behind me.

"I'm not dying tomorrow," Elora said, sounding slightly annoyed. "You have more time to learn, but you need to focus on all your training. You need to listen carefully to everything I say, and do as you're told."

"It's not that." I shook my head and stared at her. "I only just met you, and we've finally started getting along, and now you're dying?"

"Don't get sentimental, Princess," Elora chastised me. "That we do not have time for."

"Aren't you sad?" I asked, tears stinging my eyes. "Or scared?"

"Princess, really." She rolled her eyes and turned away from me. "I have painting to do. I suggest you go to your room and compose yourself. A Princess must never be seen crying."

I left her alone to finish her painting. The one consolation I had was that Elora said a Princess must never be *seen* crying, not that I must never cry. I wondered if that was why she had me leave. Not so I could cry, but so she could.

TWENTY-FOUR

tryllic

If Loki had already known about my arranged marriage, it was only a matter of time before everybody else found out. I thought it would be better if my friends learned about it from me, so I gathered them all together.

Willa and Duncan would probably be excited, but I didn't know how Matt or Rhys would take it. Probably not quite as well.

We met in the upstairs living room, which had been Rhys's old playroom. The ceiling had a cloud mural on it, and there were still old toys stacked up on shelves in the corner. Matt sat between Rhys and Willa on the sofa, and Duncan sat on the floor with his back against the couch.

"I have something to tell you all." I stood in front of them, twirling my thumb ring, and swallowed back my nerves.

The suspicious look Matt gave me wasn't helping matters. On top of that, Rhys grinned like an excited fool. He'd been so happy when I invited him here, since we'd hardly seen each other lately.

He'd been busy doing stuff with Matt, and I'd heard that he'd started dating Rhiannon.

"What is it?" Matt asked, his voice already hard.

"It's good news," I insisted.

"Spit it out, then," Willa said with a confused smile. "You've been killing me with suspense." She'd tried getting it out of me before everybody had arrived, but I wanted to tell them all at once.

"I wanted you all to know that I, um . . ." I cleared my throat. "I'm getting married."

"What?" Matt growled.

"Oh, my gosh!" Willa gasped, her eyes glittering. "To who?"

"So it's true?" Duncan gaped at me. Apparently he'd heard the rumor too.

"To Tove Kroner," I said.

Willa squealed and clapped her hands over her mouth. I didn't think she could've been more excited if she was the one getting married to Tove.

"Tove?" Matt asked, looking unsure. "That guy's a spaz, and I didn't even think you really liked him."

"No, I like him," I said. "He's a good guy."

"Oh, my gosh, Wendy!" Willa yelled and jumped off the couch, nearly kicking Duncan in the head. She ran over and hugged me enthusiastically. "This is so exciting! I am so happy for you!"

"Yeah, congratulations." Rhys nodded. "He's a lucky guy."

"I can't believe you guys didn't tell me," Duncan said. "I was with you both this morning."

"Well, we hadn't really told people yet." I untangled myself from Willa's embrace. "I'm not sure if we're supposed to tell people, but I thought you should know."

"But I don't understand." Matt stood up, clearly disturbed by the news. "I thought you were all hung up on that Finn guy."

"Nope." I shook my head and lowered my eyes. "I'm not hung up on anybody." I let out a deep breath. "That's all behind me."

I was surprised to find that that might be true. I wasn't over Finn exactly, but I had begun to realize that we would never be together. And it wasn't because of our social standings anymore. That I could fight with, argue against, try to legislate.

But Finn's unwillingness to ever try or give me credit or make any effort at all to be with me had left me exhausted. I couldn't be in love by myself.

"Your wedding is going to be so fabulous!" Willa held her hands together in front of her chest to keep from hugging me again. "When is the big day?"

"I don't know exactly," I admitted. "After I turn eighteen."

"That's less than three months away!" Matt shouted.

"We hardly have any time to plan!" Willa paled. "We have so much to do!" Then she grimaced. "Oh, Aurora's gonna have her hand in all of it, isn't she?"

"Oh. Yeah." I scowled too when I realized that I was going to have the mother-in-law from hell. "I guess she is."

"I'm so glad I'm a guy and I don't have to plan any of these things," Rhys said with a lopsided grin.

"The planning is the best part," Willa insisted and looped an arm around my shoulder. "Picking out the colors and dresses and flowers and invitations! That's the funnest!"

"Wendy, are you really okay with this?" Matt asked, looking at me directly.

"Of course she is, Matt," Willa said with an exaggerated eye

Torn

roll. "This is every little girl's dream. To be a Princess and marry a Prince in a big grand wedding."

"Technically, Tove's a Markis and not a Prince," I pointed out.

"You know what I meant," Willa said. "It's a fairy tale come true."

"Willa, stop for a second." Matt's icy stare rested on her, and she shrank back, retracting her arm from my shoulders. He turned to me. "Wendy, is this really what you want? To marry this guy?"

I took a deep breath and nodded. "Yes. This is what I want."

"Okay," Matt said reluctantly. "If this is what you want, then I'll support you on it. But if he hurts you, I will kill him."

"I wouldn't expect any less from you." I smiled. "But I'll be all right."

Willa continued her excited prattling, telling me all the amazing things we had to plan, but I tuned her out. Rhys and Matt didn't really want or need to hear all of that, so they escaped to do something vastly more fun. Duncan was my bodyguard, so he couldn't leave, but he was actually more involved in Willa's conversation than I was.

Eventually, she exhausted herself. She said she would go home and get a few things, so she could come back bright and early in the morning to plan. We left the room with her listing everything she would bring with her.

"I'll see you tomorrow, okay?" Willa squeezed my arm.

"Yeah."

"This is exciting, Wendy," she reminded me. "Act like it."

"I'll try." I forced a smile.

She laughed at my weak attempt as she departed. I leaned against the wall outside the living room door. Duncan was next to me, but he didn't say anything.

Willa was right. This whole thing was like a fairy tale. So why didn't it feel like one?

I glanced down the hall and saw Finn, doing his evening rounds. He was walking toward me to inspect the north wing, but when he saw me, he stopped. His dark eyes rested on mine for a moment, then he turned and walked in the other direction.

I woke up the next day excited to train and get my mind off the engagement, but I'd only been awake for ten minutes before Aurora burst in. She arrived even before Willa did and stole the whole thing from her. Willa was not happy about it when she found out, but she did her best to be polite around Aurora.

We met in the grand dining room because Aurora had so many papers she wanted to spread out all over the long table. She had guest lists and seating charts and color swatches and fabric material and magazines and dress designs and books and everything anyone would ever need for a wedding.

"We need to have the engagement party this weekend, obviously, since the wedding is only a few months away," Aurora said, tapping a calendar on the table.

I sat in a chair at the head of the table with Aurora standing on one side and Willa on the other. Aurora bent over the table, her green dress flowing around her. Willa had her arms crossed over her chest, and she glared down at Aurora.

"Before the engagement party, we need to have your color scheme and have the bridal party picked out already," Aurora said.

"That's too soon." Willa shook her head. "There's no way we can have all that ready, plus plan a party. It's only a few days away."

"We need to get the wedding invitations out as soon as possible. We will hand them out at the engagement party," Aurora said. "When is your birthday, Princess?"

"Uh, the ninth of January," I said.

"Why do we have to hand out the invites?" Willa asked. "Why can't we mail them like normal people?"

"Because we're not normal people." Aurora shot her a glare. "We're Trylle, and we're royalty. It's customary that we hand out the invitations at the engagement party."

"Fine, but if we have to do that, we should wait at least another week for the party," Willa said.

"I'm not going to argue with you about this." Aurora straightened up and rubbed her forehead. "As the mother of the groom, I'm throwing the engagement party. It's none of your concern. I'll plan it and set it up whenever I feel is best."

"Fine." Willa held up her hands like she didn't care, but I could tell she still was irritated. "You do what you want. That is your right."

"Let's work on the wedding for now." Aurora looked down at me. "Who did you want in your wedding party?"

"Um . . ." I shrugged. "Willa should be my maid of honor, obviously."

"Thank you." Willa gave Aurora a smug smile.

"Of course." Aurora smiled thinly at her and scribbled down Willa's name on a piece of paper. "What about the rest of your party?"

"I don't know." I shook my head. "I don't really know that many people here."

"Excellent. I've compiled a list for you." Aurora grabbed a three-page list from off the table and handed it to me. "Here are upstanding eligible young Marksinna that would make perfect bridesmaids."

"This is just their names and a few random facts," I said, looking over the list. "Kenna Tomas has black hair, freckles, and her father is the Markis of Oslinna. That means nothing to me. I'm supposed to pick strangers off a list based on their hair color?"

"If you'd like, I can pick them for you," Aurora offered. "But I did list them from most desirable to least desirable to make it easier for you, although they are all acceptable choices."

"I can help her," Willa said, taking the list from me before Aurora had a chance to. "I know a lot of these girls."

She immediately flipped to the end of the list, and I felt a small satisfaction in knowing she'd pick the ones that Aurora liked least.

"Can't I just have Willa?" I asked. "I'm sure Tove doesn't have that many friends for groomsmen either. We could have a small wedding."

"Don't be ridiculous," Aurora said. "You're a Princess. You can't have a small wedding."

"Aurora is right," Willa said, sounding sad to be agreeing with her. "You need to have a huge wedding. You have to let them know that you're a Princess to be reckoned with."

"Don't they already know that?" I asked honestly, and Willa shrugged.

"It doesn't hurt to remind them."

"Since your father is out of the picture, Noah can walk you down the aisle," Aurora said, writing something else on her paper.

"Noah?" I asked. "Your husband?"

"Yes, he's a suitable choice," Aurora replied offhandedly.

"But I barely know him," I said.

"Well, you can't walk down alone," Aurora said, giving me an annoyed look.

"Why can't Matt walk me down?" I asked. "He practically raised me anyway."

"Matt?" Aurora was confused, and when she remembered who he was, she wrinkled her nose in disgust. "That human boy? Absolutely not. He shouldn't even be living in the palace, and if others were to find out he was here, you'd be the laughingstock of the kingdom."

"Then . . . fine." I scrambled to think of someone other than Noah. "What about Garrett?"

"Garrett Strom?" Aurora was appalled, but I think it was because he was actually an acceptable candidate.

"He is nearly her stepfather," Willa pointed out with a sly smile. Having her father walk me down the aisle would give her and her family more prestige.

That wasn't why I picked him, though. I actually liked Garrett, and he was the closest thing I had to a decent father figure around here.

"If it is as the Princess wishes," Aurora said, and grudgingly she crossed out her husband's name and wrote Garrett's instead.

They continued that way for a while, and eventually I had to excuse myself. I needed a break from their subtle jabs and bickering. I wandered down the hall. My plan only went so far as to be anywhere that they weren't.

As I got closer to the War Room, I heard voices. I stopped and poked my head inside. The pasty Chancellor sat at the desk with a stack of papers spread out before him. Finn and Tove stood on the other side of the desk, talking, and Thomas was at the bookshelves, searching for something.

"What are you guys doing?" I asked as I came into the room.

"The boys here have an idiotic plan, and I'm indulging them," the Chancellor said.

"It's not idiotic," Finn said, glaring at the Chancellor, who was too busy dabbing sweat from his forehead to notice.

"We're trying to find a way to extend the truce," Tove explained. "We're going through old treaties with the Vittra and any other tribes to see if we have a precedent."

"Have you found anything?" I asked.

I went over to the desk and touched some of the papers. Most of them were written in a language I didn't understand. It was all symbols, almost like Russian or Arabic. When I looked in the library, I'd found that to be common of the older documents.

"Nothing useful yet, but we only just started," Tove said.

"You won't find anything useful." The Chancellor shook his head. "The Vittra never extend their deals."

"What kinds of things could extend the truce?" I asked, ignoring the Chancellor.

"We don't know, exactly," Tove admitted. "But often there are loopholes in the language that we can use against them."

"Loopholes?" I asked.

"Yeah, like Rumpelstiltskin," Finn said. "They usually throw in something clever like that when they make a deal. It seems impossible, but sometimes you can break it."

"I heard the deal. They didn't say anything like that," I said. "Except that the peace only lasts until I become Queen. What if I never become Queen?"

"No, you need to be Queen," Finn said and picked up a stack of papers.

"But that would make indefinite peace, wouldn't it?" I asked. "If I was never Queen."

"I doubt it," Tove said. "The King would find a way around it eventually, and it would only make him more pissed when he finally did."

"But . . ." I trailed off and sighed. "So he'll find his way around anything, including an extension. Why are you even bothering?"

"An extension isn't our goal." Tove met my eyes. "We'll settle for a temporary fix if it's all we can find, but we want to find something that will end this."

"Do you think something like that exists?" I asked.

"The only thing that King will listen to is violence," the Chancellor sputtered. "We need to attack them with everything we have, as soon as we can."

"We have tried that," Tove said, exasperated. "Over and over again! The King is immune to our attacks! We can't hurt him!"

It suddenly hit me when he said that. When Tove had talked about Loki, he'd said that only he, Elora, and I were strong enough to hold him, and he wasn't even sure if we could execute him. The King was even stronger than Loki.

Nobody had ever been able to stop him. Elora wasn't strong enough, and Tove was too scatterbrained. But I had the King's strength and Elora's power.

"You want me to kill the King," I said. "You want to extend the deadline so I have more time to train."

Tove and Finn wouldn't meet my eyes, so I knew I'd gotten it right. They expected me to kill my father.

TWENTY-FIVE

fairy tale

Thomas grabbed a large book from the bookshelf and dropped it on the desk with a heavy thud. Dust rose from the leather cover. Tove had been so busy avoiding my gaze that he jumped when the book banged.

"That might be of some help." Thomas motioned to the book. "But it's written in Tryllic."

"What's Tryllic?" I asked, eager to change the subject to something that wasn't patricide.

"It's the old Trylle language," Finn explained, and pointed to the papers I'd seen written in a symbolic language. "Only Tove is any good at reading it."

"It's a dead language," the Chancellor said. "I don't know how anyone knows it anymore."

"It's not that hard." Tove reached for the book. He opened the pages, letting out a musty odor. "I can teach you sometime, if you'd like."

"I should learn it," I said. "But not right now. We're trying to find a way to extend this thing, right? How can I help?"

"Look through the papers." Finn sifted through some on the table and handed me a small stack. "See if you can find anything about treaties or truces, even if it's not with the Vittra. Anything that might help."

Tove sat in one of the distressed leather chairs to read the book. I sat down on the floor with my stack of papers, preparing to dig into Trylle legalese. It always seemed to be written in riddles and limericks. A lot of it was hard to understand, and I had to ask for interpretations.

I didn't feel so bad about that, though, when Tove called Finn over to help him understand a passage. Finn leaned over the chair so he could peer down at the page, and he and Tove discussed what it meant.

I thought about how strange it was that Finn and Tove got along so well. Finn seemed to turn into a jealous freak whenever I flirted with a guy, but I was engaged to Tove, and he seemed perfectly okay with him.

Finn looked up from the book, and his eyes met mine, only for a second before he looked away. I saw something in them, a longing I missed, and I wondered again if I had made the right decision.

"Princess?" Aurora called from the hallway.

I'd only been sitting on the floor, reading pages, but she probably wouldn't approve of it. I jumped to my feet and set the papers on the desk to avoid a lecture about ladylike behavior.

"Princess?" Aurora said again, and she poked her head into the room. "Ah, there you are. And you're with Tove. Perfect. We need you to go over engagement details."

"Oh. Right." Tove set the book aside and gave me an awkward smile. "Wedding stuff. We have to do that now."

"Yeah." I nodded.

I glanced over at Finn. His expression had hardened, but he didn't look up. Tove and I followed Aurora out as she talked about the things we needed to do for the wedding, and I looked over my shoulder at Finn.

Aurora held Tove and me hostage for far too long, and Willa couldn't lighten the mood. It would've been so much easier if Aurora and Willa were just marrying each other. By the time Aurora let us go, even Willa was relieved to escape.

Duncan was waiting for me, and we went down to the kitchen to eat supper together. Tove went to the War Room to work, and Willa said she had plans. I knew I should be helping Tove, but I was starving. I had to get something to eat first.

I talked to Duncan about what Tove and Finn were researching, and how some of the papers were written in Tryllic. Duncan said he thought he'd seen a book on Tryllic upstairs in Rhys's living room, which made sense because he'd explained that a lot of mänks went through a phase where they tried to learn it.

I didn't really need to learn it this second, but I wanted to get a feel for the language. As soon as we were done eating, I headed up to the living room. The door was shut, but most doors in the palace were kept closed, and I opened it without knocking.

I hadn't been trying to be sneaky, but since Matt and Willa didn't hear me, I must've been awfully quiet. Or maybe they were too caught up in the moment.

Willa was lying on her back on the couch, and Matt was on top of her. She had on a short dress, the way she always seemed to, and Matt had his hand on her thigh, pushing her hem up. Her other leg was wrapped around his waist, and she buried her fingers in his sandy hair as they kissed.

"Oh, my god!" I gasped. I didn't mean to, but it just came out.

"Wendy!" Willa shrieked, and Matt jumped off her.

"What's going on?" Duncan asked from behind me and tried to push past me, so he could protect me if he needed to.

"Quiet!" Willa hissed, fixing her dress so all her parts were a bit more covered. "Shut the door!"

"Oh, right." I pulled the door shut and averted my eyes from Willa and Matt.

They weren't doing anything particularly graphic, but I'd never seen Matt in any compromising situations before. He hardly ever dated, and he almost never brought girls home. It was bizarre thinking of him getting sexy with someone.

When I glanced up at Matt, his cheeks were red, and he wouldn't lift his head. His hair was messed up, and he kept smoothing out the wrinkles in his shirt. Some of Willa's lipstick had rubbed off on his cheek and mouth, but I didn't have the guts to tell him about it.

"Wow. You two?" Duncan grinned at them. "Bravo, Matt. I didn't think Willa would ever date anyone out of her class."

"Shut up, Duncan." Willa glared at him and readjusted her ankle bracelet.

"Don't be crude," Matt growled, and Duncan took a step back, as if he expected Matt to hit him.

"And you can't say anything to anybody about this," Willa warned him. "You know what would happen if this got out."

Willa was a Marksinna, and even though her abilities were nowhere near as strong as mine, she was still one of the most powerful ones left. Matt was a human from a host family, relegating him to an even lower class than trackers and mänks. If Matt was caught defiling Willa's important bloodline, they'd both be exiled.

Considering they were two of my closest friends, I didn't want

Amanda Hocking

that to happen. Not only would I miss them terribly, but the Vittra might go after them to get to me. They needed to stay in Förening, where they were safe.

"Of course I won't say anything." Duncan crossed his heart to prove his sincerity. "I never told anyone about Finn and the Princess."

"Duncan, shut up," I snapped. I didn't need Matt to be reminded of that right now.

"Please don't be mad," Willa said, incorrectly thinking my irritation was with her. "We didn't want you to find out this way. We've been waiting for the right time to tell you, but you've had so much going on lately."

"And this doesn't change the way we feel about you," Matt rushed to explain. "We both care about you a lot." He gestured to himself and Willa, but he didn't look at her. "That's one of the things that drew us together. We didn't want to hurt you."

"You guys, I'm not hurt." I shook my head. "I'm not mad. I'm not even that surprised."

"Really?" Willa tilted her head.

"No. You've been spending so much time together, and you're always flirting," I said. "I kinda knew something was going on. I just didn't expect to walk in on you like *that*."

"Sorry." Matt's blush deepened. "I really didn't mean for you to see us that way."

"No, it's okay." I shrugged it off. "It's not a big deal."

I looked from one of them to the other. Willa's dark eyes were worried, and her light brown waves of hair cascaded down her side. She was very beautiful, and she'd already shown how kind and loyal she could be.

"You guys make sense," I said finally. "And I want you both to be happy."

"We're happy." Willa smiled, and she and Matt exchanged a look. It was one of those sweet loving ones, and it even made Matt smile.

"Yeah, we're happy." Matt nodded and pulled his gaze away from her to look at me.

"Good. But you two have got to be careful. I don't want you getting caught and banished away from me. I need you both."

"Yeah, I know you need me," Willa said. "Aurora would eat you alive without my help."

"Don't remind me." I grimaced and flopped on one of Rhys's old beanbag chairs. "And I've only been engaged for like forty-eight hours. Everyone's all afraid of the Vittra, but I swear, this wedding is going to be the death of me."

"If you don't want to marry him, don't marry him," Matt said. He sat down on the couch next to Willa, but he'd turned on his disapproving big-brother voice. "You don't need to do anything you don't want to."

"No, it's not Tove." I shook my head. "I'm fine with marrying Tove."

"You're 'fine' with marrying him?" Willa laughed and looped her arm through Matt's. "How romantic."

"You should've seen the proposal," I said.

"Where is the ring, by the way?" Willa asked, looking at my hands. "Is it out getting sized?"

"I don't know." I held my hands out to look at them, as if I expected a ring to magically appear. "He didn't give me one."

"That's horrible!" Willa rested her head on Matt's shoulder.

"We have to correct that right away. Maybe I'll say something when we're with Aurora tomorrow."

"No!" I said fiercely. "Please don't say anything to her. She'd force me to pick out something hideous."

"How can she force you to do anything?" Duncan asked. He sat cross-legged next to me on the floor. "You're the Princess. She's your subordinate."

"You know Aurora." I sighed. "She has ways."

"That's weird." Duncan looked at me as if seeing me in a new light. "I thought life would be so much different for royals. That you had total freedom."

"Nobody's really free." I shook my head. "You spend like twenty hours a day with me. You know how much of my time is free."

"That's really depressing." Duncan's shoulders sagged as he thought about this. "I thought your life was like this because you were new, but it's always gonna be like this, isn't it? You'll always have to answer to people."

"So it would seem," I agreed. "Life isn't a fairy tale, Duncan."

"And you know what they say," Willa chimed in. "Mo' money, mo' problems."

"Well, *that* was embarrassing to hear you say that, so I'm good." I stood up. "I've got lots of studying to do tonight. I'm going to squeeze in some training before I meet with Aurora tomorrow. Do you think you can keep her busy until I get there?"

"If I must," Willa groaned.

"Don't overwork yourself," Matt said as I was leaving the room. "You've got to make time to be a kid. You're still young."

"I think my days of being a kid are over," I said honestly.

TWENTY-SIX

overture

Willa bailed early on in the planning. She said she had to have supper with her father, but I suspected that she couldn't take Aurora anymore.

We were in the ballroom. The skylights were finally fixed, but a layer of snow covered the top of them, making the ballroom dark and cavelike. Aurora assured me that the snow would be removed in time for my engagement party, as if I were worried about that.

She flitted about the room, mapping out where the tables and decorations would be. I helped as often as she let me, which wasn't very often. Her poor assistant was running around like mad to do everything Aurora asked.

When she finally let her assistant go for the night, I was sitting at the grand piano, playing the opening to "Für Elise" repeatedly, since it was the only bit I knew.

"You'll have to take piano lessons," Aurora said. She had a thick black binder filled with all the wedding information, and she dropped it on the piano, making the instrument twang. "I can't believe you didn't already have them. What kind of host family did you live with?"

"You know what kind of host family I had." I continued playing the same bars, louder now since I knew it was getting on her nerves. "You've met my brother."

"About that," Aurora said. She pulled a few bobby pins from her hair, letting her loose curls fall free. "You need to stop referring to him as your brother. It's in poor taste."

"I'm aware," I said. "But it's a hard habit to break."

"You have many habits you need to break." She ran her fingers through her hair. "If you weren't the Princess, I wouldn't bother to help you break them."

"Well, thank you for your time and consideration," I muttered.

"I know you're being facetious, but you are welcome." She opened her binder, leafing through it. "We don't have time for Frederique Von Ellsin to make you a gown for the party, so he's bringing over some of his best pieces tomorrow at noon so you can be fitted."

"That sounds fun," I said, and I wasn't lying. Frederique had made my gown for the christening ceremony, and I enjoyed meeting him.

"Princess!" Aurora snapped. "Will you stop playing that song?"

"Of course." I closed the piano cover. "All you had to do was ask."

"Thank you." Aurora smiled thinly at me. "You do need to work on your manners, Princess."

"My manners are fine when they need to be." I sighed. "But right now I'm tired, and we've been at this all day. Can we regroup tomorrow?"

"You are so *lucky* I'm letting you marry my son." She shook her head and slammed the binder shut. "You are rude and ungrateful and so unladylike. Your mother has almost gotten us killed repeatedly, and my son should be next in line for the crown, not you. If he didn't have some unfounded fondness for you, he would overthrow you and take his rightful place."

"Wow." I stared at her with wide eyes. I really had no idea what to say to that.

"It's a disgrace that he's marrying you." She clicked her tongue. "If anybody found out the way that tracker Finn tainted you, he'd become the laughingstock of the kingdom." She touched her temple and shook her head. "You are just so lucky."

"You are absolutely right." I stood up, clenching my hands at my side. "I am so lucky that your son is nothing like you. I'm going to be Queen, not you. Know your place, *Marksinna*."

She looked up at me, her skin blanched and her dark eyes startled. She blinked, as if she couldn't believe what had just happened. The planning had been as daunting for her as it had been for me, and for a moment she'd forgotten her role.

"Princess, I am truly sorry," she stammered. "I didn't mean that. I've been under so much stress."

"We all have," I reminded her.

Aurora finished gathering her things and mumbled several more apologies. She hurried out of the ballroom, saying she was needed at home. I don't think she'd ever left so quickly before. I didn't know if I'd done the right thing standing up to her, but right then I didn't care.

What I did know was that I had a rare moment when I was completely alone. No guards around me. No Duncan or Tove or Aurora. And I could really use some fresh air.

I hurried before someone found me. If I waited, I knew someone would come along and want something from me. Probably a conversation, but I didn't want to talk. I wanted a moment to breathe.

I ran down the hall of the north wing, bursting through the side door onto a narrow gravel trail lined with tall hedges. It curved around the house, leading down to the bluffs before it opened onto a beautiful garden.

Snow covered everything, making it glitter like diamonds under the moonlight. The wintry weather should've killed off all the plants, but the blue, pink, and purple flowers were in full bloom. The frost on their petals only made them more beautiful.

The vines of ivy and wisteria that grew over the wall remained green and vibrant. Even the small waterfall that ran through the orchard of blossoming trees still flowed, instead of freezing solid the way it should have.

A thin blanket of snow crunched cold under my bare feet, but I didn't care. I ran down the side of the bluff, slipping in a few places, but I never fell. Two curved garden benches stood next to the pond, and I sat down on the nearest one.

The garden was a little piece of magic, and I loved it for that. I leaned back, breathing in the cold night. My breath came out in a fog, and the moon sparkled off the ice crystals in the air. I'd been locked in the house for far too long.

A snap of a twig behind me pulled me from my thoughts, and I whirled around. I couldn't see anyone, but I saw shadows moving along a hedge near the brick wall.

"Who's there?" I asked.

I assumed it was Duncan or another tracker sent to fetch me. When nobody answered, I began to worry that I'd made a rash decision coming out here alone. I could defend myself, but I didn't want there to be a need for it.

"I know somebody's here." I stood up. I walked around the bench and peered through the trees.

I saw a figure standing by the wall. He was too far away to get a good look at his face, but the moon shimmered on his light hair.

"Who's there?" I repeated. I straightened up and tried to look as imposing as possible, which is quite hard for a Princess in a dress, alone in a garden at night.

"Princess?" He sounded surprised and stepped closer to me. When he ducked around a tree and walked toward me, I finally got a good look at him.

"Loki?" I asked, and I felt joy swell inside me, immediately followed by confusion. "What are you doing here?"

"I came for you." He seemed just as bewildered as I was. "What are you doing out here?"

"I needed fresh air. But I don't understand. How did you know I'd be out here?"

"I didn't. This is how I come in." He gestured to the wall behind him. "I scale the wall. You should really get security on that."

"Why are you here?" I asked.

"Don't pretend like you're not happy to see me." His cocky grin returned, lighting up his face. "I'm sure you've been miserable since I left."

"Hardly," I scoffed. "I've been planning my engagement party."

"Yes, I've heard about that dreadful business." He wrinkled his nose in disgust. "That's why I've come to save you."

"Save me?" I echoed.

"Yes, like a knight in shining armor." Loki spread his arms wide and bowed low. "I'll throw you over my shoulder and scale the wall with you like Rapunzel."

"Rapunzel used her hair so a prince could climb into a tower, not escape it," I told him.

"Forgive me. The Vittra don't believe in nursery rhymes or fairy tales."

"Neither do I," I said. "And I don't need to be rescued. I'm where I'm supposed to be."

"Oh, come, now." Loki shook his head. "Princess, you can't believe that. You're not supposed to be locked away in a horrible castle, engaged to a boring fool, forced to sneak out in the night for a chance to breathe."

"I appreciate your concern, Loki, but I'm happy here." Even as I said it, I wasn't sure if that was true or not.

"I can promise you a life of adventure." Loki grabbed a branch and swung over, so he landed on the bench with astonishing grace. "I'll take you to exotic places. Show you the world. Treat you the way a Princess really ought to be treated."

"That all sounds well and good." I smiled up at him. I was flattered by his invitation, even if I didn't trust it. "But . . . why?"

"Why?" Loki laughed. "Why not?"

"I can't help but feel like you're only trying to get me to shirk my responsibilities as a Trylle Princess so I can aid your cause," I said honestly.

"You think the King put me up to this?" Loki laughed again. "The King loathes me. Despises me. Threatens to behead me on a daily basis. The Queen had to go against his wishes to get me. He wanted you all to execute me."

"Now I really wanna go back to that," I said with a smirk.

"Who said anything about going back? I'm asking you to run away from all of this, from all the Trylle and the Vittra, the silly royals and their silly rules." He gestured widely around us.

"Is that why you looked upset when Sara suggested I come back with you?"

"That was dreadful," he admitted. "For one horrible minute, I thought you would accept, and that would be the end of everything."

I cocked my head at him. "The end of everything?"

"The King would never let you get away again," Loki explained. "And you couldn't survive there."

"Why are you so certain I wouldn't survive against the King?" I asked. "I'm strong and smart, and sometimes I'm even brave."

"That's exactly why. Because you're good and brave and kind and beautiful." He jumped down from the bench, landing right in front of me. "The King destroys anything that's beautiful."

"Then how have you survived for so long?" I meant to keep my tone teasing, but as soon as I asked it, his eyes flashed with pain, and he lowered them quickly.

"That story is too long for tonight, Princess, but I can assure you that my survival has come at a price." He swallowed hard, then cleared his throat, and his smirk returned. "Wait. Did you just call me brave and beautiful?"

"Hardly." I laughed and stepped away from him, all too aware of his presence next to me. He seemed to exude heat as well as charm. "So, what would happen if I took you up on this offer? Where would we go? What would we do?"

"I am so glad you asked." His whole face lit up. "I have some money. Not a lot, mind you, but I've hidden some of my mother's old jewelry. I could pawn it, and then we could go anywhere. Do anything your heart desired."

"That doesn't really sound like much of a plan."

"The Virgin Islands," Loki answered quickly and took another step toward me. "We wouldn't need passports to get there, and there's no trolls of any kind. We could spend all day in the ocean, and all night on the beach." He paused, his smile painfully sincere. "Just the two of us."

"I can't." I shook my head, and I hated how tempting the idea was. To run away from all the pressure and stress of the palace. "I can't let the kingdom down. I have a duty here, to these people."

"You have a duty to yourself to be happy!" Loki insisted.

"No, I don't," I said. "I have too much here. And let's not forget that I have a fiancé."

"Don't marry him." He scoffed at the idea. "Marry me instead."

"Marry you?" I laughed. "You told me that I should only marry for love."

"That I did." In that rare moment of honesty, Loki looked almost stunningly handsome. He stepped toward me, moving so close we were nearly touching. "Wendy, marry me."

"That's . . ." I shook my head, astounded by his proposal. "That doesn't even make sense, Loki. I barely know you, and you're . . . you're my enemy."

"I know I haven't known you that long, but I've felt . . . a connection from the moment I saw you, and I know you felt it too."

I floundered, wanting to deny him, but unable to. "Loki, a connection isn't enough to build a life on."

"I don't care where I come from or who your people are," he said simply. "I can make you happy, and you make me happy. We could have a happily ever after."

His eyes were on mine, and even in the dim light they glimmered gold. A slow wave started to wash over me as relaxation flowed through me. Just when I realized that Loki was trying to knock me out, the sensation stopped.

"What happened?" I asked, as the fog lifted from my mind. Loki stood inches in front of me, and I knew I should move away, but I didn't.

"I'm not going to do that to you," he said quietly. "What I told you before is still true. I want to know that when you're with me, it's because you want to be, not because you have to be."

"Loki—" I started to protest.

He put his hands on my face, and they felt warm on my skin, even though they should've been cold from scaling the wall. He leaned in to me, but he paused before his lips touched mine. His eyes met mine, searching them for any resistance, but I didn't have any.

His mouth covered mine, and warmth stirred inside me. He tasted sweet and cool, and his skin smelled of fresh rain. My knees felt weak, and my heart battered against my chest. His hands moved back, tangling in my hair and pressing me to him.

I wrapped my arms around him, and he felt strong and powerful against me. I could actually feel his muscles, like warm marble, and I knew he could crush me if he wanted to. But the way he touched me was passionate and delicate all at once.

I wanted to give in to him, to his invitation, but a voice of reason gnawed at me. My stomach fluttered with butterflies, then twisted with knots.

"No, Loki." I pulled my mouth from his, gasping for breath. I put my hands on his chest and took a step back. "I can't. I'm sorry."

"Wendy." Loki watched me walk backward away from him.

His expression was so desperate and vulnerable, it made my chest ache.

"I'm sorry. But I can't."

I turned and ran to the palace, afraid that I would change my mind if I hesitated any longer.

TWENTY-SEVEN

sacrifice

The next few days were a blur. I did everything I could to keep my mind off the kiss with Loki, or the horrible ache inside me that I knew I might never see him again. I just had to put it behind me and move forward with my engagement.

The training with Tove left me with a constant dull headache in the back of my skull. Making arrangements with his mother left me with pain in the remainder of my head. Willa tried her best to work as an intermediary, but Aurora didn't seem ready to let our earlier conflict go.

Elora was feeling better, so she joined us one afternoon. I thought having her there would help dispel the tension, but it didn't. When Aurora wasn't busy picking at me, she was picking at Elora. And when she wasn't doing that, they were both picking at me.

I spent most evenings in the library with Duncan, studying as much as I could about the Trylle way of life. I'd found a Tryllic dictionary, and I had to keep leafing through it as I looked through older documents. It was impossible to guess what it meant, since Tryllic didn't use the English alphabet. For example, the word *Tryllic* looked like this—Трыллиц.

With the small desk lamp as the only light in the room, I sat at the desk with my nose buried in a book. Duncan was at the shelves, combing through the acres of books to find ones that he thought would be best. He did know more about Trylle history than I did, but not much more.

"Burning the midnight oil?" Finn asked, scaring me so much I nearly screamed. He stood at the edge of the desk, and I hadn't even heard him come in.

"Yeah, I guess." I stared down at the faded pages of the book, keeping myself focused on them instead of Finn.

I hadn't talked to him since I'd kissed Loki. In a bizarre way, I felt as if I'd cheated on him. That was really silly, considering I was engaged to Tove, and what little Finn and I had together was long over.

"I have something I need to go check on," Duncan said, taking his cue to exit.

He didn't need to, since I doubted that Finn and I needed privacy, but it was nice that he tried. He gave me a hopeful smile before he slipped out, leaving me alone with Finn.

"What are you looking up?" Finn asked, nodding to the stacks of books on the desk.

"Anything. Everything." I shrugged. "I figured it was about time I got to know my history."

"It's a very large history," Finn said.

"Yeah. That's what I'm finding out." I leaned back in my chair so I could look up at him. The dim light from the lamp left most of his face in shadow, but his expressions were so unreadable anyway, it didn't really matter.

"The engagement party is tomorrow," he said. "Shouldn't you be upstairs primping and preening with Willa?"

"Nope. I get to do that in the morning." I sighed, thinking of the long day ahead of me tomorrow.

"On that note, a congratulations is in order."

"Really?" I closed the book I'd been reading and stood up.

I didn't want to be that close to Finn anymore, so I went over to a shelf and put the book away. I wasn't sure if it was the right spot, but I needed an excuse to move.

"You're getting married," Finn said, his voice cool and even. "Congratulations is appropriate."

"Whatever." I shoved the book hard in the bookcase and turned around to face him.

"You can't be mad at me for being supportive," Finn said, letting disbelief tinge his words.

"I can be mad at you for whatever I want." I leaned against the bookcase. "But I don't get you at all."

"What is there to get?" Finn asked.

"You practically ripped my arm off because you thought I was flirting with Loki. But I'm getting married to Tove, and you treat us both like nothing's happening."

"That's entirely different." Finn shook his head. "The Vittra was bad for you. He would hurt you. Tove is your intended."

"My intended?" I scoffed. "Were you protecting me for him? Making sure that nobody else tainted me until Tove got me?"

"No, of course not. I was merely protecting *you*. Your good name, your image."

"Right. That's what you were doing when you had your tongue down my throat?"

"I don't know why you always resort to being so crude." He lowered his eyes in disapproval.

"I don't know why you always have to be so proper!" I shot back. "Can you tell me how you really feel for once? I'm marrying somebody else! Don't you care at all?"

"Of course I care!" Finn yelled, his eyes blazing.

"Then why aren't you doing something?" I asked as tears filled my eyes. "Why don't you at least try to stop me?"

"Because Tove will take care of you. He will defend you." Finn swallowed hard. "He will be able to do things for you, *with* you, that I never could. Why would I take that away from you?"

"Because you care about me."

"It's because I care about you that I *can't*!"

"I don't believe you." I shook my head. "You don't even care when I'm with him. How could you get so angry when I was with Loki? You admitted you were jealous when I hung out with Rhys. But when I'm around Tove, you're fine."

"I'm not fine." He sighed in frustration. "But it doesn't feel the same when you're with Tove. It doesn't bother me as much."

"How can it not bother you?" I asked, totally dismayed.

"Because he's gay, Wendy!" Finn said finally, sounding exasperated.

For a moment I was too stunned to say anything. I just played over every moment I'd ever shared with Tove until I realized that what Finn had said made sense.

"He's gay?" I asked quietly.

"Don't tell him I told you, okay?" Finn grimaced and looked

apologetic. "I shouldn't be doing that. It's his private thing, and it's not my job to be airing his business."

"Then why is he marrying me?"

"What did he tell you when he proposed?" Finn asked.

"He said . . . because he believed in me and wanted me to be the leader." I thought back to the conversation. "He did it to support me, to save our people. For the same reasons I accepted the proposal.

"He's gay," I repeated. After that sank in, something new hit me, and I shook my head. "That's why you don't care. You know that I don't love him, that I never will, so you'd rather me marry him? But you thought I loved Loki, or that I could."

"It's more than that, Wendy." Finn shook his head. "Loki would hurt you."

"But that's not why you got mad. You were jealous because I might love somebody else." Anger surged through me. "You'd rather I live a lie than find happiness with someone else."

"You think you'd find happiness with a Vittra Markis?" Finn scoffed. "He's dangerous, Wendy. I didn't trust him around you."

"You didn't trust him because you knew I cared about him!"

"Yes!" Finn shouted. "And you shouldn't. He's a bad guy!"

"You don't even know him!" I yelled back.

"Do you want to go run off with him?" His face went stony, trying to hide any hurt he might feel. "Is that what you're saying? That I prevented you from living a fairy tale with him?"

"No, that's not what I'm saying." I swallowed my tears. "I prevented myself from running off with him because I knew what was best for the kingdom was me staying here. But I can't believe how selfish you are. You say everything you do is for me, but if that were true, you'd encourage me to go after happiness, instead of trapping me here with you."

"How have I trapped you here?" Finn asked.

"This!" I gestured between the two of us. "I can't have you, and I can't be without you. And I'm stuck in it with no way out. I care about you, and I can't stop, and you don't even care!"

"Wendy." His expression softened, and he moved toward me. I stepped back and ran into the bookshelf, so I couldn't go any farther. He reached out to touch me, and I pushed him off.

"No!" I shouted, with tears streaming down my face. "I hate that you do this me. I hate how crazy you make me. I hate *you!*"

He reached out, brushing hair back from my forehead. I jerked my head away, but he didn't move his hand. He'd moved right in front of me, so his body was against mine. I tried to push against him, but he stayed firm. He wouldn't move. His hand rested on my face, making me tilt my head up toward him.

His eyes were so black and deep, and they took my breath away, the way they always had. With his fingers, he traced along my hairline. The fight inside me disappeared, but the passion still lingered.

He leaned in, kissing me. His mouth pressed hungrily to mine. An intense quivering started in my heart but radiated out all over me, so my whole body shuddered. His stubble scraped against my skin as he kissed me desperately.

His lips traveled to my neck, and I moaned, burying my fingers in his hair. His weight sent us crashing against the shelves, and books tumbled out around us. We went with them, collapsing in a pile.

"Finn!" Thomas's voice boomed, interrupting us.

Finn stopped kissing me, but he remained on top of me. His breath came out in ragged gasps, and he continued to stare down at me. Passion smoldered in his eyes, but behind that, I saw terror. He realized that he'd done something terrible and didn't know how to undo it.

"Finn!" Thomas yelled again. "Get off her before someone sees you!"

"Yes, sir." Finn clambered off me, tripping over books as he got to his feet. I pulled down my dress, and got up much more slowly than him.

"Get out of here!" Thomas barked at him. "Get yourself cleaned up!"

"Yes, sir. Sorry, sir." Finn kept his eyes on the ground. He tried to cast a fleeting glance back at me, but he was too ashamed and simply darted out of the room.

"I'm sorry," I mumbled, unsure of what else to say. I could still taste Finn on my lips, feel his stubble on my cheek.

"You don't need to apologize to me," Thomas said, and the expression he gave me was much softer than the one he'd given his son. "You need to protect yourself, Princess. Go to your room, forget this ever happened, and pray that nobody ever finds out."

"Yes, of course." I nodded quickly and stepped carefully over the books. I'd almost made it out when Thomas stopped me.

"My son doesn't tell me much about his life," Thomas said, and I paused at the doorway, looking over my shoulder at him. "We've never been close. This job is a hard one. It keeps you isolated, and that is something that you and I have in common."

"I don't feel that isolated," I said. "I'm always surrounded."

"You've been fortunate, but it won't always be that way." He licked his lips and paused. "Sometimes you have to choose between love and duty. It's a hard choice, the hardest you'll ever make, but there is only one right answer."

"And you're saying that it's duty?" I asked.

"I'm saying duty was the right answer for me," Thomas explained carefully. "And duty will always be the right answer for Finn."

"Yes." I nodded, lowering my eyes. "That I know all too well."

"Trackers are often looked down upon." He held up his hand to silence me before I could argue. "Not by everyone, but by many. We're pitied. But it's an honorable life, living in service of people. Knowing that we are essential to creating a better world for the kingdom.

"The Queen lives in service as much as a tracker, maybe even more so. Your mother's whole life has been given to the people here. There is no greater honor than that. No greater deed. That is going to be your honor, Princess."

"I know," I said, feeling even more overwhelmed by the prospect.

"In the end, you find that with sacrifice, you receive more than you give," he said. "I've enjoyed talking with you, Princess, but I will let you get to your room."

"Yes, of course," I said.

Thomas bowed before me, and I turned away. I ran all the way up to my room, lifting my dress so I wouldn't trip on my hem. My hair had come loose so it fell around my face, and I was grateful for it. I didn't need anyone to see the shame in my expression or the tears that stained my cheeks.

honor

Y ou look amazing," Willa assured my reflection for the hundredth time.

I stood in front of the mirror. Willa was at my back. I was sure I appeared as if I were admiring my white gown, but I barely even recognized myself.

Only days before my engagement party, I'd kissed two different guys. It was odd because, of the two kisses, I found myself replaying Loki's more often. His kiss felt oddly refreshing, breathing new life into my soul. Even though Finn's had felt amazing at the time, once it was over, it only seemed to drain me of the energy I had. Loki had asked me to marry him, and Finn had pushed me away, the way he always did. The way he always would.

After everything that happened, I'd wanted to cry, but in the end, the way I felt about either Loki or Finn didn't matter. Not anymore. I was a Princess, with a duty to her kingdom and her fiancé. Tove and Förening deserved more, so I had to be more. I had to become what they needed.

"Come on, Wendy." Willa grabbed my arm, pulling me away.

"The party is about to start. We don't have time for you to keep staring at yourself."

I nodded and followed her, thinking I'd have time to compose myself, but as soon as I stepped out of my room, I found Tove waiting by the door.

"Sorry," he said when he saw my expression. "I didn't mean to startle you."

"No, it's okay." My mouth felt numb, and it was hard to speak.

"I'll leave you two lovebirds alone." Willa winked at me as she walked away.

"I hope it's not bad luck to see you before the engagement party." He dug in his pocket. "I'm not sure what the protocol is, but I had to give you something. I thought it'd be better to do it before the party."

"You didn't need to get me anything."

"Yeah, I did." Tove pulled a ring box out of his pocket. "It's kinda my job. I should've given it to you when I proposed, but that was kind of a lame proposal."

"I liked it." I smiled at him. "It was sweet."

"Well, I hope you like the ring." He held it out to me, the velvet lid still closed. "My mom hates it."

"I'm sure I'll love it, then," I said, and he laughed.

I took the box from him, and with trembling hands, I opened the lid. It was a thick platinum band, designed to look like ivy wrapped around the giant emerald inlaid in the center. A few small diamonds were dotted around the band.

"Oh, Tove, it's beautiful." As I slid it on my finger, I was actually getting choked up. It was a lovely ring, and such a lovely gesture.

Even though he hadn't told me, and I didn't plan on calling

him out on it, I knew Finn was right. Tove was gay. We would never be in love with each other, but we were friends, and we could find some kind of happiness together. Hopefully.

"Yeah?" Tove had a relieved lopsided grin and ran a hand through his hair. "Good. I was really worried. I had no idea what you would think."

"No, it's absolutely perfect." I smiled up at him with tears in my eyes.

"Good." He bit his lip. "You look really beautiful today."

"Thank you. You look really good yourself." I motioned to his nice suit pants and vest. "You clean up good, Markis."

"Thank you, Princess." He held out his arm so I could take it. "Shall we head down to our engagement party?"

"We shall," I said and looped my arm through his. We walked toward the ballroom to become the leaders the Trylle needed.

GLOSSARY OF TRYLLE TERMINOLOGY

aura—A field of subtle, luminous radiation surrounding a person or object. Different-colored auras denote different emotional qualities.

changeling—A child secretly exchanged for another.

Förening—The capital and largest city of Trylle society. A compound in the bluffs along the Mississippi River in Minnesota where the palace is located.

hobgoblin—An ugly, misshapen troll that stands no more than three feet tall.

host family—The family that the changeling is left with. These families are chosen based on their ranking in human society, with their wealth being the primary consideration. The higher ranked the members of Trylle society, the more powerful and affluent the host family their changeling is left with.

mänsklig—Often shortened to *mänks*. The literal translation for the word *mänsklig* is "human," but it has come to describe the human child who is taken when the Trylle offspring is left behind.

Markis—A title of male royalty in Trylle and Vittra society. Similar to that of a Duke, it's given to trolls with superior abilities. They have a higher ranking than the average Trylle, but are beneath the King and Queen. The hierarchy of Trylle society is as follows:

> King/Queen
> Prince/Princess
> Markis/Marksinna
> Trylle citizens
> Trackers
> Mänsklig
> Host families
> Humans (not raised in troll society)

Marksinna—A title of female royalty in Trylle and Vittra society. The female equivalent of the Markis.

Ondarike—The capital city of the Vittra. The King and the Queen, along with the majority of the powerful Vittra, live within the palace there. It is located in northern Colorado.

persuasion—A mild form of mind control. The ability to cause another person to act a certain way based on thoughts.

precognition—Knowledge of something before its occurrence, especially by extrasensory perception.

psychokinesis—Blanket term for the production or control of motion, especially in inanimate and remote objects, purportedly by the exercise of psychic powers. This can include mind control, precognition, telekinesis, biological healing, teleportation, and transmutation.

stork—Slang term for tracker; derogatory. *"Humans tell little kids that storks bring the babies, but trackers bring the babies here."*

tracker—A member of Trylle society who is specifically trained to track down changelings and bring them home. Trackers have no paranormal abilities, other than the affinity to tune in to one particular troll. They are able to sense danger to their charge and can determine the distance between them and their charge. The lowest form of Trylle society, other than mänsklig.

Trylle—(pronounced "trill") Beautiful trolls with powers of psychokinesis for whom the practice of changelings is a cornerstone of their society. Like all trolls, they are ill-tempered and cunning, and often selfish. Once plentiful, their numbers are fading, along with their abilities, but they are still one of the largest tribes of trolls. They are considered peaceful.

Tryllic—An old language the Trylle wrote in to disguise their important documents from humans. Its symbols are different from those of the standard Latin alphabet, and are similar to Arabic or Cyrillic in appearance.

Vittra—A more violent faction of trolls whose powers lie in physical strength and longevity, although some mild psychokinesis is not unheard of. They also suffer from frequent infertility. While Vittra are generally beautiful in appearance, more than 50 percent of their offspring are born as hobgoblins. They are one of the only troll tribes to have hobgoblins in their population.

Turn the page for the new,
never-before-published bonus short story

One Day: Three Ways

by Amanda Hocking

One Day: Three Ways

(A Trylle Story)

1. Finn

Saturday, October 28

The fall was unseasonably cold. Sleet had been coming down hard all morning, but that hadn't stopped travelers from coming to Förening for the Princess's engagement party. From where his family's little cottage sat nestled in the bluffs, Finn had heard the cars driving up the road to the palace.

Because of the party, his father was busy working, guarding the palace from any further Vittra attacks. With the new truce in place, Finn didn't think it was very likely. That's why he'd asked to be released from the Queen's request for him to help guard the party.

He very rarely went against her wishes, but he knew he had to this time. If there was one thing he'd learned, it was that he could no longer be trusted around Wendy.

After what had happened in the library the night before, Finn was determined to end things with her once and for all. Not that they'd ever really started anything, but their relationship had gotten much more out of hand than he'd liked.

He couldn't even understand his attraction to her. She was incorrigible and defied him every chance she got. Sometimes, Finn was positive she disagreed with him just because she liked to argue. Despite being smart, she reacted irrationally at times and let her heart make her decisions far too often.

Caring about her went against all logic, and he vowed to stop. Not completely—he'd always respect her and hope for her well-being. But this game they were playing had to stop. Even if Wendy didn't see it yet, he knew she'd be happier without him. And someday, he might even be happy without her.

As soon as he got the chance, Finn was leaving Förening, moving to do work that kept him as far away from the Princess as possible.

Right now he'd have to settle for helping his mother with her goats. With the engagement party under way, he didn't completely trust the Vittra not to attack, and he didn't want to venture too far from the palace. Just in case.

Since it was so chilly out, most of the goats chose to stay inside the small barn. They'd knocked over the bales of straw Finn and his family had stacked about, and Finn was resetting them so the goats would have something to climb up on.

He heard the front door of the house slam shut across the field behind him, and his younger sister Ember stomped out to the barn, her footsteps crunching heavily on the ground.

"It's not fair," Ember whined.

Finn tossed a badly soiled bale out into the pasture and looked back at her. "I take it you didn't come out here to help me."

"Hardly," she scoffed.

Ember had taken great pains to get dressed up today, which was hard, since she didn't have many nice dresses. Annali made almost all of her clothes, and while she was a talented seamstress, Ember was a tomboy, and she preferred Finn's hand-me-downs to most anything that Annali made.

The dress she'd put on today was a bit small. The blue fabric came up just above her knees, and it pulled snug across her chest. Her black curls were still a frizzy mess, but she'd clipped them back with a few strategically placed bobby pins.

Because she was going out to the barn, she'd put on her father's oversized work boots, and they clunked heavily on the ground.

"Everybody in the whole kingdom is going to the engagement party." Ember leaned back against the wall and stared up at the ceiling, where a few pigeons roosted. "It's not fair that Mom won't let me go."

"Everybody isn't going," Finn corrected her. "I'm not. Mom isn't. Most of your friends probably aren't."

"But you *could* be going," Ember countered, and looked over at him. Her eyes were so dark they were nearly black, and they appeared almost too large for her face, making her look younger than her twelve years.

"But I'm not." He turned away from her then, hoping to avoid another conversation about the Princess, and grabbed another bale of hay.

"Right. So I should be able to go in your place."

"I wasn't invited as a guest," Finn reminded her. "I would've been there to guard, and you haven't had enough training yet to watch the palace."

"I've started my training." Ember absently petted a goat that nibbled at the hem of her dress. "It's only three more years until I graduate from the tracker program, and I'm at the top of my class."

"I'm sure you're great." He gave her a smile to show her that he meant it, but she just continued sulking. "There will be plenty of other parties for you to attend. And once you start going, you'll realize how dull and pointless they all are, and you'll wish you never went at all."

"I'll never wish that," Ember muttered.

Finn sighed and walked over to her. She lowered her eyes and kicked emptily at a rock by her feet. When she took a deep breath, it came out in a plume of fog.

"I hate to break it to you, Ember, but it's not any more of a fairy tale at the palace than it is here. Yeah, they dress nicer, but that's about it," Finn said. "It's cold out here, and I'm done cleaning up. Why don't we go inside?"

Ember shook her head. "I'm not ready to go in."

"You sure?"

"Yeah. I'd rather stay out with the goats and freeze to death than argue with Mom anymore."

Finn tried to think of something to say to her, but Ember was stubborn to a fault. Besides, she'd come in when she got cold enough, and judging from the goose bumps covering her skin, it wouldn't be that much longer.

When he left the barn, Ember followed him out, but only so she could stomp about the yard with the few goats that decided to stay outside. She jumped into a puddle of slush, splashing the icy mush out around her, and apparently working off some of her frustration.

The heat from the hearth struck him wonderfully as he opened the front door. There were many negative things he could say about growing up in Förening, but he'd never been anywhere that felt quite as homey as his cottage with his family.

Finn wasn't sure what his mother was baking, but it smelled like fresh cinnamon bread. Annali sat at the battered kitchen table, mending a few of his pants and vests that had gotten worn. Finn could sew, but his mother was a far better tailor.

"Is your sister out there?" Annali asked without looking up from what she was doing.

"Yeah. She's just playing in the field." Finn went over to the sink so he could wash the goat filth from his hands.

"Good. I was afraid she might sneak up to that party." She threaded a needle through the pants and watched her son. His shoulders tensed as soon she mentioned the party, and she frowned.

Finn finished washing his hands, then leaned against the metal basin. He stared out the small round window above it, watching Ember slosh about the field.

"You know, I could take her up there," Finn said, his words tentative. "Just so she could see what it was like."

"No," Annali said sharply and shook her head. "There are too many people, and it wouldn't be good for either of you."

"But if she saw what it was really like, how boring and stuffy everyone is, maybe she wouldn't be going on about the Princess and the palace all the time. She has them on such a pedestal."

Annali snorted. "I wonder where she learned that from."

"Oh, so this is my fault?" Finn turned around to face her.

"I never said that." She continued sewing, but she lifted her eyes to look at him. "It's not just you. Or your father. It's those damn tracker schools too. They spend so much time teaching those kids that they're nothing compared to the royal family."

"It's not that bad," Finn insisted.

Annali wasn't completely off base, but she did greatly exaggerate it. The kids were taught that the higher Trylle had more abilities, and that's what made them higher Trylle. Part of being a tracker was protecting them, but there was still honor and dignity in that.

It might be a different kind of nobility than the royalty, but tracker children were still taught that they were integral to Trylle society. They were important and had just as much value as the Markis and Marksinna did.

"It's bad enough." Annali sighed. "Some days I wish I could pull Ember out of that school and take her far away from here."

"Then why don't you?" Finn asked. He stepped away from the basin and pulled out a chair across from his mother. "If you hate it so much here, why don't you go?"

She shook her head, trying to pretend like she hadn't given it much thought. "Where would we go?"

"Anywhere you want," he said with a dry laugh. "You're not a prisoner here."

"It doesn't feel like that," she admitted.

"Why didn't you leave?" Finn asked quietly.

For a moment, Annali said nothing. Though they rarely talked of it, she knew that Finn was aware of the affair between his father and the Queen. It would've been impossible for him not to be. They lived in a tiny cottage, and Annali and Thomas had spent a good portion of Finn's childhood arguing about Elora.

"Your father would never leave." Annali stopped sewing and

simply stared down at the pants. "And despite everything, I loved him. I couldn't leave him."

"How can you still love him after everything he put you through?" Finn asked.

"Don't." She shook her head and looked up at him. "You don't need to worry about my marriage. I forgave your father, and that's all that matters."

"If you say so," Finn said, unwilling to push the issue.

"This is why it's so important that you get away from that family while you still can." She set down her needle and thread and reached across the table, putting her hand over his. Her skin was dry and callused from years of hard work.

"I know why you don't like the Queen or her daughter, but it's not the same for me," Finn said.

"No, it's worse. You have a chance for a happy life, of loving someone who can actually love you in return. But that is not the Princess. It can never be her." Annali's mahogany eyes were pleading with him. "You know that if you continue down this path it will only lead to heartbreak, both for you and the Princess. You need to move on."

He swallowed hard and lowered his eyes. "I know. That's why I'm taking the first job I can to get out of here."

"Good." She smiled tightly at him. "I'll miss you, of course, but you need to take care of yourself. Your entire life doesn't need to be in service of others."

Finn pulled his hand back from his mother, and Ember burst into the house. Being outside apparently hadn't done anything for her mood. She started to kick off her boots, but when Annali scolded her, Ember took them off carefully and set them by the door.

Even though she seemed dead set on pouting, Finn decided to

try to cheer up. He suggested she change into pants, and he would practice fighting with her. In tracker school, they learned many forms of defense fighting, including mixed martial arts.

That seemed to get through to her, and Ember hurried off to change. Her main goal in life was to become a great tracker like her father and brother, and any time that Finn spent helping her train left her elated.

So that's how he spent the rest of the afternoon. Outside, in the sleet and slush, teaching his little sister how to fight. Neither of them fought as well as they could, since both their minds were still on the engagement party. It helped distract them, though, and make them forget how badly they wanted to be somewhere else.

And sometimes that was the best Finn could do. Just distract himself until he could forget about the things he couldn't have. He had a family that loved him and a house filled with warmth, despite its history, and that was more than he could say for a lot of people.

2. Tove

Saturday, October 28

He couldn't remember anybody's names. Most of the time, Tove felt pretty fortunate that he could remember his fiancée's name. That's why, when they were introduced to people, Tove said very little, leaving it to Wendy to greet the guests at their engagement party.

At least the meet-and-greet part of the party was over, and they had moved on to eating. He glanced over at Wendy sitting next to him, her smile so wide it looked painful. Her aura was strained, looking a putrid mustard color, and he wondered, not for the first time, if he'd done the right thing asking her to marry him.

It seemed like the best thing to do when he asked her. From a political standpoint, she needed to rule the kingdom, and having the support of himself and his family behind her would help. In a personal sense, Tove didn't want to force her to do this alone.

Besides that, it wasn't like either of them could marry some-body they loved. But at least they liked each other. It would be better to marry a friend than end up in some cold prison like his parents' marriage.

But sometimes, like when Wendy smiled politely at another one of his mother's veiled insults, Tove thought he'd accidentally trapped her in this. He'd done this to help her—but maybe he'd also been selfish. Their engagement kept Aurora from asking too many questions about why Tove wasn't dating.

Tove had only briefly considered leaving Förening, accepting his fate and being banished. But he couldn't go back to the human world. His abilities made him act out too bizarrely. When they started manifesting in his early teens, he'd actually been forced into inpatient treatment at a psychiatric hospital.

Finding out he was Trylle had been such a relief for him. When Finn had tracked him down and explained that he wasn't insane, that all the things he could hear and do were real, it had been one of the happiest days of his life.

That's why he couldn't leave here. Giving up the chance at fall-ing in love was a hefty price to pay, but for him it was worth it. Living a life outside of an insane asylum was good enough.

But maybe it was unfair to ask the same thing of Wendy.

"How are you doing?" Tove asked her quietly.

"Hmm?" She'd been absently picking at the salad in front of her.

He hadn't eaten much of his own food, but events like this always made him lose his appetite. His head buzzed, even though he'd spent all morning draining his powers, and he felt a migraine growing at the base of his skull.

"How are you doing?" Tove repeated. He leaned forward, resting his arms on the table and pushing his plate away from him.

Elora made a clicking sound with her tongue when he put his elbows on the table, but she said nothing. The one good thing about the party was that Wendy had been seated next to Aurora, and Tove had been seated next to Elora, so neither of them had to make awkward dinner conversation with strangers.

Tove, Wendy, and their parents, along with Garrett and Willa, all sat at one long table in the newly finished ballroom. They looked much like the Last Supper, all sitting on one side at the head table. Partygoers were seated throughout the ballroom, their voices a dull rumble echoing through the room.

"Dandy." Wendy forced a smile at him. "How are you?"

"There's still time." He leaned in toward her, lowering his voice so it was barely audible. "We can still call this whole thing off. If you want."

"No." She lowered her eyes and shook her head, and he couldn't tell for sure if she meant it or not. "I don't want to."

"Tove, what are you conspiring about?" Aurora bent forward to get a better look at him.

"Just whispering sweet nothings to one another." Tove smiled thinly at her, and she narrowed her eyes. "You know how we young lovers are."

Wendy laughed at that, a genuine sound, and when she smiled, it was absolutely dazzling. She looked so radiant when she was happy, even he had to appreciate her beauty.

"No." She looked up at him, still smiling, and her aura lightened to more of a yellow. He'd managed to relax her a little. "I'm happy to have you here with me. Because if you weren't here, I'd have to do all this by myself. And you know how misery loves company."

He nodded. "I do."

Something must've occurred to her, because her brown eyes looked pained and her smile fell away. "Unless you're saying you don't want to do this. If you want out, that's fine with me. I was just joking about misery loving company. I don't want you to be miserable."

"No, I'm not miserable," Tove said quickly, nearly cutting her off. "And I don't want out. There's plenty of worse things I can do than marry you."

Like being banished from the kingdom and getting locked up for being crazy. That would be far worse. But he didn't say that. Instead he just smiled, and she looked relieved.

He took a long drink of his wine and settled back in his chair.

Tove tried to remind himself that he had nothing to feel guilty about. Wendy knew he didn't love her, and she didn't love him. But they were both still very young, and Wendy could eventually find someone she loved who was also suitable for marrying.

If she did that, if Tove ever found she was in love with someone she could actually be with, he would gladly step aside. That was the one concession he could make.

"You should finish eating, Princess," Aurora said.

She was speaking to Wendy, but her eyes were locked on the

engagement ring on her hand. Tove had picked it out himself, and Aurora despised it. She spent most of the evening glaring at the emerald, and Tove couldn't help but smile every time he noticed.

"I think I'm done, actually." Wendy set her fork on her plate and leaned back in her seat.

"Good. Because the dancing should be starting soon."

"We have to dance?" Tove balked.

"Of course," Elora said. "It's tradition for the betrothed to have their first dance together at the engagement party."

"Right. Because nothing says romance like dancing in front of hundreds of strangers," Tove muttered.

"Marriage has nothing to do with romance," Elora said, as if Tove needed reminding.

The server came to take away their empty plates shortly after that, and then the band started playing. His mother had gotten a small twelve-piece orchestra for the party, and they were set up on the edge of the room near the head table.

With all the tables crowding the room, there wasn't much of a dance floor. There wouldn't be enough room for more than a few couples, but that was fine, since it would only be Tove and Wendy dancing.

When the orchestra grew louder—Tove thought it was something by Debussy—Aurora gave him a stern look. Even with all the static from the crowd, he could hear her loud and clear, demanding that he ask Wendy to dance.

Sighing, Tove pushed back his chair and stood up. Holding his hand out to her, he asked, "Shall we?"

"If we must." Wendy put her hand in his, and as soon as she stood up, the crowd erupted in applause.

Tove led Wendy around the back of the table. When they walked behind Aurora, she hissed, "*Smile*. You look like you're going to a funeral."

By the time they reached the floor, everyone had stopped clapping, but all eyes were still on them. Tove could feel their stares burrowing into him, and it was rather distracting. He tried to keep his focus on Wendy and blot them out.

"I should've had more wine with dinner," Tove said as they managed a slow, awkward waltz together.

"Sorry." She furrowed her brow as she stared up at him. "Are you okay? You seem a little . . . frazzled."

"Too many people," he admitted and grimaced. "For our wedding day, I'm going to have to spend the entire night before moving everything I can so I'm completely exhausted."

"Does it help if you think of something else?" Wendy asked. "I mean, if we talk and keep your mind busy, does it help keep the noise down?"

"A little."

"Okay, so . . ." She glanced around, as if searching for something to talk about. "What should our wedding song be?"

"You mean Aurora hasn't already picked it?" Tove asked with a wry smile.

"No, I won't let her," Wendy informed him. Tove must've looked impressed because she laughed a little. "I know this is sort of a fake wedding, but it will be the only wedding I have. Aurora and Willa are picking everything else, but I wanted to have a say in the song."

He saw it then. Only for a second, but her aura darkened, going nearly black for a moment, when she said this would be her only wedding.

Her expression had remained the same, though. She was getting better at lying, at pretending to be who the Trylle expected her to be. That was for the best, he supposed, but part of him was saddened that she was losing some of her innocence.

"What song did you have in mind?" Tove asked, hurrying to erase her unease.

"I don't know, actually." Wendy laughed again. "I'd never really put much thought into my wedding until a few days ago. But I know I don't want something cheesy or super cliché."

"So 'Endless Love' is out?" Tove teased.

"I'm afraid so." She cocked her head at him. "What about you? Did you have any songs in mind?"

"No, I don't know." He shrugged. "I didn't think I'd have any input."

"Why don't we pick the song together, then?" Wendy asked. "What do you like?"

"Um . . ." Tove tried to think of music he liked that would be appropriate for the ceremony. "I've always been partial to Etta James."

"Really?" Wendy raised an eyebrow.

"Yes, really. Why do you always seem so surprised by the music I like?" Tove asked. "You and Duncan were both shocked that I liked the Beatles."

"I don't know. It's weird picturing you listening to music, I guess." She shook her head, making her dark curls dance on her shoulders. "I don't know how to explain it."

"I like music very much, actually," he said. "It helps drown out the noise."

"I suppose it would." She took a deep breath and stared up at him with the strangest look in her eyes.

"What?" Tove asked, fearing he'd done something wrong.

"There's just so much I don't know about you, and . . ." She trailed off, but he waited until she found the words to finish her thought. "And I'm spending the rest of my life with you."

"Well, that's plenty of time to learn, isn't it?" Tove tried to sound cheerful about it, but he knew what she meant.

Eventually, blessedly, the song ended, and they returned to their seats. Unfortunately, it wasn't quite the reprieve Tove had hoped for. Guests were now allowed to come up to the table, supposedly to wish them well on their marriage, but mostly they seemed to be complaining about something.

The Chancellor managed to hog a disproportionate amount of time. There was a line of people waiting behind him to get up to the table, but he continued to blabber on, oblivious to how he inconvenienced everyone else.

Poor Wendy always got the worst of it. His beady little eyes were focused directly on her. The one bright spot was that he was apparently too upset about the current state of things to be thinking anything dirty about the Princess. It was a nice change for Tove, not to see that horrible man's perverse thoughts.

"Sorry. I don't mean to bother you," Markis Bain said, pulling Tove's gaze to him. He'd been too busy glaring at the Chancellor to notice the Markis had come up to the table.

"Um, no. You're no bother." Tove tucked his hair behind his ears and leaned forward on the table. "No bother at all."

"I kind of cut in line," Bain admitted sheepishly and motioned to where the Chancellor continued to prattle on to Wendy. "But I didn't really want to talk to the Princess anyway. I mean, I did, but you were . . . available."

"I am available, so . . . that's fine." Tove smiled up at him.

Bain was in charge of changeling placement, so Tove had seen him around the palace before, but they'd never really spoken. But Tove had noticed him right away since Bain had the most brilliant blue eyes he'd ever seen—an incredible rarity in the Trylle community. In fact, it was so rare, Tove only knew of one other Trylle in the entire kingdom who had blue eyes.

It meant that somewhere, a few generations back, one of Bain's ancestors had been from the Skojare—a smaller tribe of trolls known for their affinity for aquatics. But Tove didn't care what Bain's bloodlines were. His mother would, but in matters like these, her opinions did not count.

"I wanted to wish you luck," Bain said.

"Luck?" Tove asked, unsure of what he meant.

"On your impending nuptials." He gestured over to Wendy sitting next to him, and Tove realized dismally that he'd actually forgotten she was there.

"Right." Tove forced a smile and nodded. "Thanks."

"I have to admit, I was a little surprised to hear that you were engaged to the Princess." Bain ran a hand through his dark hair and lowered his eyes, as if embarrassed that he'd said that. "Not that you're not a good choice. Because you are. I just . . ."

Tove leaned farther forward on the table, his voice hushed. "I assure you that no one else is more surprised than I am that I'm marrying a Princess."

Bain looked up at him then, letting his gaze linger a bit longer than was polite. He was only a few years older than Tove, and he was slender and almost delicate-looking, like a young Johnny Depp. That made his eyes stand out even more, and seem incredibly entrancing.

"Well, I guess I'll be seeing you around more," Bain said, taking a small step away from the table. "With you living and working here now."

"Good," Tove said, then hurried to correct it with, "I mean, yeah. I'll be seeing you."

Bain left the table then, and Tove was reluctant to look away. He leaned back in his chair and sighed, then noticed the Chancellor was still blathering on to Wendy.

"You've had your turn," Tove said, interrupting the Chancellor midsentence. "Move along."

"Beg pardon?" the Chancellor asked, his tiny eyes as wide as they could get. Aurora coughed under her breath, trying to dissuade Tove from being rude, but he ignored her.

"You heard me." Tove glared at him. "Move."

The Chancellor stammered but did as he was told, wringing his hands as he walked away from the table. A woman came up to the table after him, but before she could say anything, Wendy offered Tove an appreciative smile and mouthed the words *Thank you*.

The woman just gave them quick congratulations, which was a nice change of pace, and Tove tried to thank her for it, but he'd forgotten her name. Fortunately, Wendy swooped in to supply it, so he didn't look like a complete jerk.

While they continued with the seemingly endless procession of well-wishers, Tove found his eyes searching the crowd for Bain. Though he never found him again, it did solidify Tove's commitment to his marriage with Wendy.

It was another selfish reason, one that made him feel guiltier, like he was tricking her into this somehow. But the only way that Tove could ensure that real social change would be made to the Trylle—namely, who they were allowed to fall in love with—would be if he was in a position of power. He had to be King.

3. Loki

Saturday, October 28

The light above him flickered, and Loki glared up at it as he paced his cell. He loathed the dungeon, but not for the reasons Oren wanted him to. It just always seemed too over-the-top, with its dank bricks and dirty floors and hobgoblins at the doors. It was too predictable to be horrifying.

Not only that, the structure wasn't even very strong. Loki'd been chained to the wall, and while Oren had been smart enough to use heavy metal for the chains and cuffs around his hands, Loki had easily been able to yank them from the concrete. Now he walked around, dragging a chunk of brick behind him, but he could move freely.

The slats on the front door clicked as they slid open, and Loki groaned.

"If you're going to spend this much time with me, sire, you ought to set me up in the marital suite next to yours," Loki said as the door began to open. "It'll save you the trouble of walking all the way down here."

"Sorry to disappoint you, but it's only me," Sara said, and she came inside the cell.

Loki stopped pacing and glanced over at her. He hadn't thought she would visit. She'd sworn to wash her hands of him if he failed in his mission, and he had. Since he'd returned to Ondarike, she hadn't even spoken to him.

Now she came into the dungeon, carrying a tray with a few scraps of food and a cup of water. He eyed her, only to check for bruises or marks, but when he didn't see any, he looked away.

"What do you want?" Loki asked.

"That's no way to speak to your Queen," Sara said.

She shut the door behind her when she came in, noticing the door was dented in quite severely, probably from Loki's attempts at escape. He would say he cared nothing for his life, but he wouldn't fight so hard if he didn't want to get away.

"You're right." Loki gave her a sardonic smile. "Why don't you throw me down in the dungeon? That ought to teach me a lesson. Oh, wait . . ."

"You know I didn't want you down here," Sara said. "I never wanted to see you like this."

"No?" He shook his head. "You didn't stop him from putting me here."

"What was I supposed to do, Loki?" Sara stepped toward him, pleading with him. "You failed him, and you know it."

Loki said nothing to that. He merely stared at the ground, his jaw tense. His shirt was gone, and Sara could see the fresh lashes he had across his back. So far, he only had a few—bright red lines cut across his flesh.

But the King was only just beginning. He'd been known to drag out his punishments for months, sometimes even years, torturing his victims over and over again.

"I brought you food," Sara said quietly and held out the tray toward him.

He stared derisively at it, and for a second Sara was afraid he would smack it out of her hands. Instead, he reached over and picked up the glass of water, his chain clanking against the metal tray.

Before taking a drink, he muttered, "Thank you." He gulped it down quickly, then set the cup back on the tray.

"Don't you want the food?" Sara asked, and he shook his head. "You should eat. You'll need your strength."

"It's better if I don't have my strength." He ran a hand through his hair. "Death will come quicker then."

"Don't say that." She pursed her lips. "You don't mean that."

"I don't mean that?" Loki laughed darkly. "Of course I do! Oren is going to torture me until I finally die, so yes, I wish for a fast death. That's the only sane thing to do."

"He might not." Sara couldn't even look Loki in the eyes when she said it.

"Yes, he might not," Loki agreed with false cheer. "I might be lucky enough to be immortal like Oren, so I can spend all eternity in this dungeon. Wouldn't that be grand?"

"Why couldn't you just bring her back?" Sara spat, surprised by the intensity in her voice. She was still staring down at the floor, but when she lifted her head, there were tears in her dark eyes. "If you'd just brought the Princess back, you wouldn't be here."

He met her eyes for a moment, then shook his head and looked away. "I couldn't do that to her."

"If you care for her, then you should've done it," Sara went on. "He would've had you marry her. You could've lived forever with her, ruling this kingdom."

"First of all, you know as well as I that the King will never give up his rule," Loki disagreed with her. "He just wants her because she's a shiny new toy that the Trylle have. He'll never let her take over for him."

"Eventually he has to step down," Sara insisted. "He wants an heir."

"He wants an heir who will run things exactly like him," Loki said and began pacing again. "Wendy's nothing like him. He'd do everything he could to break her down, to turn into her a calculating barbarian. He'd destroy her."

"No, I wouldn't let him." Sara shook her head. "I would protect her."

"You mean like you protected me?" He glanced back at her with a raised eyebrow, and she bit her lip.

"I tried." Her voice broke. "But there was nothing I could do."

"I know." Loki sighed and regretted what he'd said. "I don't blame you for this. It was my choice. The King sent me to get her. I knew what would happen if I didn't return with her, and I didn't."

"You didn't have to come back." Her voice quavered, and she set down the tray on the floor so she could wipe her eyes. "After you went to Förening the other day to get her, you didn't have to come back."

"I wasn't going to." Loki paused, debating whether or not to tell her the truth. "The King sent me back to get her, knowing I'd earned her trust, but I asked Wendy to run away with me. And I meant it. If she'd said yes, I would've taken her far away from all of this."

"But she said no?" Sara asked.

He swallowed hard and didn't say anything for a minute. His shoulders slackened, and he looked more despondent than Sara had ever seen him before.

"It's for the best, though," Loki said finally. "If she'd come with me, it would've meant hell for her people. Oren would've claimed they broke the truce and were holding me hostage. He would've attacked them with everything, and the Trylle wouldn't have her to help defend them."

"That's why you came back," Sara realized. "If you stayed gone, Oren would blame the Trylle and go after them."

"He would've killed them and stolen her." Loki nodded. "It didn't seem worth it to have all the bloodshed just so I could avoid some pain."

"Loki." She walked over to him and tried to put her hand on his arm, but he pulled away from her. "You need to escape." She lowered her voice, in case the guard outside might be listening. "I can help you."

"I think it's too late for me, Sara." He smiled sadly at her. "But you should get out while you still can."

The door behind them started to push open, and Sara hurriedly stepped away from him.

Oren strode into the room, the sleeves of his black shirt rolled up and the top button undone, like he meant to get down to business. In his right hand he held a sword—the diamonds of the bell guard glittering over his hand.

"I wish you'd told me you planned to come see Loki today," Oren said, his voice like rough gravel, and smiled at his wife. "I could've saved you the trip."

"I only brought him food." Sara gestured to the tray on the ground. "I thought he should keep up his strength."

"Nah, I don't need my strength." Loki waved off Sara, making his chains rattle, and pointed to the sword. "The King's come to kill me."

Oren's smile widened and his black eyes rested on Loki. "Joke all you want, but soon you'll be begging for death."

"How would you prefer me to beg, sire?" Loki asked. "On my knees? Because I can do that right now, if you'd like."

"Loki," Sara said in a hushed tone.

"My Queen, would you leave us, please?" Oren asked, without looking at her. "I need a moment alone with our prisoner."

"Your Majesty." Sara wrung her hands and looked from Oren to Loki, her eyes wide and fearful. "Please don't do anything rash."

"I'm never rash," the King snapped. "Now leave us."

Sara glanced back at Loki, looking apologetic. He wanted to nod to her, to make some gesture to let her know that he was okay with her leaving, that he encouraged it, even. But he couldn't. If the King saw that, it would appear that she was asking for Loki's permission, and Sara would pay dearly for that.

So instead, Loki did nothing except stare stoically at the King. Sara left the dungeon without another word to either of them, and the door clanked shut loudly behind her.

"My wife cares too much for you," Oren said simply.

"It depends on what you think of as 'too much.'" Loki wagged his head, considering it. "Since you're incapable of caring because you have no heart, I suppose that any amount would seem too much to you."

The King laughed loudly, and he held up his sword, gesturing with it as he spoke, and it was a struggle for Loki to keep his eyes off the metal as it glinted in the light.

"I'll admit this to you, Loki—I did always think you were funny. I'd never say that to anyone else, but you make me laugh."

"I did always fancy myself the court jester," Loki said.

"And you were. A fine one too." Oren rubbed his chin and paced in front of Loki. "And if you'd been good at anything else, we wouldn't be here. Do you want to know the one thing I could never stomach about you?"

"My boyish charm? My stunning good looks? My untamed hair?" Loki suggested.

"You never knew when to shut up."

Oren turned on him and lifted the sword suddenly. He drove it right toward Loki, and when the tip of the blade pierced his chest directly above his heart, Loki didn't even flinch. He just swallowed hard and kept his eyes on the King, but Oren didn't push the blade in any farther.

The King narrowed his eyes at him. "I could kill you right now."

"I rather expected you were going to," Loki admitted.

"I know." Oren smiled broadly at that. "That's why I'm not." He jerked the sword back, slicing Loki across the chest, but it was nothing more than a flesh wound. Still, Loki had to steel himself to keep from reacting to the pain, and blood dripped down his skin. "I want to make you suffer the way you've made me suffer."

"This is you suffering?" Loki smirked. "You don't know the first thing about true pain. You've never gone without—"

Before Loki could say any more, the King backhanded him, so the bell guard of the sword hit him square in the jaw. The diamonds pierced his skin, and the King used such force that Loki had to use all his might to keep from falling over. But he refused to give Oren the satisfaction.

He straightened himself up, absently spitting blood on the floor, and kept his eyes on Oren. His hair had fallen forward, nearly into his eyes, but Loki didn't brush it away.

"You can mess up my face and my hair, but I'll always be more charming than you," Loki said, smiling even though it hurt like hell to do so.

Oren leaned forward, and when he spoke, his voice was low, like he was conspiring with Loki. "I know you want me to kill you. That's why I'm not going to. I also know you can barely survive without interaction. Even me, smacking you around, you thrive on that. You *crave* it."

"Aw, yes, I often long for a right hook in the jaw or a whip to my back," Loki replied. "I've written many a sonnet about the beatings you used to give me when I was a child."

"The real torture for you is being ignored," Oren went on as if Loki hadn't said anything.

"So true. That sword you have is nothing compared to being shunned. I'd take the guillotine any day as long as someone is watching."

"Make your jokes, but nobody will be around to laugh at them," Oren said, backing toward the door. "I'm forbidding Sara from seeing you or any of the guards from talking to you. You'll have nothing. When I'm through with you, you'll wish you'd never been born."

"I've always wished that, sire," Loki said and exhaled deeply.

Oren laughed as he walked out of the dungeon, and Loki could still hear him laughing even after the door had locked and Oren had begun walking away.

With no other way to express his frustration, Loki picked up the tray and threw it across the room. It crashed into the wall, denting before clattering to the floor.

He slumped back against the wall and held his head in his hands. The truth was that he had no idea if he'd make it through this. Isolation, beatings, constant threats of death—it was exactly what he'd thought it would be, but that didn't make it any less excruciating to endure.

"That Princess better be worth all this," Loki muttered to himself.

But as soon as he said it, he thought of her. The kindness he'd seen in her eyes and the fact that she'd stood up for him and fought for his life, even when his own people never had. They'd only shared a few moments together, but she'd made him feel more than he ever had in his entire life.

Without a doubt, she was worth it. No matter what the King would do to him, Loki would gladly do it all again, if it meant that he could spare Wendy the same fate.

Ascend

**If you enjoyed *Torn*, you'll love *Ascend*,
the final novel in the Trylle series.**

The first chapter follows here . . .

amnesty

I had my back to the room as I stared out the window. It was a trick I'd learned from my mother to make me seem more in control. Elora had given me lots of tips the past few months, but the ones about commanding a meeting were the most useful.

"Princess, I think you're being naive," the Chancellor said. "You can't turn the entire society on its head."

"I'm not." I turned back, giving him a cool gaze, and he lowered his eyes and balled up his handkerchief in his hand. "But we can't ignore the problems any longer."

I surveyed the meeting room, doing my best to seem as cold and imposing as Elora always had. I didn't plan to be a cruel ruler, but they wouldn't listen to weakness. If I wanted to make a change here, I had to be firm.

Since Elora had become incapacitated, I'd been running the day-to-day activities of the palace, including a lot of meetings. The board of advisers seemed to take up a lot of my time.

The Chancellor had been voted into his position by the Trylle people, but as soon as his term was up, I planned to campaign against him as hard as I could. He was a conniving coward, and we needed somebody much stronger in his position.

Garrett Strom—my mother's "confidant"—was here today, but he didn't always attend these meetings. Depending on how Elora was doing that day, he often chose to stay and care for her instead.

My assistant Joss sat at the back of the room, furiously scribbling down notes as we talked. She was a small human girl who grew up in Förening as a mänsklig and worked as Elora's secretary. Since I'd been running the palace, I'd inherited Joss as my own assistant.

Duncan, my bodyguard, was stationed by the door, where he stood during all the meetings. He followed me everywhere, like a shadow, and though he was clumsy and small, he was smarter than people gave him credit for. I'd grown to respect and appreciate his presence the last few months, even if he couldn't completely take the place of my last guard, Finn Holmes.

Aurora Kroner sat at the head of the table, and next to her was Tove, my fiancé. He was usually the only one on my side, and I was grateful to have him here. I didn't know how I would manage ruling if I felt completely alone.

Also in attendance were Marksinna Laris, a woman I didn't particularly trust, but she was one of the most influential people in Förening; Markis Bain, who was in charge of changeling placement; Markis Court, the treasurer for the palace; and Thomas Holmes, the head guard in charge of security and all the trackers.

A few other high-ranking officials sat around the table, all of their expressions solemn. The situation for the Trylle was growing increasingly dire, and I was proposing change. They didn't want me to change anything—they wanted me to support the system they'd had for centuries, but that system wasn't working anymore. Our society was crumbling, and they refused to see the roles they played in its breakdown.

"With all due respect, Princess," Aurora began, her voice so sweet I could barely hear the venom underneath, "we have bigger issues at hand. The Vittra are only getting stronger, and with the truce about to end—"

"The truce," Marksinna Laris snorted, cutting her off. "Like that's done us any good."

"The truce isn't over yet," I said, standing up straighter. "Our trackers are out taking care of the problems now, which is why I think it's so important that we have something in place for them when they return."

"We can worry about that *when* they return," the Chancellor said. "Let's deal with saving our asses right now."

"I'm not asking to redistribute the wealth or calling to abolish the monarchy," I said. "I am simply saying that the trackers are out there risking their lives to save us, to protect our changelings, and they deserve a real house to come back to. We should be setting aside money *now* so that when this is over, we can begin building them real homes."

"As noble as that is, Princess, we should be saving our money for the Vittra," Markis Bain said. He was quiet and polite, even when he disagreed with me, and he was one of the few royals whom I felt actually wanted to do what was best for all the people.

"We can't pay the Vittra off," Tove interjected. "This isn't about money. This is about power. We all know what they want, and a few thousand—or even a few *million*—dollars won't matter to them. The Vittra King will refuse it."

"I will do everything in my power to keep Förening safe, but you are all correct," I said. "We have yet to find a reasonable solution for the Vittra. That means this might very well turn into a bloody fight, and if it does, we need to support our troops. They deserve the best care, including adequate housing and access to our healers if they're injured in wartime."

"Healers for a tracker?" Marksinna Laris laughed, and a few others chuckled along with her. "Don't be ridiculous."

"Why is that ridiculous?" I asked, working to keep the ice from my voice. "They are expected to die for us, but we aren't willing to heal their wounds? We cannot ask more of them than we are willing to give ourselves."

"They are lower than us," Laris said, as if I didn't understand the concept. "We are in charge for a reason. Why on earth should we treat them as equals when they are not?"

"Because it's basic decency," I argued. "We may not be human, but that doesn't mean we have to be devoid of humanity. This is why our people are leaving our cities and preferring to live among the humans, letting their powers die. We must offer them some bit of happiness, otherwise why would they stay?"

Laris muttered something under her breath, keeping her steely eyes locked on the oak table. Her black hair was slicked back, pulled in a bun so tight her face looked strained. This was probably done on purpose to draw attention to her strength.

Marksinna Laris was a very powerful Trylle, able to produce and control fire, and something that strong was draining. Trylle powers weakened them, taking some of their life and aging them preternaturally.

But if the Trylle didn't use them, the abilities did something to their minds, eating at their thoughts and making them crazy. This was especially true for Tove, who would appear scattered and rude if he didn't find constant outlets for his psychokinesis.

"It is time for a change," Tove said, speaking up when the room had fallen into annoyed silence. "It can be gradual, but it's going to happen."

A knock at the door stopped anyone from giving him a rebuttal, but from the beet-red color of the Chancellor's face, it looked like he had a few words he wanted to get out.

Duncan opened the door, and Willa poked her head in, smiling uncertainly. Since she was a Marksinna, Garrett's daughter, and my best friend, she had every right to be here. I'd extended an invitation for her to attend these meetings, but she always declined, saying she was afraid she would do more harm than good. She had a hard time being polite when she disagreed with people.

"Sorry," Willa said, and Duncan stepped aside so she could come in. "I didn't mean to interrupt. It's just that it's after five, and I was supposed to get the Princess at three for her birthday celebration."

I glanced at the clock, realizing this had dragged on much longer than I'd originally planned. Willa walked over to me and gave the room an apologetic smile, but I knew she'd pull me out kicking and screaming if I didn't put an end to the meeting.

"Ah, yes." The Chancellor smiled at me with a disturbing hunger in his eyes. "I'd forgotten that you'll be eighteen tomorrow." He licked his lips, and Tove stood up, purposely blocking the Chancellor's view of me.

"Sorry, everyone," Tove said, "but the Princess and I have plans this evening. We'll pick up this meeting next week, then?"

"You're going back to work next week?" Laris looked appalled.

"So soon after your wedding? Aren't you and the Princess taking a honeymoon?"

"With the state of things, I don't think it's wise," I said. "I have too much to get done here."

While that was true enough, that wasn't the only reason I'd skipped out on a honeymoon. As much as I'd grown to like Tove, I couldn't imagine what the two of us would do on one. I hadn't even let myself think about how we would spend our wedding night.

"We need to go over the changeling contracts," Markis Bain said, standing up in a hurry. "Since the trackers are bringing the changelings back early, and some families decline to do changelings anymore, the placements have all been moved around. I need you to sign off on them."

"Enough talk of business." Willa looped her arm through mine, preparing to lead me out of the room. "The Princess will be back to work on Monday, and she can sign anything you want then."

"Willa, it will only take a second to sign them," I said, but she glared at me, so I gave Bain a polite smile. "I will look them over first thing Monday morning."

Tove stayed behind a moment to say something to Bain, but he caught up with us a few moments later in the hall. Even though we were out of the meeting, Willa still kept her arm through mine as we walked.

Duncan stayed a step behind us when we were in the south wing. I'd gotten talked to many, many times about how I couldn't treat Duncan as an equal while business was being conducted and there were Trylle officials at work around us.

"Princess?" Joss said, scampering behind me with papers spilling out of her binder. "Princess, do you want me to arrange a meeting on Monday with Markis Bain for the contracts?"

"Yes, that would be fantastic," I said, slowing so I could talk to her. "Thank you, Joss."

"You have a meeting at ten A.M. with the Markis of Oslinna." Joss flipped through the appointment section of the binder, and a paper flew out. Duncan snatched it before it fell to the floor and handed it to her. "Thank you. Sorry. So, Princess, do you want to meet Markis Bain before or after that meeting?"

"She'll be going back to work just after getting married," Willa said. "Of course she won't be there first thing in the morning. Make it for the afternoon."

I glanced over at Tove walking next to me, but his expression was blank. Since proposing to me, he'd actually spoken very little of getting married. His mother and Willa had done most of the planning, so I hadn't even talked to him about what he thought of colors or flower arrangements. Everything had been decided for us, so we had little to discuss.

"Does two in the afternoon work for you?" Joss asked.

"Yes, that would be perfect," I said. "Thanks, Joss."

"All right." Joss stopped to hurriedly scribble down the time in the binder.

"Now she's off until Monday," Willa told Joss over her shoulder. "That means five whole days where nobody calls her, talks to her, or meets with her. Remember that, Joss. If anybody asks for the Princess, she cannot be reached."

"Yes, of course, Marksinna Strom." Joss smiled. "Happy birthday, Princess, and good luck with your wedding!"

"I can't believe how much of a workaholic you are," Willa said with a sigh as we walked away. "When you're Queen, I'll never see you at all."

"Sorry," I said. "I tried to get out of the meeting sooner, but things have been getting out of hand lately."

"That Laris is driving me batty," Tove said, grimacing at the thought of her. "When you're Queen, you should banish her."

"When I'm Queen, you'll be King," I pointed out. "You can banish her yourself."

"Well, wait until you see what we have planned for you tonight." Duncan grinned. "You'll be having too much fun to worry about Laris or anybody else."

Fortunately, since I was getting married in a few days, I'd gotten out of the usual ball that would happen for a Princess's birthday. Elora and Aurora had planned that the wedding would take place immediately after I turned eighteen. My birthday was on a Wednesday, and I was getting married on Saturday, leaving no time for a massive Trylle birthday party.

Willa insisted on throwing me a small party anyway, even though I didn't really want one. Considering everything that was happening in Förening, it felt like sacrilege. The Vittra had set up a peace treaty with us, agreeing not to attack us until I became Queen.

What we hadn't realized at the time was the specific language they had used. They wouldn't attack *us*, meaning the Trylle living in Förening. Everyone else was fair game.

The Vittra had started going after our changelings, the ones that were still left with their host families in human society. They'd taken a few before we caught on, but as soon as we did, we sent all our best trackers in the field to bring home any changeling over the age of sixteen. For anyone younger than that, our trackers were supposed to stand guard and watch them. They couldn't take them without setting off an Amber Alert, so the Vittra avoided taking them too.

That left us at a horrible disadvantage. To protect the changelings, our trackers had to be in the field, so they couldn't be here guarding the palace. We would be more exposed to an attack if the Vittra went back on their part of the deal, but I didn't see what choice we had. We couldn't let them kidnap and hurt our children, so I sent every tracker I could out into the field.

Finn had been gone almost continuously for months. He was the best tracker we had, and he'd been returning the changelings to all the Trylle communities. I hadn't seen him since before Christmas, and sometimes I still missed him, but the longing was fading.

He'd made it clear that his duty came before everything else and I could never be a real part of his life. I was marrying someone else, and even though I still cared about Finn, I had to put that behind me and move past it.

"Where is this party happening anyway?" I asked Willa, pushing thoughts of Finn from my mind.

"Upstairs," Willa said, leading me toward the grand staircase in the front hall. "Matt's up there putting on the finishing touches."

"Finishing touches?" I raised an eyebrow.

Someone pounded violently on the front door, making the door shake and the chandelier above us tremble. Normally people rang a doorbell, but our visitor was nearly beating down the door.

"Stay back, Princess," Duncan said as he walked over to the entrance.

"Duncan, I can get it," I said.

If somebody hit the door hard enough to make the front hall quake, I was afraid of what they would do to him. I made a move for the door, but Willa stopped me.

"Wendy, let him," she said firmly. "You and Tove will be here if he needs you."

"No." I pulled myself from her grip and went after Duncan, to defend him if I needed to.

That sounded silly, since he was supposed to be my bodyguard, but I was more powerful than him. He was really only meant to serve as a shield if need be, but I would never let him do that.

When he opened the door, I was right behind him. Duncan meant to only partially open the door so he could see what waited for us outside, but a gust of wind came up, blowing it open and sending snow swirling around the front hall.

A blast of cold air struck me, but it died down almost instantly. Willa could control the wind when she wanted to, so as soon as it blew inside the palace, she raised her hand to silence it.

A figure stood before us, bracing himself with his hands on either side of the doorway. He was slumped forward, his head hanging down, and snow covered his black sweater. His clothes were ragged, worn, and shredded in most places.

"Can we help you?" Duncan asked.

"I need the Princess," he said, and as soon as I heard his voice, a shiver shot through me.

"Loki?" I gasped.

"Princess?" Loki lifted his head.

He smiled crookedly, but his smile didn't have its usual bravado. His caramel eyes looked tired and pained, and he had a fading bruise on his cheek. Despite all that, he was still just as gorgeous as I remembered him, and my breath caught in my throat.

"What happened to you?" I asked. "What are you doing here?"

"I apologize for the intrusion, Princess," he said, his smile already fading. "And as much as I'd like to say that I'm here for pleasure, I . . ." He swallowed something back, and his hands gripped tighter on the doorframe.

"Are you all right?" I asked, pushing past Duncan.

"I . . ." Loki started to speak, but his knees gave out. He pitched forward, and I rushed to catch him. He fell into my arms, and I lowered him to the floor.

"Loki?" I brushed the hair back from his eyes, and they fluttered open.

"Wendy." He smiled up at me, but the smile was weak. "If I'd known that this is what it would take to get you to hold me, I would've collapsed a long time ago."

"What is going on, Loki?" I asked gently. If he hadn't been so obviously distressed, I would've swatted him for that comment, but he grimaced in pain when I touched his face.

"Amnesty," he said thickly, and his eyes closed. "I need amnesty, Princess." His head tilted to the side, and his body relaxed. He'd passed out.

EDITOR'S PICKS – EXCLUSIVES – COMPETITIONS

INTERVIEWS – EVENTS – PREVIEWS

SIGN UP

WWW.PANMACMILLAN.COM/TORNEWS

TWITTER.COM/UKTOR

TOR®